What readers of the German version of
THE OTHER SIDE OF...

"Fantastic, unique, brilliant. This book piques your curiosity. You will want to read it and reread it!"

M.L. Fuhrer

"Max Meyer's novel combines amazing reasoning with surprising ideas. Brings Galileo Galilei and Pestalozzi into the present and has all the characteristics of a well-written thriller. A must read!"

F. Buob

"I have read the book twice. The first time, I devoured it like a thriller.... Then the second time, I enjoyed it for its numerous clues about world history, a theme throughout the novel.... It's a book for intellectuals but with the makings of a best seller."

J. Maler

"A book is only really good if you want to read it twice. I have already read Max Meyer's debut novel twice, and I just might read it a third time as well!"

J. W. Roth

"I read the book over the weekend. Interesting concepts! The physics and mathematics are explained so well that even a layperson can keep up and use them to follow the possibilities in the plot.... The book is thought provoking and encourages you to question certain "everyday" occurrences rather than just accept the world as it seems to be. Congratulations!"

F. Daniel

The OTHER SIDE of NOW

The OTHER SIDE of NOW

Max Meyer

Sumid Press

Copyright © 2016 by Max Meyer

ALL RIGHTS RESERVED

Cover design by Amygdala Design
Book design by Amygdala Design
Translated by Roger Johnson
Edited by Mayanne Wright

ISBN-13: 9781791653392

Previously published in German as *Jenseits dieser Zeit: Eine utopische Begegnung mit Gott* by the Frankfurterverlagsgruppe, 2012

Visit the author's website at: http://the-other-side-of-now.com/en

This is a work of fiction. Names, characters places, brands, media, and incidents are either the product of the author's imagination or are used fictitiously. Any resemblance to similarly named places or to persons living or deceased is coincidental.

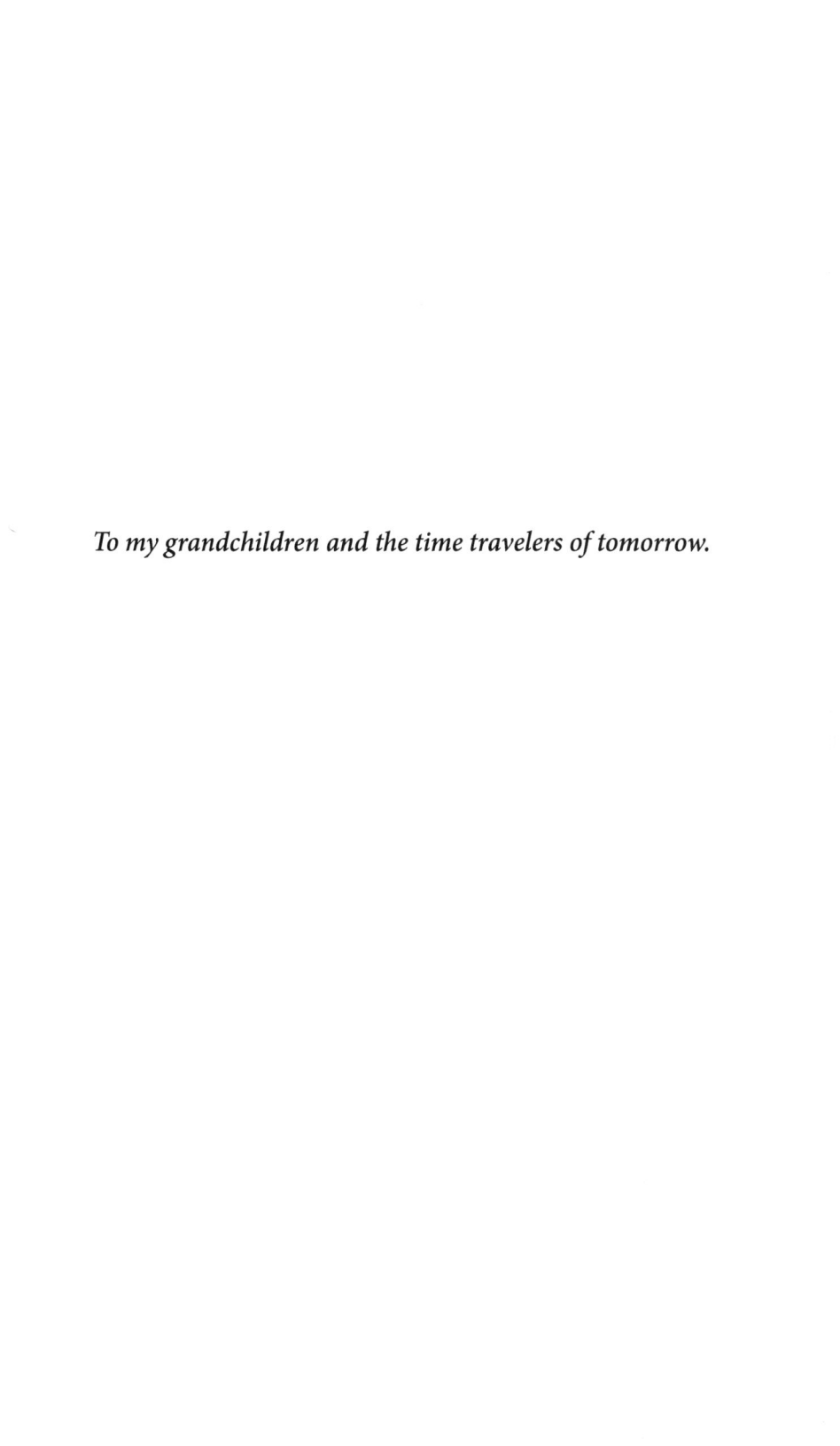

To my grandchildren and the time travelers of tomorrow.

Table of Contents

Prologue	11
The Burglary	25
Michael	52
Reading the Disk	69
Alco Sci	90
The First Disk	111
The Second Disk	122
First Suspicions	132
Pestalozzi	146
The Third Disk	178
Persuasion	199
The Vatican	211
Professor Bucher	231
Theories of Time	248
Consequences	262
This Side of Then	282
Explanations	300
Epilogue	314

Prologue

God encouraged me to write this. But he winked and said that no one would want to publish it. I wonder what instructions he would have given me if he had known that it would indeed be published. Would he have forbidden it and said that the human race wasn't ready for it yet? Or would he have said that it was high time for humans to face the full truth about their identity and thus allow publication?

Not that I was ever any kind of true believer, as you must now be thinking. Quite the opposite. Nonetheless, I knew God, and I knew him in person. You'll see.

It all began when I was twenty-one. I've grown old since then. When I look in the mirror, a wrinkled face gazes back at me. I hardly recognize it. Surely, it's not the face of that young, dynamic student I used to be. When I get up in the morning, pins and needles prick my joints, and every evening I swallow three different pills to make the next day more bearable. So I look back on my life and wonder what my duty actually is. What should I include here? Should I warn my fellow human beings? Should I recount my experiences in the hope that they will shed light on their own? Or, would it be better if I objectively and scientifically explained what actually is happening on Earth? I'm going to weigh my options—at this advanced age—in a cool and objective way. However—and this is most important—I will write in secret and tell no one until the work is published. For I have reason to believe that it would be forbidden, and I would be prevented from recalling its content, my memory deleted from my brain just like files in an out-of-date computer. I'd like to avoid that.

The story I'm about to tell you is not over but continues to unfold. Few will believe it. If I had not stumbled upon it by accident, I myself might never have seen the truth. But now that I have, I feel compelled to report it. It's as if all humanity were blind, trapped in its comfortable worldview, one shaped by the physics of Galileo, Newton, and Einstein.

This situation harkens back to the time of the Greeks, when Ptolemy gave us his view of the world. He looked up into the heavens and observed that some stars moved together, all in the same direction, and concluded they must be conjoined in a sphere. Other stars moved together in a different direction and were thus conjoined in a different sphere. Ptolemy determined that seven superimposed spheres made up the heavens, each rotating in a different direction. This Ptolemaic worldview, with Earth at the center surrounded by seven celestial spheres, held sway for centuries. It explained what people saw when they looked up at the star-filled sky. The stars moved in seven directions, so there had to be seven spheres. What they saw just had to be true. Why question it? But that's the problem. We all often see something and believe it is fact, even when our explanation for what we see is not actually true. We also get stuck in old ideas and ignore evidence of anything new. We do this even when the evidence is obvious.

This story is not made up. I lived it. Well, I lived much of it. You will forgive me for reconstructing dialog and sequences that I did not witness directly. My sources were good. But living the story makes it even more amazing. Over the course of my life, I have had many adventures. I have learned to believe only what I have observed and do only what I believe is right. I don't take people seriously when they tell far-fetched stories about ghosts, psychic phenomena, "coincidences" that are not coincidences at all, or about any other sort of superstitious or metaphysical nonsense. I simply cannot believe such stuff because in science what counts is what's concretely provable— not accepted on faith. That's why I'll understand if you choose not to take my story seriously. But, still, I ask that you hear me out. At least keep an open mind as you read. If in the end you still don't believe me, at least consider whether what I have related could have happened.

I must, however, be careful. No one must discover it is I who wrote this book. Given where I live today, I could hardly take part in discussions provoked by my story. This disturbs me. I would like to answer people's questions, and especially convince any doubters (there will always be some) with further reasoning. On the other hand, I know that my message will not have sufficient support and will cause all sorts of commotion. Sometimes, in my mind, I imagine the discussions and arguments I would conjure up to convince doubters. And in my imagination, I don't see just the scientists. They would adjust quickly to this new foundation of knowledge. No. I also imagine politicians—including great political leaders—who believe that they must invoke God in every speech to justify their own assumptions and positions. I see preachers who present themselves as God's emissaries, justifying their peculiar views with their allegedly special relationship to the higher power, a relationship only they have. And finally I see religious fundamentalists high in their pulpits, practicing intolerance, all in the name of God. I see them, all those whose worldview will collapse when faced with the truth. How pathetically they'd react if I proved to them the real nature of their business! What a pleasure it would be to watch them tumble down!

Exactly how my manuscript skipped through time and reached the hands of a publisher—well, on that subject, I remain silent. Even the publisher doesn't know how it happened.

As unbelievable as you may find my story at first, I think that some of you will quickly become accustomed to the new knowledge. The human race has often had to cope with great scientific upheaval. It will also cope with my report. With time, people may even come to find the information obvious and normal. Some will say, "How could people have been so dumb they couldn't see all that?" It will be the same as when people realized that the Earth was not flat but round. Powerful people and the vast majority of others had been against the spread of such heresy, while today we wonder how one could be so stupid back then and miss the truth. There were plenty of indications that the Earth was not flat. Ships gradually rose on the horizon as they approached land. Obviously, they sailed on a spherical Earth.

In precisely the same way, this story will make it clear that throughout history, from ancient times until today, evidence has pointed to the truth. How could people not see the evidence and then, if they did, completely misinterpret it?

***

I began to wrestle with the events I write about here after the murder of Heinz Roos, Professor Bucher's graduate assistant in the Department of Theoretical Physics at the University of Bern. My first chapter recounts this story. At the time, I worked as a graduate assistant at the law school, located in the same building, one floor up. Heinz Roos was a colleague and sort of a friend.

The first clues actually became evident during a conference before the murder. Only later, however, did they seem significant. The conference had been organized by the Department of Ethnology. It had nothing to do with the law school. I was interested in the topic, so I went over to take part in various sessions.

An American named Alco Sci also came to the conference. He had traveled to Switzerland for that sole purpose. He had a suspicion, a suspicion that later arose in me. Unfortunately, however, his motives were far different from mine.

A short, beefy man, Alco Sci had a round, thick head with Asian features. His hair was silver-gray and matched the bushy eyebrows that dominated his face. With arms that hung slightly too short, a powerful stature, and a spring in his step, he looked more like a Japanese wrestler than a scholar. He always wore a dark suit and tie and gave the impression of a relentless, hard, and mean-spirited man, an impression confirmed in my short meeting with him later. Sci came, as I later found out, from Petersburg, Kentucky. He appeared to have originally been a professor of physics but no longer taught at any university. For the life of me, I could not quite figure out what he actually did. It seemed he worked in the administration of an independent church; he was far too taciturn and too ineloquent to have been a successful preacher. Later we even wondered who had invited him to the conference in the first place. But he was there. He must have had an invitation, and someone must have paid for his trip and registration.

Knowing what I know now, this is how I reconstruct his arrival. Sci landed at Zurich airport and caught the 10:02 train to Bern. In exactly fifty-six minutes after the train began rolling, he stood on a platform in the Bern Bahnhof. He stepped out of the crowd, allowing the hurrying commuters to pass by and reviewed his invitation. It contained a small diagram with important landmarks. The University was close by, easily reached on foot.

Amazingly, Sci had come alone. He had no escort of youthful bodyguards as he did on his later visit. So he had to orient himself. He determined that he only had to walk to the other end of the underground level of the station and then take the elevator to street level. Once there, he would find himself on the right-hand side of the Institute of Science. (The train station in Bern had been cleverly built in the city center and was located, so to speak, right under the University.)

The location would be quite convenient for the international scholars attending the conference—a good thing given their disinclination to study maps.

Sci quickly traversed the length of the underpass. Several people were waiting in front of an elevator. He joined them and entered the elevator as soon as the door opened. Surprised, he studied the walls on the ride up. They were full of smudges and graffiti, confirming his view that a decadent generation was coming of age in the western world. Today's youth lacked ethical backbone. They had no standards by which to make value judgments such as those provided by his religion. *Ora et labora*—pray and work—was the motto of medieval monasteries. Sci had also made it his own. Switzerland, once the cradle of Calvinist values, had lost its work ethic and its will to produce, just as in parts of his own country, the East Coast and especially the West Coast. Calvinist values were those that suited him most, and he displayed them with his entire demeanor.

Reaching street level, he oriented himself once again and walked toward the building where the conference would take place. He found the big auditorium right away.

Some participants had traveled with him from the Zürich Airport to Bern. Most did not know each other, so they had boarded different cars in the train and made their way individually to the University. Other participants had arrived on earlier trains and killed time by taking an impromptu tour of the city before heading on to the University. Still others had come by train from Geneva or had arrived a day earlier.

Altogether about fifty scientists from around the world had gathered for two days. So it was not a big event and consequently made no headlines. Most participants were relatively young biologists and anthropologists who studied the history of the Earth. Their primary interests revolved around how life originated on Earth, how today's life forms developed, and especially how such a complex creature as a human being came into existence. The purpose of the conference was to promote the exchange and discussion of the latest scientific findings in this area. Neither the conference nor the subject was extraordinary. There would be no pronouncements with significant consequences. But for me this conference is where it all began because the conference brought two important people together, even if only for a short time—Alco Sci and Edward Bucher.

***

Darwin's theory of evolution served as the foundation for discussion at the conference. The theory had long held sway in the scientific world, given its clear support in nature. Most scientists believed that the development of different species could not have taken place in any other way, and, for the scientists present at the conference, it formed part of the basic premise on which they based their ongoing research.

However, debate continued over the details of how evolution actually played out. There were two serious and clear theories about the evolution of life from single-celled organisms to human beings. One theory claimed that the original life form, single primitive cells, developed more or less by chance. These cells then changed over time through a series of random mutations. According to the law of "survival of the fittest," certain mutations prevailed over other competing life forms within a particular environment, and through this process more complicated beings evolved. After millions of years of this sort of evolutionary development, human beings eventually came into existence. The theory of "natural selection" had many followers among scholars and was widely accepted.

The other theory was based on statistical calculation and claimed that not enough random mutations could have possibly occurred between the appearance of the first life form and the present day. There was simply insufficient time. Thus, other factors must have existed in the selection process and influenced development. These factors corresponded to mechanisms found in nature. They steered evolution in a specific direction, namely toward intelligent forms of life. Of course, not all these factors were known and thus posed major and continual research challenges for scientists.

Some scholars seized on the fact that we do not know all these steering mechanisms and interpreted human ignorance as evidence suggesting the work of a higher or divine power. In their minds, it is this power—God—that had steered evolution toward intelligent life. Of course, such scholars did recognize the findings of scientific research, but they also posited the presence of a divine hand where science could find no explanation.

Scientists no longer took seriously anyone who rejected Darwin's theory of evolution. Such people were mostly religious fundamentalists who believed in the literal truth of the creation story as recorded in the Bible and claimed that life began a few thousand years ago through an act of God. Some also rejected as blasphemy the idea that humans descended from apes. Surprisingly, even a few isolated university graduates supported this view, as if none of the previous research and findings existed. At the conference in Bern, no one even discussed these fundamentalist views.

However, participants did address a different set of questions that interested me: Would life continue to develop in the future? Would, for example, human beings continue to change and adapt to the ever-changing conditions of life? And if they did, which direction would this change take? Participants were searching for clues that pointed to an ongoing evolution of life forms, especially among people over the last few decades or centuries. They wanted to know, in this context, what had actually brought about human progress over the last few thousand years—from cave dwellers to our present communication-based society. Had sly mutations come into play? Such matters, when discussed impartially, proved especially difficult for religious people. Among scientists, however, these were burning issues.

**

The conference auditorium could accommodate far more than fifty people, so the few participants left big spaces as they sat down. In general, they didn't know each other personally and only greeted one another in passing. When Sci walked into the auditorium, he hesitated a moment in the doorway. Running a hand through his close-cropped hair as though slightly embarrassed, he surveyed the room. He then sat down in the row next to the rear entrance. He knew from the program that the session would be interpreted into German and English. He knew no German. English was his native tongue. However, he had no intention of participating in the discussions or of speaking his mind and challenging others. This group of people would not accept his opinions, and anything he said would only serve to provoke them. At any rate, he had no fondness for these modern, informal discussions that had replaced traditional lectures at the universities these days. Therefore, he had chosen the back row. He waited there motionless during the fifteen minutes before the initial presentation. He did not look around or talk to anyone.

Professor Bucher came in a few seconds before the speaker began. Although the topic had little to do with his discipline, he had decided to attend the session for the same reason I had. The subject interested him, and he could simply walk from his office nearby. Or had Bucher come because Alco Sci was there? At any rate, he took a seat in the back row because he was late.

Bucher and Sci sat next to each other during several presentations without exchanging a word. Bucher, a stylishly dressed, tall man, looked energetic and likeable, a stark contrast to Sci. It was Bucher who finally took the initiative to address his somewhat strange neighbor. His attempts received no response, however, and he eventually gave up. He turned his attention back to the speaker.

"The mutations of one life form to another take place in very small random steps. We can count these random coincidences over a rather long period. We also know from probability statistics how many coincidences are needed for an advantageous mutation. We therefore also know that the length of time that has passed between the appearance of the first single-celled life forms to the emergence of humans has been insufficient."

The speaker obviously supported the second theory cited above, that the development of life must have been controlled or "steered" by factors existing in nature. The speaker went on by citing examples present in nature that have influenced the evolution of life in a certain direction—population growth during times of plenty, changing weather patterns, the need to develop social groups for hunting and protection of the young, and planning to accommodate migratory food sources. Sci listened intently and shook his head from time to time in disagreement. After the presentation, he suddenly turned to Bucher and expressed his displeasure. The two began to talk.

As I came to realize later, no one overheard their complete discussion. Thus, I could not reconstruct it at the time of my investigations. This is unfortunate, for its content would have greatly increased my understanding. I did learn something, however, from other participants—that the discussion between Professor Bucher and Alco Sci became fairly intense and lasted into the break. Bucher seems to have tried to sound Sci out to determine what the burly man really knew. His gestures had even drawn the attention of another participant, who later told me that Sci had said, "Could it be that human beings have really controlled their own evolution from their future? A scary thought! A downright ridiculous explanation of progress!" Sci had hesitated and then continued, "Nonetheless, there might already be scientific knowledge, theoretically, to make such a statement credible. Can you tell me more about it? Could you explain your theory in detail?"

Professor Bucher apparently gave no further explanation. As if he had already said too much, he brusquely terminated the discussion, turned away, and disappeared during the break. Sci shot him a hostile glance and is reported to have muttered, "Now I know exactly who you are, Bucher. And I know that you know more about our subject than any other person in this room. We'll be talking to each other again sometime soon."

Then, I heard, he left the room and wasn't seen in the other sessions.

No one seemed to have paid much attention to what took place between the two men. However, I claim that Alco Sci understood at that moment exactly what I intend to describe in this book—human beings have managed their own evolution! If only Sci had been a scientist willing to communicate instead of someone solely set on pursuing his own interests!

***

Subsequent inquiries revealed that Sci was a "creationist," as the Americans call them. He believed in the biblical doctrine of creation, according to which, everything—including human beings—was created by God several thousand years ago in the perfect form that they retain today. That is, he pretended to believe in this doctrine, at least in public. Today, I doubt whether he truly did. After all, he had a solid scientific education, and it is quite possible he used his "religion" to pursue his more secular interests. But Alco Sci did come from Petersburg, home of the Creation Museum, a hotbed of those subscribing to the biblical narrative of creation.

Although science had repudiated the theory of creationism

based solely on the Bible, amazingly enough, many people still believed it. In Europe, the vast majority of the population believed that Darwin's theory of evolution was essentially correct. The same held true for Canada and Australia. The United States was blatantly different. According to several surveys, about half (!) of the population said they believed God created humans in their present form about 10,000 years ago. Any other view was blasphemy to them. In the land where independent churches had become big business with expensive buildings and private television channels, many benefited from religion. Religious leaders kept beliefs alive in order to support their business. Sci benefited from such a religious enterprise. That may be why he defended the biblical doctrine of creation.

The Burglary

The morning when it all began started out like any other. I woke early, had a cup of coffee, and ran down the stairs of my apartment at about 6:30. As always, I took the steps two at a time. After a few months of living there, I had become sure-footed with practice even though I was often rubbing sleep from my eyes. I had rented the small two-room apartment in the university district, where I lived my bachelor life alone. No longer a student and now making a bit of money as a graduate assistant, I could afford the apartment. It seemed an enormous luxury after such a long period of living in a residence hall, where I had only a single room.

Downstairs I opened the front door. It was still dark, but a faint light shown on the horizon. Back when I was a law student preparing for the bar exam, I used to get up even earlier. I could study better in the morning and had never counted myself among that breed of student who hovers over books all night long. After the exam, I continued to rise early, although I did not crawl out of bed quite as quickly as before.

As I passed my mailbox in front of the building, I stopped to check for mail. I didn't expect anything since I had emptied it the night before. I just couldn't go by the mailbox without opening it. Much to my surprise, it contained a single small envelope. I pulled it out and dropped it in my pocket. I'd open it later at the office. It was still too dark on the street to read. I went to my car, an old blue Fiat with dents here and there and some rust. It was not going to pass the next annual inspection, but so far it had served me well. I sat behind the wheel, turned the key, released the hand brake, and let the car roll down the slightly sloping street. Once I had enough speed, I engaged the clutch. The car jerked and started. To this day, I don't think much of expensive cars or other status symbols. Back then, however, I had hoped that, as a lawyer, I would be able to afford a decent car, at least one with a working starter.

***

I lived very modestly. Money doesn't mean much to young people, and I really didn't want to make a show of my new salary. I also studied hard and passed all my tests with high marks. I should have been a good catch for a woman. But I just couldn't make it happen. Most of the women I found interesting had values very different from mine. They lived on dreams and preferred hippie types. They had little interest in a man like me, who spent his time working hard and focused on his economic future. They preferred men who enjoyed staying up all night discussing the world's problems, problems that held no interest for me back then. In fact, women seemed hardly to notice me at all. So, not lacking in self-confidence, and especially since I still had my entire life ahead of me, I punished these women by ignoring them. Every now and then, I had a girlfriend, but never the right one. Looking back, I see that I was inexperienced and downright naive compared to my older male colleagues and even to the women themselves.

Despite my self-confidence, my early academic career had been unexceptional. I graduated from the Gymnasium without any major difficulties, but I had been a mediocre student. I had too many other interests. I read a lot and tended not to focus on much of anything in particular. Moreover, school hardly monopolized all my time, so I spent it playing chess and studying the intricacies of history and mathematics. But I was particularly keen on science and liked conducting my own experiments, even if I did not apply myself in a methodical manner. Teachers only asked that I achieve a C each year, which I managed without difficulty. So I found no good reason to make any extra effort. Over the holiday breaks, however, I did take several courses in areas of Switzerland where a different language was spoken. I learned French and Italian this way.

After the Gymnasium, I went straight to the university. Initially, I couldn't decide between medicine and history. I looked into both and then went in a third direction—law. Unlike in secondary school, I concentrated on my studies and graduated in five years with good grades. I was offered a position as a graduate assistant but decided not to take it right away. Instead, I went to the United States for a year to study

Anglo-Saxon law and learn English. I proudly returned home with a Master's degree in law from Stanford University. Back at the University here in Bern, I obtained an assistantship and viewed the job as a continuation of my education. But for the first time in my life, I had a salary.

***

    I decided to open the envelope while waiting at a red light. Inside was a note from one of my girlfriends. Marianne had come to see me last night, but I had already gone to bed and didn't answer the door. At any rate, I didn't really want to make a commitment, so I didn't care if I snubbed her. Only now do I realize how easy it would have been to have acted a little nicer and maybe enjoyed life more. I had such different values and priorities back then.

    When I reached the parking lot of the University, I tucked the tail of my red-checkered shirt back into my jeans. It had come loose on the drive. I walked quickly to the main entrance. I opened the door, entered the foyer, and took the elevator to the fourth floor. It was still dark. But at the end of the hall, an overhead light leaked out from behind a door, indicating that someone was already working. I walked halfway down the corridor and stopped, surprised that the light came from my office. Had I forgotten to switch it off last night? Or had the cleaning lady gone in after I left and failed to turn it off? I went up to the door. As usual, it was not completely shut since there were no valuables in the room, and my legal work held no secrets. I opened the door and stood on the threshold.

***

"Next item, Security." Police Kommandant Herbert Stucki looked up from his agenda. A tall man in his fifties, he exuded authority. It generally fell to him to lead the division heads of the Bern City Police in their weekly meeting.

Stucki looked around the sparsely furnished conference room of the main station. He studied the faces of the six department heads, the Kommissars, checked that his assistant was keeping the minutes, and made sure that the two specialists he'd brought in to address specific issues were paying attention. All were dressed in civilian clothes except for the head of Transportation Services, who wore his police uniform. The mood was sober, matter of fact, and as ordinary as the room itself. Routine. They had run through the weekly events in the usual order and had now reached Security, which as a rule meant providing protection for political activities or groups having a demonstration or rally. Security was particularly important in the capital city, given the many events that took place here.

"The farmers plan to demonstrate," remarked the Kommandant's assistant, a young lawyer.

"Another demo," said the Kommissar of Transportation Services, rolling his eyes. Paul Lack had worked in Transportation Services ever since joining the police force. He knew his duties inside and out and had little time for people who, in his view, made his job unnecessarily difficult. Such people included protesters, for whom he had to redirect traffic all over the place.

The assistant continued. "The organizers got in touch with me a few days ago. They want the Bundesplatz for the entire afternoon, beginning at one o'clock."

"What're the farmers protesting this time?" asked the head of the Criminal Division in a monotone. The matter did not really concern him.

"The use of genetic engineering in agriculture," said the assistant. "Parliament is debating a law about it."

"Why are the farmers against genetic engineering?" asked the Kommissar, looking down at his hands.

"They're probably worried about competition from cheap industrial production. If people get scared about genetic engineering, they're more likely to protect the farmers' current vested interests." The young assistant had sounded sarcastic. Demonstrations just meant more work for him.

"Stop it," ordered Stucki. "It's not the job of the police to make policy, but to make sure others can exercise their political rights." He paused for effect. "Will you set up the usual detours, Paul?"

Lack was not happy. "We've been having three to four demonstrations a month. This month we've had the Kurds and the Croats protesting the war in their homelands. Women twice—for or against something. I can't remember any more. Greens opposing the nuclear power plants. When will it end? No good comes of it all. These protesters just make it worse on themselves. They don't help their cause by harassing people and causing traffic jams. Demonstrating against nuclear power or some other new-fangled technology isn't going to stop progress, and making us block the streets certainly won't, will it, Herby?"

Stucki liked it when his colleagues called him "Herby" in English.

"Certainly not. But that's beside the point. We can talk about it sometime after work. For now, I just need to know your plan of action. You'll organize the usual traffic detours?"

"Of course, Herby. I suggest . . . ." He went over the usual measures.

When Lack had finished, Stucki took up the last item on the agenda: "Other Issues." This time Kommissar Erb spoke up. "We've had another death threat against our local 'science star.' " Everyone knew whom he meant.

Nevertheless, Stucki stuck to routine, "Against Edward Bucher?"

Lack stood and took his leave. He had nothing to contribute when it came to death threats. Two other attendees also took the occasion to leave the room.

"Yes, against Dr. Bucher. He's once again received an anonymous letter asserting that what he does is the 'work of the devil' and must be stopped. Naturally, he contacted us."

Rarely did the University's faculty members gain fame outside of Switzerland. Bucher was an exception. Having received numerous awards and additional honorary doctorates from three different universities, he had gained ultimate renown by winning the Nobel Prize four years earlier. The police referred to Bucher as their "science star" because his work provoked such strong political opposition that he occasionally needed police protection.

"An anonymous letter? Not much we can do about that."

"But the writer has also phoned him twice, without

revealing his name of course. He asked if the letter had arrived and warned that he meant business. The second time, we were able to trace the call to a group of religious zealots."

"Christians?"

"Fundamentalist Christians."

"Are they dangerous?" asked the Kommandant.

"Well, they need to be taken seriously," replied Erb. Kommandant Stucki knew that he was about to enter the realm of politics, but wanted to make sure he understood the situation. "So, once more, we've got people who condemn the advancement of science because they are afraid of its consequences."

"What do you mean 'once more'?"

"Well, they're not unlike the old-fashioned farmers who plan to protest. Forward-thinking farmers don't argue with new technology. They use it."

Erb nodded and Stucki returned to the business at hand. "Do you plan to monitor the fundamentalists?"

"Sure, I have to," confirmed Erb.

"And inform Professor Bucher?"

"No. It'll just distract him. Incidentally, he seems to be working on something very big."

"What you mean?"

Erb nodded. "Apparently significant." The Kommissar checked his notes. "According to the border police, some suspicious people have come to Bern. They came as tourists but seem bent on something else. The police believe this group may be after Bucher's research findings. One of them could be our caller."

"I see," said Stucki. "If this continues, we'll have to create a special unit just to deal with matters concerning our Professor Bucher."

***

Heinz Roos lay motionless on the floor of my office. Dead. Dr. Bucher's studio-office was one floor below mine, and Roos had no reason to be in my office or even on the fourth floor. I looked past him. My stomach tightened. Two men in tight-fitting black suits were busy coiling a rope at the window. Black stockings covered their heads. A third man, identically dressed, was climbing through the window into the room. Where could he be coming from? My office was fairly high up. Nobody could just climb in from outside. Instinctively I drew back into the corridor. My first impulse was to gain some time and figure out what to do. But just as I was ducking away, one of the men saw me.

He looked me straight in the eyes, then lunged across the room and struck me on the side of the head. I crumpled to my knees. He grabbed me under the arms and pulled me back inside. Then he dropped me in a heap. I knew that I didn't stand a chance against all three. So I kept quiet and pretended I had lost consciousness.

Sure that I had been knocked out, the men again busied themselves with the rope. Once they had finished coiling it, one man took the bundle and slung it over his shoulder. As they passed my body heading out of the room, I convulsed involuntarily. If only I had remained still! I ended up kicking one of the men in the shin. He tripped and two tiny disks slipped unnoticed from his pocket onto the floor. From out of his jacket, one of the other men pulled a pistol with a silencer attached. He pointed the gun directly at my abdomen. I rolled to the side just as he pulled the trigger. I twitched and groaned, then lay still. The three hurried out the door.

A stinging pain ran up my left thigh. Slow and uncertain, I ran my hand down my pant leg till I found the spot where I had been hit. I was bleeding. Remembering the two disks, I groped along the carpet until I found them. With difficulty I placed them in the breast pocket of my shirt. Touching my wound, I could feel where the blood had spread. Struggling to reach the phone on my desk, I rose up on one elbow and had just managed to prop myself up when everything went black.

**

Dr. Edward Bucher entered his study well before eight o'clock that same morning. He unlocked the reinforced door with an ordinary key, and then entered a code on an electronic keypad to release a deadbolt that secured his office and adjoining studio both from the inside and out. This was the only security system of its kind in the building. He stepped into the room and gasped. Shards of glass glittered on the floor beneath a broken window. Drawers had been pulled out and papers scattered all over his desk. He closed the door, steadied himself, and looked around, noting each detail. Walking carefully to the window, he peered down to the pavement three stories below. No ordinary ladder could have reached this high. The walls on either side of the building were sheer and flat, no ledges. He glanced up, but he could see nothing of the facade above him. The intruder must have come down from the roof.

Bucher ducked his head back into the room and went to his computer. The screen was in sleep mode; someone had turned it on. Anxiety tightened his chest. He sat down with a thump. He pressed the space bar and the computer woke up. Eyes never leaving the screen, Bucher's fingers flew across the keyboard. He held his breath. Minutes passed. Finally he stopped typing and sat back, satisfied. He stared into space for a second, then reached up to the shelf above the monitor, took a disk, and inserted it into the drive. He entered a series of commands and waited. He leaned back again and smiled. No one had cracked the code, nothing had been erased, and the files containing his work remained untouched. He sighed and looked around the room again. The mess was not all that bad—a broken window to repair and half an hour of tidying up should suffice to put things back in order.

He went through the collection of disks again, pulling out one after another to determine whether each disk was in its proper sleeve. Hmm, he thought. Two disks were missing, the two that he had not yet labeled. Had he placed them on the shelf? No, he'd left them on his desk yesterday. Bucher chuckled. The content of each disk had been coded and compressed using a protocol that only he knew. So whoever had taken them would have to spend a fortune in order to break the code, if that was even possible. But if some hacker did succeed, the information would be worthless, unless . . . the thief could somehow put it together with Bucher's youth and career. Bucher shook his head, thinking the scenario highly unlikely.

Bucher pushed away from his desk and returned to the broken window. He looked down into the courtyard directly below and saw nothing unusual. Then the sound of hurried footsteps and muffled voices floated upstairs. He popped his head back inside to listen. The sounds disappeared. Then he heard footsteps and voices from outside. He looked through the broken window again. Over to the side of the building, in front of the main entrance, sat an ambulance with back doors wide open. Two medics loaded a stretcher with a portable IV dangling over it. Then they jumped back out to help two more medics load a second stretcher carrying a sheet-covered body. The ambulance sped off, sirens blaring. Bucher turned away from the window and headed out of the studio office, leaving everything the way it was.

"Dr. Bucher," someone said. "I have some terrible news."

Bucher waited.

"Heinz Roos is dead."

***

In an apartment on the outskirts of Bern, three burglars hunched around a scarred table eating breakfast. They still wore black pants and turtleneck sweaters. A half-empty jar of instant coffee, three cups, a plate of yellow cheese, a package of smoked ham, and a loaf of bread sat before them. The other furniture in the room consisted of two chairs and an old sofa, where they had slung two gun belts and a coiled rope. Pale sunlight and a humid morning breeze came through the single window.

One man rubbed his eyes. "Who the hell woulda thought somebody'd come to work so early?"

"Ya never know what a pointy-headed intellectual's gonna do," said the second man. He spoke flippantly but did not feel good about what happened.

"Don't worry, he didn't recognize us," said the third.

"Ya sure, Gus?"

"Jeez, Stan. No way he can finger us. You and Leroy're such pussies."

"Who's callin' who a pussy?" growled Leroy. "You shoulda bumped him off like that first guy."

The phone rang. Gus picked it up, "Yeah." His face grew tight as he listened. He shifted from one foot to the other.

"Naw. Too bad. We didn't get what you wanted. Wasn't no files like you said they'd be. Besides, it was gettin' light fast."

Again Gus listened. His jaws clamped tighter. "Nope, sorry," and after a long pause he said, "No idea if there's gonna be complications. We had to get rid of one guy. He showed up out of the blue when we was 'bout to go down the rope. The other one we just worked over a bit on account of we still had our masks on. He couldn't see nothin'."

The room grew still. Gus turned pale and croaked, "Naw, the second one ain't likely dead." He listened hard for a moment. The phone clicked and the caller hung up.

Gus sat down at the table, relaxed, and took a sip of lukewarm coffee. "That was the boss. By the way, I snatched two disks that ain't in my pocket no more. You seen 'em?"

"What disks?" asked Stan.

"Computer disks. Two without labels. They was just layin' there on the desk."

"You reckon they have som'um to do with this job?" asked Leroy, scratching the stubble on his face.

"Maybe."

"If they was important, why was they left laying around. Don't make sense." Leroy continued scratching.

"Got a point," Gus said. "But ya never know."

"Well, I ain't seen 'em," said Leroy.

"Me neither," added Stan.

"Oh well. Maybe they'll turn up. Anyway, we got some work to do today, boys."

"Shit."

"We gotta go back, normal like, so we don't stick out. Maybe pick som'um up. Maybe pay a visit to that second guy in the hospital. Supposed to listen to the news and read the papers, too."

***

My pulse raced. Wild images flashed through my brain. I flew through the air, swooped down, and landed on a branch. I lay in bed, and beneath me the Earth burned. Through the flames, I saw my mother's face. I said something to her, but in mid-sentence, everything went black. I heard the howl of a siren—far, far away. Something pushed me against straps, as if I were in a race car hugging the outer lane in a bend of the track. The flames came back; I raced through them feeling nothing. I had to pack. I was leaving. What was I trying to pack? I couldn't see. The flames turned blue, engulfing everything around me. I kept racing through them. Had to move forward. Eventually I slowed down, and there was nothing.

When I came to, hours later, I kept my eyes closed. But I felt comfortable and warm. I was in a bed. Light pressed against my eyelids, and the darkness grew brighter. I gingerly opened my eyes and scanned the room without moving my head. Everything around me was white—the bedding, the walls, and the light coming through the window. My head spun. I closed my eyes and tried to remember. The images of the last few minutes before I fainted slowly emerged. I had been on the floor, in pain, and had kept silent. A man dressed all in black had tripped and half fallen near me. Another man had pointed a pistol at my abdomen and shot me. I had rolled and the bullet had lodged in my leg. The man's mask had slipped up, and I saw the stubble on his chin. I opened my eyes. A leather strap with a handgrip hung over the bed. I'm in a hospital, I thought, and fell asleep again. A powerful sedative was doing its work.

***

Kommandant Stucki stood at his desk and looked out the window. Thousands of protesters marched down the street past the main police station to the Bundesplatz, the huge square in front of the Parliament Building. The farmers, spanning all ages, wore heavy, dark brown clothing and work boots. Many of the women had donned traditional peasant costumes. Some farmers pulled carts and farm wagons behind them. Others drove goats or carried piglets in their arms. Herbert Stucki's attention was drawn to the flowers. They were everywhere. Women carried bouquets or dressed their hair with them. The carts were decorated with flowers, and some of the banners were adorned with them. He read, "A Healthy Economy Means a Healthy Food Supply" and "Agriculture Serves Everybody." Other texts were more militant: "Death to Genetic Engineers" and "Overproduction Leads to Devastation."

Transportation Kommissar Lack must be pretty busy now, thought Stucki and sighed. Lack had to block off the inner city from traffic, organize detours in the outer districts, provide parking spaces for demonstrators, and along with the municipal transportation authorities, ensure that the public transportation system remained as effective as possible. The inner city functioned as a kind of regional shopping center and was already overloaded by morning.

Poor citizens of Bern. I pity them having to put up with these demonstrations every Saturday, thought Stucki. Then he began to wonder why so many people had trouble accepting something new, why they fought so hard to maintain their comfortable bourgeois status quo. If I were a farmer, he thought, I wouldn't demonstrate. I'd study the modern techniques, apply them on my farm, and make a lot of money.

Someone knocked on the door. Stucki returned from his thoughts and called, "Come in."

The door opened, and Police Kommissar Erb walked in. He looked at his Kommandant standing at the window and said, "Nice event out there. I bet Lack is having a field day."

"Sure."

"The riot police are standing by. But we're keeping them in the barracks. Don't want to stir things up. I don't think there'll be any incidents though."

"Hardly."

"That's not why I came."

The Kommandant stepped away from the window and asked, "What's up, Erb?"

He addressed Erb as he did all colleagues, by his last name, even though they were friends outside of work.

"We had a burglary and worse at Bucher's office. Someone, probably more than one person, broke in and killed his assistant. Also somebody else got shot."

"Oh my! Any leads?"

"Not yet, unfortunately. We just began the investigation. At any rate, I don't think it has anything to do with what's going on in the city."

"Does the shooting victim know anything?"

"I couldn't speak with him. He's in the hospital so hasn't been interviewed yet."

"Who is it?"

"A graduate assistant at the law school. He has an office directly above Bucher's and apparently left his office door open. The burglars rappelled down from there. He surprised them as they were making their escape back through his office."

"Will he come through?"

"Oh, yes. He lost a lot of blood, but there's no permanent injury. He'll be out of the hospital in a few days."

"You said a burglary. What's missing?"

"Apparently nothing is missing. Anyway, nothing important according to Bucher. We don't know what they were looking for. I'm thinking that they were some kind of obstructionists wanting to interfere with Bucher's research, maybe even religious fanatics, or it might have been some sort of economic espionage."

"Let's focus on the economic espionage angle," responded Stucki. "Usually there's money involved when this kind of violence occurs."

"Okay, Herby. I just wanted to get you ready for when the press gets wind of this."

***

I awoke the next day when the door to my hospital room opened quietly. Someone came in. Still groggy from the sedative, I allowed moments to pass before I realized it was Marianne. She sat down on the bed beside me and took my hand. I felt her closeness and her touch in a particular way, quite the opposite from the way she appeared—like an image on a faraway movie screen. I focused on the touch. It felt warm. Finally she spoke.

"How are you?"

I nodded, unable to speak.

"Whatever did you get yourself into?" she asked, looking at me tenderly.

"I don't know." My voice shook.

"You don't need to explain. It's all in the newspaper."

She took a newspaper from her purse and held it out to me. I didn't even try to read it. I had eyes only for her. As I looked at Marianne, my perceptions and thoughts became increasingly clear.

"Glad you came. I actually feel pretty good," I said, my voice firmer. I didn't feel much pain, only fatigue. But when I moved, something didn't seem quite right with my left leg. I patted my thigh and felt a thick bandage.

"The newspaper said you got shot in the thigh and bled a lot."

"Oh," I said. "Nobody bothered to tell me why I'm here."

"Well, you've been asleep the whole time."

Marianne told me that I had received only a flesh wound and no bones had been hit. The doctor had told her that I would soon be released. "You were lucky," she concluded.

"It's so sweet of you to worry about me," I said softly, and I probably meant it at that moment. I was aware, however, that my emotion was more likely due to my physical weakness.

"Poor Roos," Marianne said. "Did you know him?"

"Roos?" I then remembered that he had been lying beside me on the floor. "What?"

"The funeral is tomorrow," she said.

"Tomorrow?"

"Yes. It seems he heard sounds coming from your office, went to investigate, and the burglars shot him. That might have happened to you. You were lucky," she said again.

After Marianne left, I sat up in bed and looked at the newspaper. The haze before my eyes was gone, and I could think clearly again. The front-page headline read, "Nobel Laureate Robbed." Below that: "Graduate Assistant Dead, Another Wounded." In addition to the article, there was a picture of my office, with chalk lines outlining where Roos's body had lain. The text indicated that burglars had entered through my office to gain access to Professor Bucher's, but no one knew what they were looking for or if they'd found it. A subtitle in the article read, "Graduate Assistant Killed," the text below giving a summary of Heinz Roos's short life. Another subtitle read, "Graduate Assistant Severely Injured." The paragraph said that the burglars had shot me, but I was out of danger. It was unlikely that the perpetrators were looking for valuables or money but had been seeking something else. Finally, it stated that Professor Bucher was working in the field of theoretical physics and had made groundbreaking discoveries that had earned him the Nobel Prize. At present he was occupied with new research.

Apparently his work was of the utmost importance to industry. The newspaper hinted at industrial espionage. Until now such spying had generally been carried out without violence, but nowadays there were more and more vicious industrial criminals who resorted to arms to get what they wanted.

I put down the newspaper. Obviously, the aggression had not been directed specifically at me. I found it annoying that I now had to suffer. Then it came back to me that two disks had fallen to the floor. Where were they now? I looked around. Where was my shirt? I'd put the disks in the breast pocket. I thought to get up, but of course I couldn't. I sank back into the bed.

***

The three burglars, Stan, Leroy, and Gus, once again sat around the ugly kitchen table in their apartment. They were drinking beer. Leroy peered at an English language newspaper, *Swiss News*, but it was all about wine and concerts, no current news. Picking up the *Berner Zeitung*, he scanned, just looking for key words like "Roos" and "Bucher," but he couldn't spot them in the jumble of German words. The phone rang. Gus answered.

"So," said the caller, "you found out anything?"

"No sir."

"I've been thinking. The newspapers have spilled all the details. The cops won't be expecting a second hit, so I'd like you to try again, but not until I give the order. Got it?"

"Yes, Boss."

"In the meantime, get ready for more action. Survey the entire target area. Keep an eye on the professor. And for heaven's sake, make sure that all of you keep quiet and stay out of trouble."

The caller talked a few seconds longer and hung up. Leroy put down the newspaper and groaned. "We gotta find out if that damned kid can eye-dee us. And we gotta find them disks. Hey, you ain't said nothin' to the boss about the disks, have ya?"

"Naw, ya know all what I said. Our surprise boy is actually what they call a assistant. The Boss says we gotta be sure everybody what could be dangerous don't have no chance to talk."

"What's he mean by that?" asked Stan.

"Just what I said. For any asshole what saw us, it's 'Auf Wiedersehen, Baby.' " Gus laughed.

"Tricky," muttered Leroy and bit off a hangnail.

"I didn't sign on for no contract killing, and this ain't Alabama," Stan whined.

"Yeah, okay. But we gotta take out any risk. Or we're screwed."

Gus took the last swallow of his beer and crushed the can between his palms.

***

The day was eventful for me. Before lunch, the doctor came to visit. Accompanying him were three interns, a supervising nurse, and a regular nurse. The six of them came just to examine me and ask how I was doing. It felt like an inspection one might have in the military. Nonetheless, I learned that there were no complications. I was on the mend and could leave the hospital in a few days.

Later I asked the nurse who brought me lunch where my clothes were.

"Over there in the closet," she said.

I was tempted to ask her to bring me my shirt but didn't because she would certainly have thought the request strange. I would look for the disks later.

In the early afternoon, the door opened again, and a stranger entered.

"Daniel von Arx?" he asked, closing the door behind him. I said I was and looked at him expectantly.

"I got your room number in the lobby."

The stranger put a small box of chocolates on the bedside table. "Something to sweeten the introduction," he said.

He pulled out a press card and held it in front of my nose.

"I'm from *Berner Zeitung.* How're you doing? I was wondering if I could ask you a few questions."

I had to laugh. "Seems I'm suddenly famous. What would you like to know? How can I help?"

The journalist wanted to know exactly what happened and what I, the victim, had experienced. "That's what interests our readers, something more than the bare facts."

I described the scene I had interrupted in detail. He jotted down a few notes and looked up.

"Could you please describe the burglars?"

"I'll do my best. There were three. All of them wore black and had stockings pulled over their heads. I did get the impression that they were foreign."

"Foreign?"

"Yes. Medium build, at least one of them unshaven. Maybe one of them, not the one who shot me, wore a belt with a big, fancy buckle. But that's only an impression. I didn't really get a very good look at them."

"Thanks. You're the only one who saw the burglars. A real coincidence that you came to work so early."

"Yes, just my bad luck," I said, irritated. "But hardly a coincidence. I often go to work early because nobody bothers me then and I can get things done."

We chatted a while about fate, what might have been the motive for the break-in, and about Professor Bucher's work. When the journalist said goodbye, he was obviously satisfied, and his thanks sounded sincere.

I was half-asleep when, thirty minutes later, the door opened again. Once more, the visitor was a stranger. I wished it had been someone I knew, like my brother Michael. It would have been great to see him.

Without hesitation the stranger pulled up a chair, sat down by my bed, and, like the reporter, showed me some sort of identification that I couldn't quite bring into focus.

"Did you know that you can ask for a patient's room number at the reception and then just come up?" he asked, scowling.

"So? What's wrong with that? Who are you anyway?" I asked.

"Police," he said. "I am Police Kommissar Erb. May I ask you some questions?"

"Yes, of course," I said. "The press was already here."

"The press always beats us by a nose," Erb grumbled.

I described my office, the three burglars, the scuffle, and all the other details. I didn't mention the disks. Just why, I couldn't say at the time.

The Kommissar took notes and threw in a question once in a while.

Shortly after Kommissar Erb had gone, Susanne came in. A law student, she was in one of my post-grad seminars, and we had become friends. She had her hair up, wore her jacket open, and looked delightfully saucy. Although I was tired after the exhausting interrogations, I really enjoyed the fact that two women were worried about me. Susanne was a little different every time I saw her. Unlike Marianne, she was full of surprises, and I liked that.

She told me that she had to show her identification at the hospital reception when she asked for my room number. "Strange, don't you think, Danni?"

"Why did you even have to ask for the room number? I'm sure you could have read it in the newspaper," I joked.

"Just to be sure you and Elvis hadn't left the building," she joked back.

I got to thinking. The police must have asked reception to put a new policy in place.

"Looks like the police are protecting me," I said, and I told her about my previous visitors.

Susanne studied me a minute. "Those visitors tired you out, you poor baby! Telling the same story over and over. That would have been too much for me." She kissed me on the forehead. "I'll leave you alone now. But I'll be back." I watched the swing of her hips as she walked out the door, and I sighed.

***

After two hours of sleep, a nurse woke me up. She had slipped in to bring me dinner. I felt strengthened by the nap. The sun was still shining, and through the open window I could hear birds chirping and the distant hum of the city. A clock on the wall opposite my bed indicated 5:30.

"Wow, you sure bring dinner early," I said to the nurse.

"Have to start early. Otherwise we'd never get through," she said.

I laughed. "You sound disciplined."

"This is exactly why our patients recover quickly. Discipline and good food on a regular schedule."

Up to that point, whenever a nurse had come in, I had noticed only the bright green uniform. This time I saw the young woman herself. She had a slim figure and a warm, friendly face under the white cap that hid her hair.

"Under your care a man could recover even without eating," I said, feeling a bit fresh.

"Your mistake." She smiled. "Food is an important part of any treatment. You can't imagine how many patients have to follow a special diet. Why there are . . . . "

A knock at the door interrupted her.

I was annoyed. I wanted to flirt with my amiable caretaker, and precisely at that moment somebody had to come and interrupt us. We both looked at the door, which opened slowly.

***

Gus had parked unobtrusively with a view of the main entrance to the University and the entire side of the building where he and his fellow burglars had had their misadventure. He sat behind the wheel with a bag of candy open on the passenger seat. Bored, he stuck another piece in his mouth. As he sucked on it, he looked across at the gray stone facade of the building. The occasional pedestrians—mostly students—ignored him, and he paid them no attention.

His mobile phone beeped. Holding it to his ear, he listened and said, "No, nothin' new. His ass is still parked at a desk by the window." He hung up, yawned, and continued watching.

Just over an hour later, the window on the third floor closed. The man in the car looked up, but the sun reflecting on the windshield caused a glare, and he could see little. He turned to stare at the main entrance of the building. Bucher appeared after a few minutes. He walked down the stairs and out between parked vehicles to his own car. The watcher already knew which car belonged to Bucher and had placed himself so that he could keep an eye on it. He punched a number into his phone.

"He's gettin' in his car," he told the person on the line. "I'll tail him and report in."

He started the motor, waited until Bucher had driven past him, and followed at a distance.

Michael

It was Michael at the door. He was three years younger than I but stood taller by almost a head. He had a lanky frame and a slight stoop. We'd had a good relationship since birth. Because of the difference in our ages, we hadn't discussed certain things as we grew up. That reticence changed when our parents were killed in an avalanche in the Engadin near St. Moritz. I was in my fourth year at the University, and he was just beginning his studies. The tragedy brought us close, and I became more than just an older brother. Like me, he had attended the Gymnasium in Bern but had then gone off in a completely different direction, preferring to study mathematics and physics.

Michael was smart but undisciplined. Through many serious talks, I tried to help him find a direction for his life.

Perhaps I succeeded to a small degree. We discussed our career choices thoroughly and tried to foresee what the future held for each of us.

I still had an interest in scientific matters, especially those pertaining to physics. I was looking for answers to questions about the nature and origin of the cosmos, Earth, life, and human beings. But I had never wanted to make physics my profession. I considered its theoretical problems only suitable for young scientists. They might have success early in their careers but would burn out later and thus have no opportunities for the type of advancement and personal satisfaction I was looking for.

Michael was aware of my objections to his choice of study. But he was not ambitious in the same way I was. He was passionate about the issues physics addressed and wanted to learn all he could. He simply wasn't all that concerned about having a career.

"You got it pretty good here," he said as he walked into my hospital room. "Bright, private room with a view of the city." He brought two issues of *Scientific American* and laid them on the stand beside my bed. He knew I enjoyed reading articles in English.

The nurse busied herself laying out my meal, wished me "En guete," nodded to Michael, and disappeared.

"Of course, I've got it great here," I said. "I have good health insurance."

"So, how are you? I tried to visit yesterday, but they said you were sleeping and shouldn't be disturbed. This afternoon I had seminars back to back. But I've been reading a lot about you in the newspaper."

"Well, I'm okay, at least under the circumstances. As you undoubtedly read, I got shot." He could hardly miss the irony of my words.

"How on earth could such a thing happen? In this highly civilized and unexciting Switzerland where we live, you got yourself into a shootout? Geez, I never imagined you as a gunslinger."

We both laughed, and relief spread over my brother's face. He went to look out the window. The slanting rays of the sunset made the city glow. He turned back toward me and pulled up a chair just as Kommissar Erb had done earlier.

"You were lucky, Daniel, fortunate in spite of everything," he said. "I suppose your guardian angel was standing by." He smirked. Neither of us put much stock in angels.

We chatted casually about the incident. Once more, I went over the whole affair in detail. Michael told me what he had learned from the newspaper and speculated on the burglars' motive. He also filled me in on everything he knew about Edward Bucher and his work. Bucher was maybe the best theoretical physicist in the world. An amazing thing was that he had not accomplished his seminal work as part of a team but, like Albert Einstein and most of the great physicists, quite alone. If he had discovered something new, it could well be that someone might want to steal his findings before he published them.

"Do you think the Mafia or somebody like that did it?" I asked.

"Hardly," said Michael. "The Mafia always wants to make a quick profit. That's not possible in science. The road to the Nobel Prize is long and arduous."

"So what did Dr. Bucher actually do to win it?"

Michael hesitated. He knew I was sincerely interested, so he began at the beginning and gave me a mini-course in the history of physics. He told me that the rules governing moving objects and the forces that act on those objects have been known for a very long time.

"In fact, it was roughly three centuries ago, when Isaac Newton formulated his laws governing the interaction between mass and movement. Newton's Law of Gravitation states that the gravitational force between two bodies decreases as the distance between them grows and increases as their masses increase. Newton also explained how velocity influences energy."

I knew all of this, but I let Michael talk. His passion for the topic was palpable, and he was just getting started.

"Newton described the movements of the stars and created a physical model for the universe, one that allows us to make predictions about what will happen in the real world of the universe. Specifically, Newton's formula allows us to calculate the trajectory of celestial bodies and to determine where the moon or a star will be in the future and where it's been in the past. However, any model only has validity as long as it withstands the crucial test—whether the predictions are accurate."

Michael explained that the Newtonian model had to be corrected by modern physics. "The model predicted that, because of gravity, celestial bodies would ultimately crash into each other. But this is not the case. We now know the opposite is true. The universe is expanding, not collapsing."

Michael continued in full lecture mode, his voice rising with enthusiasm. "Einstein offered another model at the beginning of the twentieth century. He brought together gravity, time, and the speed of light to formulate his theory of relativity."

Michael glanced at me, "Are you with me so far?" I nodded in the affirmative.

"For observers moving at different speeds, the velocity of an oncoming object will be different. If I am moving slowly or standing still, then the relative speed of an oncoming object will be different from the relative speed if I am moving fast. This is, however, not true for an object moving at the speed of light—and here, dear brother, is the correction to Newton."

His eyes caught mine and I watched as he punctuated his sentences with gestures mimicking objects moving in space.

"In the case of objects moving at light speed, velocity is independent of the situation of the observer and is always the same. As Einstein said, the speed of light is absolute. No matter from what vantage point it is measured and no matter how the observer is moving, the speed of light will always be exactly the same."

Michael smiled triumphantly as if he were explaining his own theory. I grinned back, ignoring the food on my tray.

"Einstein concluded that, because the speed of light is constant, time cannot be constant for all objects. Thus, he devised his famous formula, $E = MC^2$, energy equals mass times the speed of light squared. And so, intervals of time between two events will be different for observers moving at different speeds. The rule is this: time passes more slowly the faster you move. An observer traveling at the speed of light would not experience the passage of time at all."

Michael paused to watch my reaction. Apparently satisfied,

he explained that scientists include the variability of time when calculating travel in outer space. "Because time is running at different speeds on the moon or a satellite, the variability of time becomes a factor in calculating the paths of rockets. If this variability weren't taken into account, and calculations were based on Newtonian physics, errors would occur, and points in space at a future time would not be where they were supposed to be."

He absentmindedly took a carrot from my plate and popped it into his mouth. Wiping his fingers on my napkin, he then turned his attention from the macrocosm to the microcosm. "What do you know about microcosms?" he asked.

"Refresh my memory."

"The behavior of particles smaller than atoms—you know—protons, electrons, and neutrons, is much more difficult to study because measurements on such a tiny scale would not be accurate. If we examine subatomic particles, for example, we have to be aware that light itself consists of particles that will encounter the particles we intend to measure. So light will act on the particles and influence and distort each measurement.

"Some physicists in Copenhagen developed a new theory of the microcosm, called quantum theory. The new model relates to the Heisenberg uncertainty principle. According to the principle, the position and velocity of a particle can't be measured precisely at the same time—thus the 'uncertainty.' The more exactly the position is known, the less exactly the speed can be measured."

He took another carrot, pausing before taking a bite. "The converse is also true. The more accurately velocity is measured, the more uncertain is position. For any particle in motion, the exact position can never be determined, only the probability of where it is located. And because of the uncertainty principle, several positions are possible. This means that each particle, depending on the assumed probability, is here or there, or—now this seems even crazier, Daniel—partly here and partly there. So an event of any sort, like the collision of two particles, may or may not have occurred, and for any event several variants are possible. The uncertainty principle contains an element of chance. An event might run its course randomly and differently, and there is even the probability of parallel events that are temporally different, or several parallel paths for a given particle to follow."

"So a particle can be in two places at once," I said, thinking to make a joke.

"Ha! You got the picture," said Michael. "For example, an object can be in one place with a thirty percent probability, and in another location, at seventy percent. We can only talk about the probability of where the object is located. According to the choices the observer makes, the particle might be located here or there, or anywhere, but with a quantifiable probability. However, here's the problem. Quantum theory contradicts certain parts of the theory of relativity."

"Then one of the theories must be false," I ventured.

"The word 'false' is way too harsh. The situation is sort of like language, which was in practical use before anybody came along with rules and grammar. Physical reality was already there, and of course scientists had to formulate their theories so that they corresponded to reality. Quantum mechanics is just such a theory, but it applies only to the microcosm. It has only limited applicability when gravitational forces come into play. Insofar as it contradicts some of the theory of relativity, quantum theory is incomplete, but not false."

Michael continued in a serious voice, "This is where Bucher's research comes in. He's working to formulate a theory regarding the microcosm that locates each particle in a specific location. He is, in fact, seeking to apply the basic laws of physics within the microcosm in a way consistent with how the laws are applied to objects subject to gravity."

"And this work is significant?" I asked, leaning forward.

"Absolutely. This would be a theory that connects everything—the ultimate unified field theory, what some people call 'the theory of everything.' It's also what Einstein spent the last part of his life trying to formulate."

"Didn't Einstein live for a while in Bern?"

"He sure did. He developed the theory of relativity here while working in the federal patent office on the corner of Speichergasse and Genfergasse. You know, he was also a lecturer right here at the University."

"Interesting. Bern is the home of both the theory of relativity and Bucher's unified field theory."

"Yes."

"A coincidence?"

"I guess so."

"But strange. Now, Michael, who would gain the most from Bucher's theory?"

"You mean, who might have an interest powerful enough to steal and commit murder?"

"Yes."

"Any industry that deals with matter on the microcosmic

scale. Any number of entities might have that level of interest—the nuclear industry, the laser industry, the electronics industry, among others. Anyone in the field of nanotechnology would have a vested interest."

"So, lots of people."

"You bet."

***

Marianne walked through Old Town, which wasn't far from the hospital. She enjoyed strolling through the arcades, looking into windows, aimlessly wandering. But on this occasion, she walked right into her favorite shop, found the blue sweater with the V-neck she had tried on a week before, and bought it. Next she walked into Adriano's, bought an espresso, and carried it to a table in the corner, where she sank into a chair.

She felt confused and a bit tired because of all the excitement over the last few days. She held the little white cup with its black liquid between her fingers but did not drink. She stared into space and thought about Daniel. I hope he'll be okay, she worried. It wasn't like him to put himself in danger.

The coffee smelled wonderful. She took a sip. She was glad he was out of harm's way. Maybe this experience would change him, make him think, and they could grow closer. She stopped herself. No, he wasn't ready for any serious commitment. But then . . . . She had to be patient. She took another sip. Actually, she admired him, so energetic and hardworking, and he had shown such courage. She had never thought of him that way before.

A middle-aged man came up to the table and sat down

across from her. She looked up surprised. He carried nothing to eat or drink. There were plenty of vacant tables. He sensed her annoyance, and said, "Sorry, to bother you . . . ." He pulled a badge from his breast pocket and continued, "I'm Police Kommissar Erb. May I speak with you?"

Marianne frowned. "You want to talk to me? Why?"

Erb put his badge away. "You're Daniel von Arx's girlfriend, right?"

She nodded. "Yes, one of them. He has many friends and several girlfriends."

"Well, I'd like to ask you about him. Let me be direct. Do you think he might be more deeply involved in this matter than he lets on?"

"What makes you say something like that? I don't understand what you mean."

"You should tell me if you know anything."

"What do you think I might know? I really can't add anything. Besides, I can't imagine that Daniel knows more than what he's telling you."

"Are you aware that you might be able to help him if you cooperate with the police?"

Cooperate? Marianne resented the implication. "He's old enough to know what he's doing," she said.

"Sure." Erb leaned back and paused. No one in the cafe seemed to notice them sitting in the corner. "All right then. If you have something you want to tell me, or if you need help, please call me at this number."

Erb took out a card and held it. Marianne took it without

thinking. She still couldn't get over what the policeman had implied. Erb pushed back his chair and stood up. He hesitated, as if he had something else to say.

"How did you find me here?" she asked. She ran a hand through her hair. "Are you watching me?"

"You're not under surveillance. I just happened to see you come in here. Look out for yourself, and don't hesitate to call me if you have something on your mind."

He nodded to her in a way that was almost fatherly and walked away. Marianne watched him leave. Her hands trembled. Creepy. Had he really just happened to see her? She looked down at the rest of her coffee, now cold.

***

I put down my knife and fork. I had no appetite.

"You've barely eaten," said Michael. "You have to get your strength back after all the blood you lost."

"Don't worry," I said. "The doctors have everything worked out. I'm going to live, although apparently without the benefit of carrots."

Shamelessly Michael returned to our earlier discussion. "Hey, you're familiar with the theory that the Earth's atmosphere favored the emergence of life, aren't you?"

"Sure, I've read that."

"It was in that atmosphere where the first living molecules appeared, strictly by chance, maybe because the lines between solid, liquid, and gaseous states of matter were less distinct and matter was subject to frequent electrical stimulation."

"You think? Really?"

"Well, it's a theory."

Michael paused and went back to the incident at the University. "Did you know that Dr. Bucher's work has helped us understand exactly how our planet has evolved?"

That got my attention. "No, tell me. I want to know all about it."

Before Michael could answer, the nurse came in again. She carried a glass of tea and two pills. "Your dessert, Herr von Arx," she said, smiling, and picked up the tray.

"What are these pills anyway?" I asked.

"They're what the doctor prescribed," she said with mischief in her eyes.

"No kidding. But I want to know what they're for."

"The white pill is for pain and the reddish one strengthens your blood."

"Well, thank you, Nurse. Come on. Can't you tell me the names of the drugs?"

"I'll let you know on my next visit." She smiled.

"Are you mad at me?"

"No, what makes you think that?"

"You sound so strict."

She laughed softly. "We have to be strict so that patients like you behave." She picked up the food tray and left.

"You seem to be hitting it off with the nurse," said Michael. "With attention like that maybe I should get myself shot."

I laughed and swallowed the pills with the tea. "Where were we?" I asked.

"Talking about the formation of the Earth and the evolution of life and humans."

Michael resumed his animated discourse. "About fourteen

billion years ago—that's how old the universe is—all energy was compressed into a single point. It exploded, and the universe as we conceptualize it today was born. We call the explosion the Big Bang. In a fraction of a second, matter came into being and began to expand. In other words, the universe expanded from the size of a single atom to an entire galaxy and continues to expand today. From that point on, the physical laws we are familiar with came into play. Studying these laws has enabled us to understand and trace the history and expansion of the universe."

Michael's eyes widened, and their focus moved to a place beyond the room.

"Then, when the universe reached about the size of our solar system, the expanding particles formed the first atomic nuclei. But it was still too hot for the nuclei to transform themselves into elements. This finally occurred after a period of cooling and expansion, which took some 300,000 years, while the universe was still a thousand times smaller than it is today. At this point, atoms started to attract each other and form gas clouds. These clouds later became stars, which in turn came together to form galaxies. Our own solar system is relatively young, about five billion years old. It originated when the universe was about two-thirds of its current size."

"Michael, how do we know all this?" I asked.

"Well, the galaxies are at different distances from the Earth, and their light only arrives here after millions or even billions of years, depending on the distance. Thus, we see how the universe looked when the light was sent. We know what the oldest and youngest galaxies look like and the stages of development in between. So when we look out at the universe, we are looking at various points in time. Light that has traveled the farthest is coming from the oldest celestial bodies. We can tell a lot about the composition and form of any galaxy that emitted the light. Younger formations are closer, so the light we gather from them gives us information about the composition and form of the cosmos at a later point in time. Since galaxies have predictable stages of development, we can place our own galaxy at a particular stage because of its composition and form.

"A star like our sun has a lifespan of about ten billion years. We can estimate its age based on how much internal energy it has. Five billion years have passed since the creation of the sun, so it has reached the halfway point of its lifespan. The Earth is also about five billion years old. It was formed from cosmic dust that coalesced into clouds of particles that became ever denser under the influence of gravity. The clouds came together with other dust clouds and later with fragments of coalesced matter, smaller meteors and planets, eventually forming larger and larger clumps. About four and a half billion years ago, the Earth had gathered enough material to begin to form a core. Although the bombardment of meteorites from space did not stop, the collisions became weaker because there was less unattached material flying around. Matter was being captured by other stars and planets."

"So when did life appear on Earth?" I asked.

"Life forms appeared just a short time after the Earth formed. The first single-celled organisms spread rapidly over the entire planet, and, since they secreted oxygen, they created an atmosphere favorable to later forms of life."

"So these organisms built the environment," I injected.

"Right. That's exactly what happened. We got our atmosphere because an army of primitive organisms produced oxygen—just as some life forms do today. The history of the Earth is filled with examples of how living organisms influence our environment. Over and over again, living beings have created conditions that serve as the basis for their further development."

He paused.

"Well, you know the rest. Through mutation, living things have become more and more complex. It's gone on for millennia and continues today. We contemporary humans constitute just one example."

"All by chance mutation?"

"What do you mean by 'chance'?"

"Hasn't some entity or force helped it along, intervened in evolution and controlled it?"

"No. At least science hasn't found any evidence to suggest control from the outside."

"So there's nothing to suggest that human beings developed as a result of some single act of creation?"

"Of course not. It's clear that humans are the product of a very slow and well-documented series of random mutations, each of which could have been different. Our history on Earth might have taken a completely different direction than it did."

"So, again, randomness. And chance plays a big role in quantum theory as well?"

"Exactly."

"But why has chance led to the evolution of such complex creatures as humans? Is there some law of nature that favors complex life forms?"

Michael shook his head. "Probably not. But there are explanations. First of all, Darwin found that, for a life form to survive, it needs to be stronger or more adaptable than other life forms competing in the same environment. Another explanation comes from statistics. After the first appearance of life, all sorts of mutations occurred. Some mutations are simple in nature, others more complex. If the mutation is of a lower order, then it is likely that the environmental niche of that particular mutated organism has already been filled. Nothing particularly advantageous occurs as a result of the mutation. The Earth is full of such creatures. However, if the mutation has a higher degree of complexity, the creation of something potentially more successful is possible. So, statistically and over time, the evolution of life forms tends to flow in the direction of more complexity."

"So, no creative force?"

"I can't be sure," Michael mused. "Basically, our findings are piecemeal. The universe is monstrously huge. We've only explored a tiny part of it. But listen, there's a particular application of mathematical statistics which gives me pause."

"Go on."

"Based on successful random mutations, I calculated how long it would take for human beings to evolve."

"How long?"

"Well, much longer than the four to five billion years since life appeared on Earth."

"You mean you figured out, based on random mutations, it's not possible for humans to evolve in the time elapsed?"

"That's about it."

"Michael, whatever made you set out to calculate something like that?"

"Don't you see?" he replied. "This is mathematical proof that some ordering principle has helped evolve Earth's inhabitants. This is proof that God exists."

"Oh, you mathematicians. You want to prove everything—even that God exists."

I was tired. I wanted to end the conversation. I asked Michael to get my shirt from the closet. I needed to see if the disks were still there.

Michael got up and brought the shirt. The two disks were still in the pocket where I remembered putting them. I handed them to Michael.

"The burglars dropped these disks. I picked them up off the floor."

"I gather you didn't tell the police."

I nodded. "Would you mind checking out what's on them and let me know once you find out?"

"Sure." He grinned.

"Oh yeah, and could you bring me some clothes from my apartment?"

Reading the Disk

As Michael approached the door of Daniel's building, he had the feeling that someone was watching him. He looked around but saw no one and walked on quickly. My brain is probably playing tricks on me, he thought, and ascribed the uneasy feeling to the excitement of the last couple of days. He fumbled in his pocket for the keys to the door and looked around again. Then he laughed at himself, "I'm behaving almost like a criminal."

He shook off the feeling, entered, and opened the mailbox. Inside were stacks of brochures and junk mail that he glanced through and tossed in the trash bin. A foresightful janitor had set it up next to the mailboxes. He pocketed two letters, opened the foyer door, and climbed the stairs. Eleven steps in one direction, eleven steps in the other to reach the second floor, and another two sets of eleven steps to reach Daniel's apartment door on the third floor.

He let himself in, took a look in each room, picked out the clothes that Daniel had asked for, and watered the plants. A half hour later, he left. Back on the street, he once again felt as if someone was following him. With growing anxiety, he looked around, saw no one, and reprimanded himself for his uncontrolled imagination.

Michael returned home and locked the door. Just after he kicked off his shoes, the doorbell rang. Looking through the peephole, he spied a middle-aged gentleman wearing a gray raincoat and a hat. Michael cracked the door cautiously.

"My name is Erb, Police Kommissar Erb," the man said and showed Michael his badge. Michael opened the door wide and let Erb in. On the one hand, he was relieved that someone trustworthy was standing there; on the other, he wondered why a police officer was paying him a visit.

"To what do I owe the honor?" Michael asked. "Have I done something wrong?"

"No, not at all," Erb answered. "I'm investigating the murder of Herr Roos, Professor Bucher's assistant, and I'd like to ask you some questions.

"Okay. Come in and have a seat."

Erb took a straight-backed chair across a table from what appeared to be Michael's usual spot. "You're a student at the University. You knew the murdered man?"

Michael sat down. "Yes, of course. But I don't know anything about his murder."

"Don't worry. I'm just gathering information."

"So what's this about?"

"Actually, I'd like to ask you about your brother. Have you noticed anything different about him?"

"Of course. He's in the hospital. He's been shot."

"I know. I wasn't asking about his injury. I was just wondering if he seemed unusually distraught or . . . ."

"Of course he's distraught. Wouldn't you be?"

"The police investigators think this crime had nothing to do with Herr Roos. He was there by chance. It had to do with Professor Bucher himself."

"Could be. But I can't help you there either."

Erb shifted his weight. "What I mean is . . . do you think your brother knows something he's not telling us?" Erb waited.

"I have no idea."

"Has he told you anything unusual? Anything about Dr. Bucher or his assistant, for example?"

"No. He was friendly with Roos, but they weren't buddies. Just colleagues."

"I see. Does your brother seem to be under any pressure or acting like he's keeping a secret?"

"I didn't have that impression."

"Might I ask you to let us know if he does say anything or if something strikes you as odd about his behavior?"

"What makes you think he's under pressure or hiding something?"

"We don't think anything yet. I just don't want something to happen to him, something like what happened to Bucher's assistant."

"What's going on? Is my brother in danger?"

"No, I don't think so. We just need to investigate all possibilities. Here's my card. Please call if you notice anything."

"Absolutely. May I ask you something now?"

"Sure."

"Did you have me followed from the hospital to my brother's apartment and then here?"

"Why do you ask?"

"I had the impression I was being followed."

"Not by me and not by the police. You can be quite sure of that. I came directly from another meeting to your apartment."

Michael paused. "Strange."

"Watch out for yourself." Erb shook Michael's hand and turned away, leaving Michael perplexed.

***

After Michael left, I thought about our discussion. The last rays of sunset shown through the window, creating shadows in the room. The mountains outside grew darker and nondescript against the fiery backdrop of sky. Red. Good weather tomorrow.

The word "God" popped into my head. I did not consider myself a religious man, yet I had always believed that some regulatory force, some higher power, must exist. Something must be influencing the phenomena around me. But lately I had discarded even this notion and tended more and more to believe that there was no God. I could find no evidence of God's existence. Why didn't he reveal himself? Why didn't he just show up? Why did he leave so much unfinished? Why would he create something as imperfect as my teeth? I chuckled to myself. My teeth are striking proof that a human being is not a perfect, fully realized, and divine creation. And why was there so much evil in the world? Preachers claimed that God was good. All that evil made the claim hard to believe.

Then I thought about Michael's mathematical "proof" that God—or something like God—did indeed exist.

Michael and I grew up somewhat in the Protestant tradition. Maybe we didn't live quite as puritanically as our ancestors did, but we still adhered to the Calvinist traditions of hard work and modesty. To our way of thinking, every problem could be solved eventually with the human mind, and every process in nature could be explained rationally. Whenever we couldn't find a solution to a problem or we couldn't explain something scientifically, we didn't automatically ascribe the event to the supernatural. Rather, we believed that science simply wasn't there yet. We didn't believe in miracles or in mystical forces. We even questioned philosophy. We tended to think that philosophers were good for holding the empty spaces open with their cogitations until science could fill the spaces up. At some point, we were confident, a scientific explanation would exist for every problem. Superstitions would eventually come to an end and so would religion. The explanations religious people provided about the world were often inaccurate. The case of Galileo Galilei was a classic example. The Church later had to move away from its worldview, despite having defended it with persistent intolerance. Here science filled the gap with real knowledge and superseded faith, as it has for so many other false religious assertions.

Still, my ancestors had been devout Protestants. They found Catholicism contrary to their nature—the pomp of the Church with its colorfully illustrated medieval stories about Heaven and supernatural beings and its vivid conception of Hell. Yet, over the years, the family had lost its devotion, modern science having pushed our faith further and further to the back of our lives. My generation no longer believed much in the constant presence of God as creator and personal guide for each person. For us, God served at most as an ordering principle, one quite far removed from the individual. Our notion of God scarcely resembled the omnipresent and omnipotent God of the Middle Ages, a god who influenced the fate of his people. Direct communication from man to God, as the early Protestants believed, was no longer conceivable and thus led to the kind of atheism we have today. Anyway, an intellectually oriented religion and atheism are not far apart.

Now Michael had claimed that he could mathematically prove the existence of God or at least of an ordering principle. What I found attractive about this claim was that it was based on reason and derived from science. It therefore fit into Michael's and my sensible view of the world. The existence of God was not emotionally asserted—but in a way proven. That was worth thinking about.

I remembered a conversation with Michael that we had had some time ago. He had said, "The evolution of human beings continued long after their first appearance, and they became increasingly more complex over time. Today we know that the ancients did not look the same as we do now. They were physically smaller and had a different brain. That explains scientific progress. And human civilizations have developed in different ways and at different speeds across the world, resulting in great cultural diversity."

"How do you know that?" I had asked back then.

"Research based on intelligence quotients, so-called IQ tests, has shown that different regions of the Earth may have different average levels of intelligence—as measured by the tests, of course. People have evolved differently under different circumstances."

"Besides," Michael continued in that distant conversation, "these tests have shown that a mix of diverse people can lead to far higher intelligence and far better human characteristics than closed gene pools can, provided that the favorable properties are passed on to descendants. That happens whenever ethnic groups interbreed."

In any case, Michael believed that the Church was just plain wrong when it claimed that all human beings were created "complete." Furthermore, humans were still evolving, so only a dynamic concept of humanity could possibly be accurate. Michael had cited the ancient Egyptians as an example. The Egyptian civilization lasted about three millennia, such an enormously long time—with the same social structure: a pharaoh at the top, clear hierarchies, and a static religion. During that long period, virtually no progress was made.

"Would that even be possible today? Three millennia of oppression?" Michael had asked. "I wonder why, when that civilization came to an end, there was finally a breakthrough and progress was made. Could it be that humans had evolved? That they became, as it were, wiser? That a gene mutation led people to redefine themselves?"

Michael had paused, his mind jumping from one era to the next. "In any case, the jump to Greek civilization was enormous. Shortly after their rise, the Greeks were establishing democracy." I remember Michael waving his arm about with a student's zeal. "Take a look at them. The images we have of ancient Egyptians and those of the Greeks. These are not the same people. The Greeks seem intelligent, similar to us. The Egyptians look like they are from an earlier stage on the evolutionary path from ape to homo sapiens."

"That difference you see in their appearance may be due to the drawings themselves," I had thrown back at him.

***

I flipped through one of the *Scientific American* magazines Michael had left me. An article about the human brain caught my attention.

The author wrote that the organ had evolved over millennia in small mutations from its animal origins to become the human brain. Some neurons disappeared, while others appeared. Different parts of the brain were disposed quite randomly, some parts used only slightly in comparison with other parts. The existence of lesser-used structures could be explained only in terms of the brain's long history of evolution. Humans have leftover structures in the brain that are no longer needed today.

In some ways, the brain could be compared to a computer, claimed the author. However, a computer can only work linearly by carrying out a sequence of operations with terrific speed. It calculates every step in sequence and proceeds to a result. Therefore, a computer must be able to process information very quickly, or it is no good. A fast computer at the beginning of the twentieth-first century could make thirty petaFLOPS per second. In contrast, the brain does not work in linear fashion. The nerve cells communicate simultaneously through multiple paths. In some respects, the brain is slower than a computer because a single cell can only process a few hundred operations per second. In other respects, it is faster because it performs multiple calculations or operations simultaneously. People can make a decision after weighing various factors, all of which are simultaneously processed. The brain is like an advanced parallel computer, one just theorized at the time of the article.

Of course, the author's explanation at that time held true for only a short while. What we used to call computers has evolved into fully functioning beings with artificial intelligence.

I continued to read. Consciousness, I learned—the phenomenon that distinguishes humans from animals—derives from a special short-term memory function, the anatomical location of which is known. Those particular neurons allow us to be aware of the events around us and know who we are.

And the soul?

I got an answer in the next section.

Science has no evidence of a soul, at least in the sense that scientists cannot distinguish between body and soul. There is no scientific reason to believe that, when the body dies, a soul lives on, whether in some heaven or in another human or animal body. The "soul" as well as human emotions and perceptions are based on a specific function of the nerve cells in the brain. The "soul" dies just as soon as the neurons cease their activities, that is, when they die.

I sighed and eased myself away from that thought. Despite

Michael's materialistic attitude, which was based purely on science, he had spoken of God. Did statistical probability really provide scientific proof of God's existence?

On that thought, I closed my eyes and quickly fell asleep.

***

The receptionist seated behind glass near the main entrance of the Universitätsspital was busy inputting data for new patients admitted that day. She also kept an eye on a seating area. It was her responsibility to watch over the people there and provide assistance if someone had any difficulty. She was near the end of her shift. The door opened, and Gus approached the counter. He wore black jeans and a dark jacket.

"Good evening, ma'am," he said in English, smiling at her. "I was wondering what room Daniel von Arx is in. Be much obliged."

She understood the gist of his request. The hospital had about nine hundred beds, and the name meant nothing to her. She turned to the computer and typed in the name. An alert popped up on the screen. She could give out no room number without proper identification and administrative approval.

She looked up at Gus and asked, "Please you show me your Ausweis? Umm. Identification?"

"How strange. Got to?"

"Not always," she answered.

"Why you think I got to now?"

"Who knows? Maybe just for this patient. Of course, you maybe know better why than I do. You know him."

She smiled.

"Oh yeah, I know 'im good. We're friends. But I don't understand the requirement."

"Sorry. I mean to you no inconvenience."

"I don't have no identification with me. Can't you make an exception? Bitte," said Gus.

"I am not authorized."

The man scowled. "I just wanna go up for a couple minutes. Come on. Help a guy out."

"I cannot. We have instructions. But I ask my supervisor." She picked up the phone and began to punch in a number.

"Whoa, that's okay." Gus stepped back. "I'll come back tomorrow with my passport." He thanked the receptionist, turned around, and hurried back out the door.

The receptionist watched him leave, shaking her head but proud of her language proficiency.

The appearance of the name Daniel von Arx on the receptionist's computer screen alerted a plain-clothes police officer working for Kommissar Erb. Nursing a cup of cold coffee, he sat in a canteen area behind the receptionist. He stared at his laptop, which was linked to the receptionist's computer, peered beyond her, and spotted Gus. The officer closed the laptop, stood, and strode through the lounge. He opened the main door and scanned the access road to the hospital, the street running in front of the building, and then the line of parked cars. Not seeing anyone, he headed back inside. There was an unguarded side entrance to the hospital around the corner.

I've got to get to von Arx's room before the guy in black does, he thought. He hurried to the elevator and pressed the button. An eternity seemed to pass before it arrived, and when it did, two medics emerged, pushing a stretcher. He shoved his way past them, punched the button for Daniel's floor, and rode the elevator up. As the doors opened, his eyes swept the corridor. He spotted Gus talking to a nurse. She pointed to Daniel's room. Before Gus could enter, the policeman caught up with him.

"Stop!" he cried. "Police. Step back to the wall, and put your hands where I can see them!"

Instead of following the order, Gus ducked, charged the policeman, and bowled him over with a powerful shoulder to the chest. He then turned and sprinted in the opposite direction. The officer lay on the floor, stunned, losing precious time as he regained his breath. "I'll never catch him on the stairs," he muttered to himself. He walked painfully to a window, looked out, and after a moment saw Gus running to a car. The officer called Kommissar Erb and told him what happened. Erb told him to head straight to the hospital administration offices.

***

Out of a deep sleep, I was suddenly awakened. Night had fallen. Two nurses had entered my room, making no effort to be quiet. They began packing my belongings. They laid them all out on the foot of my bed, acting as if I weren't even there. Neither one even looked at me. They jerked out the electric lines running from the wall to the bed, released the brakes holding its wheels, and pushed me out the door.

"Hey! What's going on?" I finally managed. "What're you doing? Where are we going?"

"We have to move you to another room," said one of them.

"Why? Can't it wait 'til tomorrow?" I said, my voice rising. "You can't just storm in here and haul me off."

"Sorry about that," the nurse said. "but have to. Orders."

"Someone tried to get into your room without authorization," the other nurse added. He was about to open your door when a police officer stopped him."

I was speechless. But then I said, "Oh," as it hit me that I really was under police protection.

The next four days passed without incident. I spent most of the time reading. Often I caught myself letting my thoughts just wander. I looked out the window a lot. My recovery continued on schedule, and the wound healed without the slightest complication.

***

In his one-room apartment, Michael sat down at his computer. The first menu appeared. He inserted one of the disks into the drive and attempted to transfer the contents to memory. The screen displayed an error message. He patiently took the disk from the drive and reinserted it. Again "Error" appeared. He hesitated and then tried two other drives. Each time "Error" appeared.

Strange, he thought. He slid one of the disks behind some books on his desk and put the other in his pocket. He left his room and walked to the scooter rack in front of the house, mounted his motorcycle, and rode toward the city. The largest computer discount store was only a few kilometers from the

Köniz exit to Bern. He rode his bike to the store and parked in front of the entrance. Once past the large glass doors, he found a salesperson and showed him the disk.

"Do you know what brand it is?" asked Michael.

The salesperson shook his head and said, "Beats me. I've never seen a disk like that."

"Is it unusual?"

"I don't know. Anyway, I don't know the brand. Here, let me see."

The salesperson looked more closely, turning the disk over in his hand. The letters PK were printed on one side, followed by "double-sided, ultra-high density." Inscribed on the protective sleeve were the words "In remembrance, J. Newton." The salesperson carried the disk to a sales counter. On the store computer, he searched for the letters PK and waited. There was no disk manufacturer by that name. He then took out a large catalog and searched through it. Again, he found nothing.

"I'm afraid I can't help you," he said.

"What's to be done?" Michael asked, more to himself than to the clerk. "Any suggestions?"

"Hard to say. I guess it's from some small Asian manufacturer that hasn't made it into our market."

"Do you think there's a chance to read the disk or copy it onto something readable?"

"We do mainly hardware here. Don't know much about software."

"Who would?"

"I'm not really sure. But maybe you could try a company called SoftBau. I hear they have all sorts of exotic equipment and experience with difficult problems."

Michael asked for the address, thanked the salesperson, and left.

SoftBau turned out to be housed in an old warehouse in a nearly deserted area close to the freight station. No place for a reputable service company, Michael thought, as he rang the bell. The door opened, and an unshaven young man stood before him. He wore a shirt that looked like it had been slept in.

"What d'ya need?" he asked.

Michael briefly explained the problem. The young man nodded and invited him in. He led Michael to a room with a concrete floor and flickering florescent lights. Dozens of computing devices and strange pieces of apparatus were strewn pell-mell on benches and tables.

"My name is Michael von Arx," he said. "I could use your help."

"I'm Heinz," replied the other. "What can I do for you?"

Michael explained the problem and told Heinz he studied mathematics and physics at the University. Heinz's face lit up. Like a kid with a new toy, he took the disk Michael handed him.

Heinz and his partner studied computer science and had opened SoftBau six months earlier. They specialized in debugging applications written by amateur programmers and smaller software companies. Sometimes they solved difficult problems by re-conceiving problematic applications. The two students loved to tackle the unusual, using their expertise and unorthodox approaches. They worked—or rather improvised—with great dedication and enthusiasm. They earned little, just enough to finance their studies.

Not a single drive in any of the computers could read the disk. Heinz eventually put it on the turntable of an old record player. With a laser beam, he scrutinized and scanned the surface of the disk. Then, using various switches, he changed the rotational speed of the turntable and varied the distance between the laser and the disk surface. He adjusted the laser's intensity and beam width. His eyes continually returned to the monitor connected to the laser. Ten minutes later, he nodded his head and confirmed that the disk did indeed contain information.

He watched the screen, eyes carefully scanning each new section of data that appeared. "Codes. I'm seeing code strings like you would find on an optical disk."

"You mean images?"

"Yes. Well, sort of. Some kind of optical information is stored on this thing. I'm gonna try to read the strings at slow speed. If I can do that, maybe I can write an application to output the data to another site. If that works, we can probably pull out associated color and light intensity. But all that's gonna take some time. You want me to try?"

"Is it expensive?" Michael asked.

"Depends on how quickly I can extract and arrange the data strings and then put together a program to translate them."

"Hang on a minute." Michael looked at the display. He turned on a PC that was sitting on the floor next to him, waited for it to come to life, and entered a series of commands. A mathematical formula had crossed his mind. Maybe he could use it. Heinz leaned forward with a big grin on his face. He saw what Michael was doing, grabbed a cable, and connected the two computers.

Four hours later—it was dark outside—Heinz and Michael were still working to decipher the disk. They had long since realized that they had run the turntable much too fast and that the information was far more compact than on any disk they had ever seen. This meant that they had to play everything in extremely slow speed. First, they had tried to load the data strings onto other disks. Then Heinz came up with the idea of using a digital audio-video recorder with editing and dubbing capacity. It was a sophisticated machine used to produce video and sound for commercial broadcast. He connected it and began dubbing. An advantage of the machine was that they could continuously modulate its speed.

At 11:00 p.m., the two decided to call it a night. Michael stretched and yawned. He thanked Heinz for his help, and they agreed to continue their work the next day. Michael pocketed the disk and drove home. Neither had brought up the cost of Heinz's time.

At 4:00 p.m. the next day, Michael went back to SoftBau, this time with the two disks. He and Heinz quickly reconstructed the set-up they had used the evening before. Heinz moved the impromptu drive to a table in the middle of the room, connected it to his computer, and plugged in the digital editor into the computer. At first they played yesterday's recordings from the editing device. On the screen, a hazy and distorted picture appeared.

"Hey! It really is a movie after all," Heinz said. "But a recording that's so compressed is almost unbelievable."

"Yeah, it's a movie," Daniel said. "Let's see if we can make sense of what we have."

They continued to work doggedly and enthusiastically.

After another three hours, they had progressed to the point where they were producing a reasonably good picture from the editing machine. After more experiments and adjustments, Heinz was able to transfer the content of both disks, in readable protocol, to a standard video tape. A movie flowed onto the screen.

***

"Fools! Blithering idiots! Dumbass rubes! Y'all don't have the sense God gave a cognitively challenged cow!" said the voice on the phone.

Stan and Leroy sat at the ugly table, and Gus stood nearby holding the phone to his ear. His face froze. "Now the police know who you are. The guy you shot but didn't kill gave them your description. Not to mention that brawl with a cop in the hospital. He most certainly got a good look at you! Now, listen to me, and listen carefully! I want you to stop everything. Don't leave the apartment, at least until tomorrow morning. It's way too risky."

Gus listened, a blank expression on his face but with a growing queasiness in his belly.

"Got it? Then, tomorrow, I want you to get up really early and go to the train station. Take the first train to Paris. Buy your tickets on the train, not at the station. Assuming you idiots make it to Paris, call me so I can give you further instructions." Sci was not aware that taking the TGV to Paris would require a reservation—one of several miscalculations.

The line went dead.

***

A couple days later, the hospital released me. I was still a little weak and needed a few more days to recover, but I didn't want to waste any time. So, instead of taking the days off and going to the mountains as the doctor recommended, I went straight home, fully intending to resume my work at the University. I also wanted to find out what was behind the break-in at Bucher's office. All that time for reflection and speculation in the hospital left me eager to uncover the truth. I had been shot. I had a right to know why.

Without delay, I went over to Michael's. He told me what he'd been doing with Heinz. The disks were not the least bit ordinary but apparently had an ultra-modern design quite unknown even to Heinz. They contained information in a highly compressed format. Not without pride, Michael described how he had succeeded, with the help of Heinz, in deciphering the disks. He told me about the reader they had cobbled together from an old turntable and a digital audio-video editing device.

"You want to see what we found?" Michael asked.

"Do I ever! Have you already looked at it?"

"Of course. Content on the first disk lasts twenty minutes, the second, forty minutes."

"What are they about?"

"They seem to be some sort of documentaries that show staged scenes from different periods in history. However, the filming is amateurish, in fact, downright miserable. The scenes definitely weren't recorded by a professional."

"Any clue why they were stolen?" I asked.

"You mean, are they hiding something so valuable or earth-shattering that someone would steal and commit murder to have it?"

"That's the question, Michael."

"If there's anything, I don't see it. I can't imagine the two movies being valuable to anybody. Nothing worth industrial espionage, much less violent crime. But, you know, I did notice something strange. Although the filming itself is amateurish, I mean really bad camera work, the actors have wonderfully authentic costumes and expertly applied makeup. And the set is perfect. The whole episode is filmed as if some spectator had made a secret recording."

"Why would such a thing be recorded on a disk, especially one so hard to read?"

"You've got me there. These disks have enormous capacity. I've never seen anything like them before. Heinz either."

"So the disks aren't full?"

"No, a long way from it. They still have plenty of space."

"And except for the documentaries, they're empty?"

"Yes, as far as we could tell," said Michael. "We played them a while and didn't find anything else."

"Okay, enough talk. Let me look at them," I said. "This is all so hard to believe."

Michael turned on a small combined unit consisting of video playback and a television, practically an antique, and put the tape into the slot. The screen flickered. Then a fairly good picture appeared. It lacked high contrast but was easy to make out.

"At first we thought there was no sound to go with the

image," Michael said. "Only after poking around for a long time did we identify the audio codes among the different data strings."

"See," I said, "persistence pays off."

"It sure did in this case. Only we didn't manage to make the voices sound natural when we amplified. They sound hollow and metallic."

"Never mind. We just want to understand what they're saying."

"By the way, there's something else that doesn't add up. On the first disk there are no recordings of the actors' voices. All you can hear is voice-over commentary."

"How about the second disk?"

"It's got both commentary and some live audio."

"So the unknown film maker must have picked up some skills."

We settled in and got ready to watch the film.

Alco Sci

After the conference in Bern, Alco Sci caught the next train to the Zürich airport, asked how he could get home quickest, and bought a ticket for the Cincinnati-Northern Kentucky International Airport with a change at JFK. Landing in Cincinnati, he took a cab to his office in the Petersburg complex of the Gospel Church of True Christians.

The complex had a large meeting hall called the Cathedral. It looked more like a luxurious theater than a house of worship, however. In the front, there was a semi-circular stage. Curved rows of comfortable chairs filled the rest of the room, which could easily hold over a thousand True Christians. Next to the Cathedral, on the ground floor, was an administrative center connected to several retail outlets selling religious objects. The workshops where artisans created those objects were located just behind the outlets. The complex also housed radio and television studios. Alco Sci strode into his office on the top floor and slammed the door.

"Those idiots!" he muttered, still fuming over the burglars' misadventure back in Switzerland. He certainly hoped they'd made it to Paris and would soon be on their way home. At any rate, he would have to tackle the matter differently.

He sat down to go through the mail and documents on his desk. In the stack of letters, two caught his eye. Both concerned members wishing to discontinue their affiliation with the Church. He pulled them from the stack. The first case of apostasy concerned a certain Brent Scott who wanted to leave the Church with his wife and two children because, as he claimed, he lacked the religious conviction to continue participating. Sci knew that a desire to leave was rarely due to lack of faith but rather lack of willingness to contribute the ten percent tithe on income required by the Church. Scott would save a bundle by leaving the Church. Sci's administrative assistant had attached to the letter a confidential file on Brent Scott. It contained information regarding Scott's income and the amount he had tithed to the Church over the past five years. The file also contained a notation: "Having an extramarital relationship with Linda Ernst." Her address was included. A second notation read, "Received a one-time compensatory reimbursement ($33,200) from the Abost Company headquartered in the Cayman Islands (not declared)."

The Church collected data on all its members. The information was useful in cases like this. The files on some members contained information so explosive that the members would do anything to keep it hidden. Only Sci and his assistant, who maintained the files, had access to them. Sci studied the document carefully. In the "Action" section appeared the handwritten notation: "Anonymous letter sent" and then "C had success with the Abost compensation."

Satisfied, Sci sat back in his swivel chair. So someone wanted out of the Church, and as usual the apostate had received an anonymous letter. In this case, the sender mentioned the compensation from Abost, which had not been declared to the Internal Revenue Service and of course would not be reported because both Scott and the writer were members of the Gospel Church of True Christians. Sci read the details.

C, who, like the three idiots in Switzerland, was a member of the internal enforcers, had later accosted Brent Scott on a dark street corner. C wore the standard black stocking over his head. It prevented recognition and instilled fear. He warned that if Scott left the Church, the details of his unreported income would be leaked to the IRS and Scott would no longer be protected by the Church. Such tactics usually worked and seemed to have done so here. Scott had immediately revoked his declaration of separation and was once again an honorable member of the Church. The file also noted that the extramarital affair had not been brought up. It could be used later if Scott ever needed to be reeled in again.

The other letter declaring a desire to leave the Church was signed by one A. E. Adams. Again, a copy of Adams's file was attached although it contained nothing compromising. Apparently, Adams had always behaved impeccably. Under "Action" appeared the note, "Anonymous letter sent." The letter presumably came from a church member who expressed concern that some harm might befall Adams if he left the protection of the Gospel Church of True Christians. The anonymous letter was always supplemented with quotations from the Bible and religious exhortations. The file also contained a question, "Pass on to C?" Sci wrote "Yes" next to the question and put it in his outbox. He would not have to concern himself over this fellow if C succeeded.

Without pausing, Sci took a document from the pile, "Membership growth this month: 123." He leaned back in his chair, thinking. The number was low. A few months ago, someone had told him about this Professor Bucher and how he and his colleagues were undermining religion in Europe. In order to get a better picture of the situation, Sci had gone to Bern to that damned conference. His worst fears had been confirmed. People like these men had been active on Earth for centuries—long before Sci's Church had been founded. And they grew stronger every day. In Europe, the importance of religion had decreased significantly, and only a few people even bothered to attend church. Belief in the theory of evolution was so prevalent in the old world that hardly anyone took seriously the story of creation as decreed by the Bible. Even the Pope, considered a real authority on faith, had implied, using tortuous rhetoric, that evolution was compatible with religious doctrine. Now books written by these Europeans who denied outright the existence of God were being published in the U.S.

Sci had to do something. He wanted to know where Bucher and his tribe came from, how they were educated, and especially what motivated them. What kind of people believed as they did? Sci did not see Bucher as a scientist. For him, he was simply someone who undermined the religiosity of people and made assertions that shook the foundation of every church. Bucher had to be stopped. The very existence of Sci's Church depended on the credibility and authority of its religious doctrine. Under no circumstances could these heretical doctrines be permitted to spread in the new world as they had in Europe. He had to rip the evil out at its root, starting with Bucher.

***

The Gospel Church of True Christians, known also by the initials GCTC, had been founded by Rod Hammersmith in the 1930s during one of America's "Re-Awakenings." Near the end of the century, it had about 70,000 members. The GCTC had spread principally through the Southern and Midwestern states but also had a sizeable concentration in Arizona. Members called themselves "True Christians" or simply "Believers." Hammersmith had written a book entitled *Foundations of a New Faith*, which served as the basis for the Church's beliefs and rituals. Each member received a copy and underwent weekly religious instruction via television satellite broadcast or in classes at the Cathedral. For Believers, the book held the same importance as the Bible, if not more.

The preachers of the GCTC declared over and over that theirs was a Christian church—truly Christian. But they differed from other Christian churches on various issues of faith. One such distinction concerned the status of Mary's mother. She was not the grandmother of Jesus, because Jesus, the Son of God, could not have human ancestors. Nonetheless, she belonged to the family in which Jesus grew up and was particularly revered. The True Christians stressed the importance of family, and of course grandparents provided the foundation. All family members had to treat grandparents with particular respect. This requirement was similar to the practice of some groups of Native Americans, who gave great importance to the council of elders. In fact, elders made all important decisions. So it was in the GCTC. Elders were treated with deference, and the importance of grandparents could not be overemphasized. Preachers often picked out those passages from the Bible that spoke of grandparents, and Mary's mother was included in this veneration. The contradiction, that she was not a progenitor of Jesus, seemed to bother no one.

Another difference between the Church and other Christian communities was the notion of Heaven. Nowhere in Christendom was the concept very clear. The Bible did not consistently describe how Heaven was created; what Paradise really looked like; and where the angels, archangels, and God lived. So, often, religious communities ran into trouble by promising their followers a special paradise if the adherents behaved according to the dictates of church leaders.

The True Christians believed in a Heaven with seven levels, which Hammersmith described in his book. Ascending from level to level, a Believer might come closer to God and inhabit an ever more beautiful and privileged place in Paradise. Gaining new levels required hard work, but the right to a higher level could be assured in advance through special actions undertaken on Earth. Hammersmith was not specific about the special actions, but it was understood that they pertained to spreading the true faith, that is, missionary work. A Believer could reserve a higher place in Heaven by recruiting new members or by providing the Church with a means to gain a foothold in new geographic locations. Almost any deed that increased the renown of the Church would be effective so long as it resulted in increased membership.

In his time, Hammersmith was the only person who had reached the seventh stage, the level closest to God. His two current successors would inhabit the seventh level when the time came. Only those who resided at this top level had the power to acknowledge and authenticate the special actions that other Believers undertook on Earth in order to assure themselves a higher level in Heaven.

Despite an emphasis on the family as an institution, a family unit as such could not achieve a given level of Paradise. Only individuals could rise from one level to the next. Thus, there was always the risk that family members would not see each other in Heaven. Such separation throughout eternity would be terrible. Thus everyone worked hard to make sure that no family member would fail to be transported upward. By these means, Hammersmith and his two successors hoped to guarantee that good deeds would flourish.

Each elevation in the Paradise-to-come was celebrated with a Mass. Celebrations for an ascent to one of the first three levels could take place in a local church. Ascent to the fourth or a higher level had to take place in the main house of worship, the Cathedral in Petersburg, where a particularly elaborate ceremony took place.

Finally, the GCTC differed from other Christian churches with regard to certain rituals. For example, becoming a member could only occur through baptism by water brought to Kentucky from the Jordan River. Also, before each sermon, the faithful had to recite a kind of liturgy, during which they stood up, then dropped to their knees, then sat, then stood up again—repeating the exercise for seven cycles. This ritual was sometimes difficult for older people, but the preachers insisted that they also comply. It was God's command. The exercise would strengthen their health and prolong their vitality within the family.

The True Christians believed, as did most Christian denominations in the United States, in the biblical account of creation. They believed it a sin to say that humans evolved from a lower life form through a series of mutations that took place over several hundred thousand years.

***

Hammersmith had been a talented preacher. He could easily cast a spell over his audience—even evoking a kind of delirium. He also knew how to do business and managed to build a significant economic empire. Each Believer had to tithe to the Church. With this money, Hammersmith built the Cathedral and all the adjacent rooms, much like those found in an administrative center. As the number of members increased, he built other meeting places. He founded companies that manufactured religious objects like statues and framed portraits of Mary and Mary's mother. He set up his own publishing company, its only product the book he wrote. He made all these goods available to the public through small retail outlets, which the Church also owned. Eventually, an entire industry developed to produce and sell all manner of religious objects, products vital for Believers and indispensable in exercising their faith. As the financial resources of the Church grew and became increasingly important to Hammersmith, he began to engage in secret transactions that had nothing to do with the Church. He speculated in the stock market, bought a company in the automotive supply industry, purchased a drilling company, and even acquired and managed real estate.

Back in the 1940s, Hammersmith founded his own radio station so that he could spread his word and stay in constant touch with his extended congregation. His successors added a television station that included studios using the latest technology. With various TV shows that supplemented the sermons, the Church's programming achieved high ratings across the nation. Politicians dared not say anything negative about the stations or the content they broadcast for fear of offending the voting public and risking re-election.

When Hammersmith died, Alco Sci, a young scientist turned entrepreneur, had been the founder's right-hand man. He ran the commercial side of the church and did not hesitate to step in and appropriate the entire business enterprise for himself. He reorganized it professionally as a corporate group. He founded a holding company, moved all financial investments of the Church to it, and made himself president. In legal terms, the Church itself became an entity without monetary value.

Since Sci was a poor preacher—his speeches were dry, colorless, and uninspiring—he teamed up with an accomplished orator. Mel Court had been preaching a good deal in local meeting halls and had given a few sermons at the Cathedral. Eloquent and popular, he could preach without notes and keep the crowd under his spell for hours. This made him Hammersmith's logical spiritual successor. However, Court knew nothing about business. So Alco Sci dealt with the money and wielded the power; Court delivered the sermons. Sci kept close control over everything, even where and when Court would preach and how often he could appear on his own television show.

Yet the Believers hardly knew the actual Alco Sci. He remained in the shadows, and only vague rumors circulated about him. The more rumors, the better, thought Sci. In fact, he purposefully encouraged them, ordering his troops to plant stories about him surreptitiously. This resulted in the faithful now claiming, albeit furtively, that a man like Alco Sci was unique on Earth. He had intimate contact with God. Others were convinced that Sci could not die and often journeyed up to Heaven to visit God. One day he would simply remain there. Still others concluded that Sci had supernatural powers. He could read minds even over long distances and influence the thoughts of others. As chief minister, however, Mel Court was quite visible. He alone presided over the ceremonies in the Cathedral to celebrate ascensions to celestial levels four through six. Sci, of course, decided who would rise. To be sure, both Sci and Court would attain the seventh level of Heaven.

Although Sci did not strictly control what Court told Believers, especially during services, he did control his remuneration. Court received a wage only somewhat above the average of ordinary people, a wage that allowed for no luxuries. On the other hand, Sci allotted himself a mansion on a nearby hill, all paid for by Believers supporting the Church.

Sci had conceived the idea of systematically glorifying the late Rod Hammersmith by granting him sainthood, thus making the founder someone to whom the faithful could relate. It would set the GCTC apart from other Christian churches and give it a special spiritual dimension. Sci had an elaborate ceremonial tomb for Hammersmith constructed in the Cathedral, albeit without the bones of the deceased, which remained where they had originally been buried. Of course he told nothing of this to the public. But he did order Court to mention during services not only God the Father, God the Son, and the Holy Spirit, but also Rod Hammersmith and, of course, the mother of Mary. He noted with satisfaction how the faithful came in droves to crowd around Hammersmith's false grave, standing in awe before its splendor, showing it to their children, and praying before it.

A large picture of Hammersmith hung in each local congregation. Pictures and figurines of Hammersmith were produced and sold. They found their places in the homes of the faithful. All were embellished with the Christian cross, although Sci would have much preferred a special symbol, one associated only with his GCTC. That made more business sense. He had seen many powerful symbols, like the eye on the temples of the Cao Dai, the Star of David of the Jews or the star affixed to Chrysler automobiles, the swastika, and the stylized fish of the early Christians. He would have liked to provide his followers with a new icon to distinguish them and the Church from other Christians. But Hammersmith had retained the cross, and any change would prove difficult.

Still one idea remained that he had not yet implemented—staging a resurrection of Rod Hammersmith. The plan was ready. One evening during services, the preacher would look up toward the sky through the Cathedral's retractable ceiling and say nothing. After a moment, he would suddenly point upward with an outstretched arm and cry, "There he goes. I have seen him. He is risen!" Sci was convinced that most Believers would turn their gaze upward to look for Rod Hammersmith. Some would later claim to have seen him. While all eyes were directed upward, the door to the ceremonial tomb would quietly open. The mechanism was already in place. All the preacher had to do after proclaiming the resurrection would be to hit a switch. Then everyone could see the miracle of the open tomb. The body would not be there.

But the spectacle called for a preacher to play the starring role. Court simply could not pull it off. A preacher usually had to believe what he preached, and Court did. It was the rare person who could convince others of something he himself did not believe. Unfortunately, Court was too sincere.

Alco Sci was not a believer. He knew, however, that the primitive yearning for spirituality and religiosity felt by many people formed the foundation for success in any church. He therefore encouraged people to form small groups to pray and enact rituals that resembled the early medieval mysteries. In fact, he had copied these traditions as closely as he could. He orchestrated celebrations to further satisfy this yearning, sponsoring great spiritual revivals where people sang religious songs and moved rhythmically to the music, creating a trance-like state among the Believers.

Sci also made sure to satisfy the intellectual needs of Believers by having his preachers underscore the purity of their true faith. By "purity of the true faith," he meant the doctrine that distinguished the Gospel Church of True Christians from other churches, the doctrine delineated in Hammersmith's *Foundations of a New Faith*. Only when his True Christians separated themselves from other churches, accepted their theological differences, and professed the differences to others, could they expect special treatment in Paradise. Sci regularly had his preachers stage "Disputations," as they were called, which were broadcast publicly on the Church's television station. Hammersmith's concept of faith was the controlling vision of Sci's enterprise. The religious disputations about this vision within the Church and with representatives of other faiths emphasized and clarified their common values. They thus strengthened the Believers' sense of solidarity and served Sci's business interests.

These were the ways Alco Sci struggled to grow his church, thus his business, and ultimately his power base.

As a church leader, however, Alco Sci was not satisfied with holding on to his people through the mechanism of a common faith. Sometimes special measures were needed. So he had trained a number of people to carry them out. He called them the "Troops for the True Faith," the TTF, a church police that he commanded himself. Typically, members of the TTF wore discreet dark clothing with neckties—as was appropriate for people of the Church. But they also had specially fitted black uniforms for their operations. One special unit kept order during official Church occasions. This unit wore distinctive uniforms during official functions and was known to all. Other units of the TTF were secret.

Like many churches of revealed religions, that is, religions that sprang from a Messiah or similar guru, the GCTC divided people into three categories—namely, that of Believers who had joined the Church, potential Believers who might be converted, and people who would never join because they already belonged to another religious denomination. For each of these three categories of people, the TTF had a specific set of orders. The first group, the Believers, had to be kept in line. The Troops' task was to keep them from leaving the Church so as to maintain the member base. The archive of confidential files was useful to accomplish this task. At one time Sci had thought about introducing confession, as in the Catholic Church, in order to learn and record any wayward behavior of Church members more efficiently, but he ultimately dropped the idea. Instead, Sci authorized other dissuasive actions. Almost no method was too extreme to prevent members from leaving the Church.

The second category, those people who might convert to the Church, rarely received the TTF's attention. Here is where the imperative for members to recruit came into play. Every Believer had to proselytize, painting the Church in its best light in order to bring in as many new members as possible. Winning new Believers was the best way to rise to a higher level in Paradise, so members were motivated to do their duty.

Finally, the third category of people, those who would never become Believers because they already belonged to a religious denomination competing with the GCTC—this group had to be opposed by force to curb its influence. Unfortunately for Sci, options for opposition were extremely limited, given United States law. Sci would have gladly started a holy war if he thought he could get away with it. However, he limited himself to organized propaganda campaigns against "wrong thinkers."

Alco Sci had studied the structure of successful Western churches since the times of antiquity. They not only had priests to serve the faithful and hold them together but also some variation of the Inquisition, an authoritative group empowered to enforce orthodoxy. In addition, they had missionaries charged with the task of spreading the faith. In building his Church, he copied such earlier structures. There was no reason to invent something new when he could borrow from tried and true organizational schemes from the past.

The GCTC maintained a close relationship with government authorities. Locally, many Believers had bureaucratic or official status, and some Believers had achieved offices at the national level. The police worked hard to foster good relationships with them, and each side supplied information to the other with the rationale of helping to maintain public order. A police crackdown on the Church was unthinkable. In the U.S., freedom of religion was unassailable, enshrined in the First and Fourteenth Amendments of the Constitution, and any police action against a church would be seen as an attack on this fundamental right. The internal structure of a church had to be exclusively determined by that church, and no governmental agency could control it. Nor, in practical terms, was the government very likely to investigate abuses.

The situation was different in Europe, where religious wars have taken place into modern times. Much blood had been spilled because of various churches' desire to spread their "true faith." Therefore, in most of Europe, strict laws for the conduct of religious communities were passed in order to preserve religious peace. Both officially sanctioned and independent churches were subject to these rules and could be forced to comply.

The Gospel Church of True Christians from Petersburg had had a painful experience in Germany. One of the Believers had emigrated there and attempted to set up a mission cell. German State Security learned of the cell's illegal recruitment methods and began monitoring it. Of course this action had offended those at Church headquarters in Petersburg. At the Church's insistence, the U.S. State Department had been asked to intervene with Germany and demand that it uphold the Church's right to freedom of religion. On another occasion, when a Believer from the United States was sentenced by a Swiss court for proselytizing unscrupulously and thereby interfering with religious peace, the U.S. government had felt compelled to criticize the lack of religious freedom in Switzerland.

***

Alco Sci still sat at his desk. He had reviewed all of his mail, made notes on some documents, written instructions on others, and put them in his outbox to be distributed to his employees, who now would have to deal with the issues themselves. It was getting dark outside, and the first street lights came on. He turned on his desk lamp. A single cone of light illuminated the papers, throwing the rest of the room into further darkness.

He considered reviewing the videos from the last few sermons in order to discuss them with Mel Court. Court needed a certain sort of guidance. Generally Sci checked every sermon via video when he could not attend in person. His thoughts then slid over to the conversation he had had with that man Bucher. He went through it again, trying to remember each word. His conclusions disturbed him and brought up a memory from the past.

Years ago, an elderly man had visited Sci to tell him

about a possibility that now dominated Sci's thoughts. Sci remembered only vaguely what the old man looked like. He'd dressed poorly, worn glasses with enormously thick lenses, and covered his scraggly gray hair with a black stocking cap—something a bum might wear. The man's name had slipped Sci's mind. He had seen him only briefly, and the visitor had not left an address.

The old man had claimed that he was visiting selected church leaders in order to warn them about a series of events that might endanger religion. He had quoted Bible verses one after another. Sci had not taken him seriously but had listened quietly since he considered this one of his duties as a leader of his Church. The visitor claimed to have found irregularities in the personal histories of several great physicists. He said that some of their experiences could not have been possible, could not have happened as recorded in their biographies. He had researched their lives in great detail and summarized his findings, which he insisted on sharing with Sci.

At the time he had handed Sci the stack of papers, the old man's claim seemed so far-fetched and vague that Sci had dismissed him as a deluded fanatic. He never read the material. He didn't even remember if he had thrown the papers into the trash or had stored them in the archives. But when he'd read an article in which Bucher casually dismissed the biblical account of creation, he remembered the old man's assertion. Was there a connection or was it just a coincidence? He had pondered the matter a long while before deciding to go to the conference in Switzerland and perhaps learn more about this Professor Bucher. That he had actually met Bucher personally had exceeded his expectations.

The conversation with Bucher in Bern had reinforced Sci's suspicion. The old man was probably long dead now, but perhaps he was right about something being amiss in the life histories of great physicists. Bucher had said things that would not have attracted the attention of any ordinary person. Sci, however, understood the implications of what Bucher had said. One statement in particular Sci found especially alarming. In Sci's mind, it had grown in importance, but he still wanted to study the issue a bit more before taking action. Bucher had claimed there was evidence of intervention from an outside force throughout the entirety of human history. All one had to do was read between the lines. This intervention was particularly evident in the mythology of classical antiquity.

Did Greek mythology have something to do with Bucher's scientific work? What a far-fetched notion! He went to the bookshelf and retrieved two books on ancient Greece. He began reviewing the creation myths and legends.

He knew the basic creation story, that it was several centuries older than that of the Bible, and that in some respects had served as a model for subsequent religions, even though monotheism—the belief in only one God—had not yet taken root. Thus, he could skip over some of the text. He flipped quickly through the pages on the first generation of gods even as he recollected the familiar stories.

The first Greek gods rose out of chaos—the god of the sky, Uranus, and the goddess of the Earth, Gaia. Uranus came to Earth every night, to Gaia, and fathered the Titans. The Titan Cronus, however, defeated his sky father and became the father of gods. With his victory, a second generation of Greek gods came to power. The sky did not have to fertilize the Earth every night; spontaneous generation ceased; and the happy age of the Titans began.

The second generation of Greek gods did not pertain to Sci's questions either. The Titans Cronus and Rhea produced several children, one of them Hera, later the wife and sister of Zeus. Hera became the mother goddess who protected marriage and, in particular, childbirth. Cronus and Rhea also produced Hades, god of the underworld; Hestia, the goddess of family, hearth, and fire victims; Demeter, the goddess of grain and fertility; and the sea god Poseidon. Their youngest progeny was Zeus.

Because Cronus feared his children would defeat him as he had once defeated his father, Cronus devoured all of them immediately after their birth. So Rhea secretly gave birth to Zeus in a cave and left him to be raised by nymphs. When Zeus was old enough, he sneaked up on his father Cronus and forced him to vomit out the children he had swallowed. Then, with the help of Poseidon and Hades, newly vomited out, Zeus defeated Cronus and became the father god. This third generation of gods moved to Mount Olympus, a high mountain in Greece, and from there conquered all earlier gods until the Olympians alone ruled.

This third generation of gods ruled at the time of classical Greece. These were not featureless, legendary gods like the primeval gods and the Titans. Mount Olympus was real. It stood there before everyone's eyes. And its residents, the ruling gods, were very much present in people's lives. If someone in the street had been chosen at random and asked if he or she had ever encountered a god, the answer might have been, "I myself haven't, but I know someone who has." These stories circulated until people really did believe the gods existed. They must have, for many people had seen or spoken to one of them.

Alco Sci felt he was on track. Could these gods have been Bucher's interveners in human history?

Zeus, the father god, had several children, many who became gods in their own right. Of course, they were not all borne of Hera. He had countless love affairs with other women. Hephaestus, the god of the forge, did come from Hera, the official wife. But with Leto, a daughter of one of the other Titans, he fathered Apollo, the god of light and the sun, and Artemis, the goddess of the hunt and the moon. Many other nymphs and mortal women attended to Zeus. His love affairs never lasted long, however, because of Hera's extreme jealousy.

Sci was especially interested in Zeus's dalliance with mortal women. From such couplings came demigods—heroes and kings, like Perseus, one of the most famous heroes of antiquity; Minos, King of Crete; Helen, the most beautiful woman in the ancient world and the immediate cause of the Trojan War; and Heracles, one of the bravest heroes of ancient mythology. They were all the offspring of Zeus and a mortal woman, and they were well known and revered in ancient times. The love children of gods and mortal women were thus by no means bastards or outcasts, as such children were in Christian cultures but, on the contrary, highly respected. Of course, they did not grow up in an intact family. They lived at the margins of society and were thus more or less free of inhibitions. It was precisely this freedom from social conventions that gave them the latitude to develop new ideas. The demigods initiated free thought in Greece. More importantly, however, they became highly respected heroes. The ancient Greeks recognized their extraordinary powers and gifts, which the Greeks attributed to the demigods' divine conception.

Alco Sci had already pulled lessons from human history when organizing the Church. He was convinced that the intervention of the gods and Greek society's acceptance of demigods and heroes did much to eliminate the rigid structures present in earlier cultures, like that of the ancient Egyptians. This was how a new society, one that produced the first great philosophers and first democracy in history, could develop within such a short period of time.

Although Sci had no trouble grasping these relationships, he still could not see what Greek mythology and Bucher's comments had in common. Any possible connection seemed so remote that ordinarily he would have rejected the notion outright. Yet a connection could exist. The issue niggled at him. Maybe there were correlations that had escaped human notice? Sci decided to travel to Switzerland again. This time he would take only his best people and prepare them appropriately for the task. He would not travel immediately, however. He wanted to prepare himself well this time. He wondered whether others shared his thoughts, like that graduate assistant, Daniel von Arx. What did that kid know?

The First Disk

Michael lived among books, electronic equipment, and dirty dishes in a tiny studio apartment. He'll probably never have a female visitor, I thought, for no woman would feel comfortable in a place like this. When I was a student, I had lived in a similarly tight space, but I liked order and cleaned up occasionally. Michael didn't bother. He felt at ease with things just the way they were.

A small combined unit consisting of video playback and a television stood on a wobbly stool beside the bed. I pushed it to the foot of the bed, moved books and papers to Michael's untidy desk, and propped two pillows against the wall. Michael set things up so we could watch the first film. I leaned back and made myself comfortable. He adjusted the volume on the playback machine and sat down on the bed beside me.

White speckles appeared on the screen. Then a fuzzy image

distorted by flickering white lines emerged. Michael jumped off the bed and adjusted a knob on the unit. The image became noticeably sharper, and the lines disappeared. I focused on the image, which appeared to be a group of about twenty primitive men. They moved rhythmically around a roughly hewn stone in the middle of an open space of trampled earth, as if dancing to musical instruments neither seen nor heard. On their heads they wore leather helmets supporting curved cow or antelope horns. Some sort of military decoration? The men had long, straggly, unkempt hair. Around their waists, they wore animal skins held in place by leather straps. On some, the garment covered one shoulder, leaving the other bare. Other men wore tunics of rough cloth. Their burly and hairy legs were bare. Each dancer carried a spear in his right hand.

For a long time, the camera lingered on the scene. Then it dipped to show the dancers' feet. Clad in leather sandals, the feet whirled and stirred up dust. A tinny voice emerged.

The Alaker War Dance. The Alaker were a prehistoric people who lived in the twentieth millennium BCE. Warlike and superior in size and mental ability, they subjugated all their neighboring tribes.

The commentator paused before continuing.

The Alaker believed they were the chosen people of the gods and could therefore defeat all other tribes.

The camera zoomed in on a single dancer. In contrast to the others, his face was smeared with red and yellow pigment.

Instead of a helmet, he wore a colorful wooden mask with feathers and beads, as well as a sort of hat. The voice spoke again.

The Shaman of the Alaker

The shaman interrupted the dance with an imperious gesture and walked to a large fire, where he sat down. The men followed and settled into a circle. Women and children, who had apparently been watching, also sat and formed an outer ring. The commentator resumed his intonation.

The shaman knows that his nation was chosen by the gods. This knowledge was passed on by his father, who was also a shaman, and who had in turn heard it from his father. He also believes that his family is directly descended from the god of the hunt, who is also the god of warriors. This must be so because the hunting weapons brought by the god to his people were also useful in wars against other tribes.

After a while, the commentator continued.

The shaman will now recount the story of his people.

The camera panned out. Most of the tribe members seemed to enjoy listening to the shaman's stories, but what else was there to do sitting around a campfire in the evening? The camera zoomed back in, focusing on one face after another. They were weather-beaten, bearded faces of fearless men at home with nature. They had learned to think for themselves, make decisions, and to act, often alone in the wilderness out on a hunt.

These men do not doubt that the gods exist. They know the gods, honor them, and bring them offerings. Some of them even claim to have encountered a god on a hunt or in the forest. Because the gods direct people's destinies and influence their lives, the gods must be present everywhere. Why would they not encounter a god in the forest? Why would a god not come to them in the village or even in their huts? However, the idea that a god might come to a people, live among them, teach them personally, give them advice daily, speak to them, and touch them—that was beyond the imagination of these people. So if the shaman claimed such a thing, the tribespeople interpreted the story for what it was, a legend or myth.

The camera turned again on the shaman. He sat motionless before the fire. Only his lips moved as he talked calmly to the people. The commentator continued.

But the shaman is not like the others. He believes the god of the hunt was his ancestor, and this fills him with pride. This belief is, in fact, what makes him who he is.

The commentator fell silent. Michael stopped the tape recorder and looked at me. "Well, what do you think? Does this shed any light on why these particular disks were stolen during the break-in at Dr. Bucher's office?"

"No, I can't see any connection," I had to confess.

Michael turned the tape player back on and said, "If I understand the story correctly, now comes the tale of the shaman."

The screen flickered, stabilized, and showed a man wearing an open shirt, long pants, and hiking boots. A revolver was stuck in his belt, a semi-automatic rifle hung from one shoulder and a portable tape recorder from the other. A pair of binoculars dangled around his neck. The irritating metallic voice made an announcement.

Several hundred years earlier.

The camera panned out to a wide angle. A man stood in a forest clearing among clumps of purple thistle reaching up above his knees. A hunter on a beautiful spring day, I thought. Then my eyes moved to the edge of the forest. Surprised, I looked at the massive trees. They reminded me of Sequoias I had seen in a California park.

"The trunks had diameters measuring up to three meters," our tour guide had explained. "These Sequoias were part of the original forests that once covered much of Asia, Europe, and America. With time they began to die out, giving way to more adaptable trees like firs, oaks, and beeches. But in the park, these very old trees have been preserved."

The film must have been shot in a park in the U.S., I mused. Perhaps this was a clue. "A primitive and spooky backdrop," I said to my brother. "Probably Sequoia National Park."

The camera panned to a slope in front of the man. Three figures lay on their stomachs. The camera zoomed in. Were they monkeys? Apes? Or maybe people? The hunter motioned for them to get up. Two remained lying down. Only the one in the middle got to his knees, trembling with fear. He was much smaller than the hunter, naked and hairy all over. Not an ape, I thought. However, the narrow forehead and hairy face indicated little intelligence. The characters reminded me of Cro-Magnon people—prehistoric homo sapiens, whom I had once seen modeled in a diorama at the Naturhistorisches Museum in Bern.

"I remember seeing a film once about the way prehistoric people used to live," Michael said. He had had the same thought as I. "This film reminds me a lot of that film."

The man turned around, motioned the three figures forward, and walked to the edge of the forest. The scene ended.

Several different scenes followed. Each featured the hunter with the primitive people.

In the first, they walked in single file across a field. There were five of the ape-like people, the hunter walking second in the line. Suddenly, all five dropped to the ground in the knee-high grass. The first in line pulled the hunter down, pointing ahead excitedly. A large feline creature resembling a tiger strode in front of them. It had enormous teeth that extended some twenty centimeters down from its jowls and dark brown fur. The hunter straightened up and unslung the gun from his shoulder. He took careful aim at the mighty beast and dropped it with a single shot. He walked over to make sure it was dead. The primitive people lay still and watched from their cover in the grass. They dared to stand only when the hunter placed a victorious foot on the head of the big cat. Hesitant and cautious, they advanced and knelt down in front of the hunter.

In the next scene, the hunter sat in front of a cave. Behind him, three women were cooking on an open fire. Three small children played around him, their faces resembling his more than the faces of the primitive people. Apparently he had mated with female cave dwellers.

The picture flickered again. When the image came back, we saw the hunter again. He was driving an ox that pulled a kind of plow fashioned from a sharp, curved stone attached to a strong tree branch. The plow was quite primitive, and the people with him helped as best they could.

In the fourth scene, the hunter was surrounded by a dozen children. This time he sat in front of a wooden hut, not a cave. A dog and some goats lolled in the dirt outside the hut. The hunter fumbled with the device that looked like a portable tape recorder. Some of the children were teenagers, and all of them seemed to be his.

These scenes made no sense to Michael or me.

One snippet led back to the shaman sitting by the fire. Only now did I notice the resemblance between the shaman and the hunter's children. One young man in particular, one who had approached the hunter at the end of one of the scenes, looked like the shaman. In general, the people sitting around the fire appeared more like the hunter's children than the primitive people in the previous scenes.

The commentator resumed his metallic monotone.

Shamans recount the story of their ancestors, which they learn by heart and pass on from generation to generation. So this shaman knows exactly what his father had learned from his grandfather. He knows his people descended from the god of the hunt. The god had come to them many years ago to teach them.

He had not only given them strategies for a successful hunt but also showed them how to build wooden huts and cultivate fields. He fathered numerous children who grew into demigods. Consequently, their tribe was now wiser and stronger and could conquer other peoples. They were the master race because the hunting god had willed it so. That is why the god had come to them in the first place.

The screen flickered and went blank. Michael and I looked at each other.

"What's going on here? What's this movie mean?" I asked.

"Movie?" Michael replied. "Do you really get the impression it's a movie?"

"What else?"

"Well, it's not a movie. More like some poorly made piece of propaganda," said Michael.

"What makes you say that?" I asked, puzzled.

"We've heard this stuff before in Europe. It's all about a master race and the subjugation of inferior peoples. This one guy claims to be descended from a god and superior to everybody else," Michael argued.

"Fascist propaganda then? Did Fascists already exist in prehistoric times?"

"The film is about today. The scenes are just re-enactments," Michael said.

"Throughout history there have always been people who claimed to be chosen by God or the gods. They believe they are better than everyone else. Is that what the film is about? Is it just propaganda to promote the idea of a master race?" I asked.

"If it is, it's awful propaganda. This film's so naive, it would backfire."

"Maybe that's the idea behind the film." I laughed. "Fascism originated with primitive peoples." We were talking again in that familiar ironic tone we sometimes took on.

"Nonsense. In Greek mythology, there were gods who came to mortal women and fathered children with them."

"Right. And that's a similarity I find strange. Never mind. What's clear to me is this film doesn't tell us anything about why someone broke into Bucher's office."

"I guess you were shot for no reason at all then," Michael just had to say

"And you sacrificed two days of your life trying to decipher the disks," I retorted

He ignored my cynical response, picked up the second disk, and looked at it thoughtfully. "In remembrance, J. Newton," he read aloud. "Newton . . . Newton . . . ," he repeated the name.

Michael stepped back onto solid ground in full lecture mode. "Don't you remember, Big Brother? I mentioned him in the hospital when we were talking. Isaac Newton was one of the most important physicists ever. He lived in the second half of the seventeenth century and established the laws of mechanics, which led us to calculate planetary orbits and explain the tides, among other things."

"But who is the Newton who gave Professor Bucher this disk 'in remembrance of' "?

"You'd better ask him about it. How'd I know? A descendant of Isaac? That's not likely. Newton is a common enough name."

Meanwhile, the screen flickered and turned white. Neither of us had shut off the tape machine.

"What's going on?" I asked.

"No idea," replied Michael. "I copied the whole disk onto the tape, but I didn't watch after the film ended. I thought it was finished."

We heard the tinny voice again.

Eve and Adam Hamilton. The last pictures we have before losing contact with them.

A two-person tent appeared on the screen. It was about a meter high, and staked to the ground, not unlike those used by the military. It was pitched by a rushing stream in a forest full of head-high ferns and mighty trees. Outside the tent sat a man. He waved at the camera while a woman peeked out from inside. They seemed to be on a camping holiday but did not look very happy. The man got up, crawled into the tent, and returned with an electronic device that resembled the one the hunter had in the scene with the Alaker. He began to fiddle with it. Then suddenly the movie stopped.

I cleared my throat and asked, "Are there any more pictures on this disk? And who are Eve and Adam Hamilton?"

"I have no idea. I honestly didn't know there were other scenes on the tape. I searched through everything on fast forward and saw nothing."

"Maybe it's worth the trouble to look again."

***

Kommissar Erb stood on a platform in the train station contemplating the reflections in a display window. As the train to Paris opened its doors, he turned around and watched the passengers boarding. Three men wearing black pants and dark jackets attracted his attention. Unlike other travelers, they had no luggage, but each carried a black briefcase. Their appearance was so striking that Erb and his surveillance team had no difficulty following them. Erb wondered why tailing them was so easy. Did they want to give the impression that they had nothing to hide? Or were they just amateurs?

Erb walked up to the three. Plainclothes police emerged unobtrusively from the crowd and surrounded them. Gus, Leroy, and Stan surrendered without a scuffle. The police officers handcuffed them, took their black briefcases, and led them off. Erb knew he had caught only the small fish. The big ones were probably already abroad. The case file on the murder and burglary was far from closed. He wondered what the three would reveal during questioning.

The Second Disk

We settled ourselves on the bed to look at the tape recording from the second disk. The first disk had been short, so we weren't tired and didn't require a break.

"The second disk is about twice as long as the first," Michael told me. He had already viewed it. "It's another film with actors, but this time the sound is synchronized. So our film-maker has made some progress. Still, it's no masterpiece."

"Let's watch," I said.

A title flashed across the screen: "The History of Amat the Sumerian." An emaciated boy appeared, all skin and bone. He wore a loincloth, and sat at a rough wooden table, holding a stylus in his hand. The scene took place in a rather primitive mud hut. The only light came through an open door. Other than the table and stool, the room contained no furniture. Stacks of clay tablets lay on the dirt floor in the background.

Behind the skinny boy with wavy brown hair and oval eyes stood an older, well-nourished man wearing a brown robe and leather sandals. He stood erect and solid. His bearing suggested that he was accustomed to command. We later learned that his name was Posthup.

The story unfolded, partially told by a narrator and partially through the actors' dialogue. The film was more like a documentary with re-enactments and voice-over as one sometimes sees on television. The authoritative man began.

POSTHUP: Sumid the Wise not only knew things that no one had known before him, but he also was the one who showed my ancestors how to write on clay tablets and read script.

NARRATOR: The boy Amat had never heard Master Posthup speak of the great sage Sumid before. When he had been ordered to the writing room, he had not known what would await him there. He had no idea, therefore, that his life was about to change, that the teachings of Sumid the Wise would come to occupy all of his time and, in the end, become his passion.

POSTHUP: Now listen, boy. The great sage Sumid, whom my ancestors knew, has now risen up to the gods. You, Amat, were brought to the scriptorium so that another slave scribe might rise up and thereby serve his king in the spirit of Sumid the Wise. You should be grateful and prove yourself worthy. You should take pains to incise the correct character for each word but, most of all, be obedient in every regard. Otherwise, you'll be kicked out of the scriptorium and probably castrated and sold as a eunuch in the slave market.

Michael and I watched as Amat trembled. The narrator resumed his part.

NARRATOR: If that happened, he would go beardless all his life, have soft cheeks and a high-pitched voice. Amat worked diligently in the scriptorium, the words of Master Posthup never leaving his mind. But soon the words lost their effect, and after a few months of training, he began to feel that Posthup was a kind man at heart even if he appeared loud and rough. In fact, Posthup never carried out his threats. Amat no longer toiled in fear. Instead he worked harder and harder because he had become fascinated by the art of writing. He began to excel but, like all people, not because he had been forced to excel through external pressure. No, his success was only possible because of his interest, his disposition, and an inner fire to achieve something—a fire that had been kindled by the deep injustices done to him in his short life and by the early recognition that only the successful evade injustice while the inept and unfortunate constantly face new injustices.

Despite the poor quality of the film, the boy's story fascinated me.

NARRATOR: When Amat was seven years old he lost his parents and everything that had been important to him. Marauders had attacked and burned his village, herding the survivors into a cow pasture and tying them together in a long line with ropes around their necks. Amat was among them. The first prisoner on the line was tied to a horse mounted by a beefy warrior. Every time Amat or the others stumbled or hesitated, the rope tightened around their necks, forcing them to move on.

For eight days, the column agonized its way through the region. Semi-conscious, Amat tried not to stumble and to keep marching. He had barely enough strength to fight for his survival. Only when they arrived in a town and he gained a few hours' rest, did he realize that his parents and siblings were not among the prisoners. Where were they? Did anybody know? The captives before and behind him were so preoccupied with themselves they did not bother to answer. What could he do? Exhausted and frightened, he looked around. When a group of men approached, he desperately wanted to ask them what had happened, to untie him and let him look for his family, but he remained silent. The men looked at him, talked a bit, and walked on. He was a commodity on the slave market.

After a while, which seemed very long, a well-fed man approached. He bore himself with authority. In any case, the overseer who accompanied the man acted deferential, almost submissive. They stopped in front of various prisoners. Each time, the overseer demanded that the prisoner stand up, and the well-fed man spoke a few words to the prisoner. When they came to Amat, he also stood up. The man looked him over and asked where he was from and how old he was. Amat could not answer either question. Then the well-fed man asked him if he knew what clay was. Amat had heard of it and said so. The two walked on. Amat saw that they continued talking with other prisoners. Then a guard came back and untied him. He had been purchased, as he later learned, by Posthup, the Master of the Royal Scribes.

Writing for the king took place next to the royal palace in the capital. Eight scribes worked there. Posthup's father had trained some of them. Posthup himself had trained the rest. In most Sumerian garrison towns, there were scriptoria with two to four writers who had been sent out from the capital. They remained on station for a few years to record events in the province and report to the king. Because of their position, linked to the king, and because the commanders could neither read nor write and were dependent on them, the scribes enjoyed considerable authority, even though they were slaves. They belonged to the king himself.

Master Posthup had the sole right to take on slave apprentices. Each scribe had two or three apprentices. If the boys distinguished themselves, the apprentices were purchased by the king at the conclusion of their training. They thus rose to the rank of scribe. After a few years on temporary assignment to a garrison town in the provinces, however, trusted scribes were transferred so they would not develop a close relationship with local commanders and would remain loyal to the king. After they returned from the field as experienced scribes, they took up residence at the court, where they received important special tasks—until some of them rotated out to another garrison town in the provinces.

Each writing center had assistants who produced clay tablets, watched over the drying process following inscription, and made the tablets ready for transport. A writing center required many people and was thus actually a small industry.

Posthup now spoke directly to the camera as if to his protégés.

POSTHUP: Sumid the Wise is the father of writing. My father, may the gods have mercy on him, claimed Sumid was a human being as we are, but I disagree. Not all gods have the same powers. The small gods can affect only certain things and must obey the greater gods. Even the sun god, from whom all power comes and on whom all depend—even he is bound by laws. He has to get up every day, travel his predetermined path, and go down again in the evening. Sumid was a god because he was spiritually superior to men and he gave us writing. That he behaved like a man does not prove anything. We know that all the gods harbor feelings like lust, greed, and envy, just as we humans do.

NARRATOR: Posthup demanded that his followers go every day to Sumid's shrine and honor him. The shrine was a room in the writing center with a larger-than-life statue of Sumid.

POSTHUP: Often the gods come to us because they want to teach us something or because they want to satisfy their desire for our valuables—eat good things or enjoy our women. Sumid also came to us, to teach us writing, and those who knew him have passed on to us that he could speak at any time with the supreme god through a big black box. Sumid had golden hair and was not dark as we are. You know, thinking about it, something makes me believe Sumid was afraid of the sun. The sun gives strength and life, but it had the opposite effect on Sumid. It made him tired and turned his skin unnaturally red and burnt. So Sumid the Wise went out of his way to avoid bright sunlight. This is not so unusual. We know that the gods may feel resentment and hatred towards one another and even make war. If the moon and the stars avoid the sun god, perhaps it is not so strange that Sumid did too.

NARRATOR: Amat was a bright boy. Initially, he awoke at night and cried for his mother. But memories of his previous life faded with time. That life had been shallow and careless, with no purpose, and therefore left few strong impressions. Only the raid came back repeatedly to haunt him. Thanks to his new job, however, he learned to control his emotions. He had even almost forgotten the long march after the slaughter. Since he had experienced the march in a semi-conscious state, his impressions blurred soon enough.

Sumid the Wise had introduced the art of writing not much before Amat's time during the reign of the previous king, so few people had mastered it. In four years, Amat had learned the art so well that Master Posthup came to him one day and addressed him in a kindly manner.

POSTHUP: I had a good eye when I bought you in the slave market. The king has refunded me the price I paid for you.

NARRATOR: This meant that Amat was no longer an ordinary slave, but one of the king's apprentice scribes. The news made Amat happy and proud.

AMAT: So I can now receive and write down orders from the king?

POSTHUP: Later perhaps. You have to practice patience, Amat.

NARRATOR: And because his pupil, of whom he was very proud, often seemed impatient, he emphasized his admonition.

POSTHUP: You can't do or know everything at once. The water in the water clock is going to drip for a long time, and you still have much life before you and much to learn. You see, a man never stops learning. Even at my age, I am always learning new things. Patience means that you come to terms with your position and are satisfied with it. Those who are impatient always strive for more and desire a position the gods have not intended for them. Such people remain unhappy and dissatisfied. Impatient people also provoke the indignation of others, who will despise them as over-ambitious. But, worse, impatient people arouse the wrath of the gods, who establish the eternal order that no one should presume to overturn.

AMAT: I will abide by your wisdom and try not to be impatient, Master. But allow me to say that the king himself is sometimes impatient.

POSTHUP: Great men—keep this in mind, Amat—are always impatient. The gods made them so, and it is not for us to criticize them nor, most certainly, the gods. Impatience is a characteristic of the lords whom we must serve.

NARRATOR: It took another three years before the king appointed Amat as scribe in a garrison town. As custom dictated, Amat celebrated this event and invited his friends to a feast. It took place in a tavern, where they enjoyed a sumptuous meal. Then came dancers, and Amat felt an exciting temptation. He struggled against it initially, but the wine took away his inhibitions. He spent a wild night and woke up at noon the next day. Posthup gave him salt water to drink to help him recover.

POSTHUP: Let that be a lesson, my son.

NARRATOR: This was the first time he had called Amat "my son."

POSTHUP: A scribe should never drink beyond the point of

satisfying his thirst. Like a priest, he is among the elect. Scribes are the only people who have mastered the art of writing, and that gives them power. Scribes owe good behavior to the king so that he may reign as no other.

NARRATOR: Amat drank the salt water and felt better.

POSTHUP: With the experienced drinkers of the Royal Palace, who spend each night in such revelry, salt water is of no use anymore. The next morning they drink a jug of beer. It's the only thing that wakes them up and puts them in a tolerable mood. I wouldn't be surprised if the king drank a glass of beer each morning.

AMAT: The king is a noble person and free of such cravings.

NARRATOR: Clearly Amat had not mastered the virtue of patience, but he caught himself before continuing to argue with Posthup. Besides, he had now come close to those in power and knew how human they could be. But he also was human, and a wave of melancholy swept over him.

AMAT: I'm about to go to the provinces and will not see you for years.

POSTHUP: All young men must go away. Anyone who wants to learn must see the world. It will be good for you take a post of responsibility in a distant part of the kingdom. There you can continue to educate yourself in the art of writing.

AMAT: Yet it pains me to go to the provinces.

POSTHUP: Writing is becoming increasingly important to the king, my son.

NARRATOR: Again he called Amat "my son," and that filled Amat with pride.

POSTHUP: We have become essential to him.

AMAT: Wouldn't it be good if more people mastered the art of reading and writing?

POSTHUP: Writing is a secret art, and nothing gives more power than secret knowledge. Imagine if the knowledge came into the hands of our enemies. They could use it against us. So it's good if only a select few know how to write and they agree among themselves to keep the secret. In fact, you must take an oath to guard this secret before leaving.

NARRATOR: Without saying it, both knew that their knowledge of writing gave them power, and Amat was easily persuaded not to share it with others.

The screen started to flicker, and the picture disappeared.

"Over?" I asked Michael, who was operating the tape player.

"Yes, it's done. I've played this tape through," replied my brother. "There's nothing more on it."

I shook my head. "I don't understand. What's so important about a Sumerian boy becoming a scribe?"

"That's a question for Professor Bucher."

"But I need to know now," I said. "I was shot because of these disks."

First Suspicions

Michael steered his motorcycle onto the road leading to downtown Bern. I sat behind him as we cruised along at the limit of 50 kilometers per hour. We both wore jeans, leather jackets, and helmets. I had the disks in my pocket. We were on the way to the University, where, for the first time since my hospital stay, I planned to pay a visit to my office. I also needed to pick up my car from the parking lot in front. We had decided to return the two disks to Professor Bucher. After all, they belonged to him, and we had no right to keep them. Moreover, returning them would give us an opportunity to chat and get to know him better. We were determined to find out what the motive might have been behind the burglary. Why on earth would someone want to steal these disks?

I enjoyed the ride on the bike. My recovery had been rapid, and I felt really good. The sun was shining. Being outdoors and experiencing the buzz on the street brightened my spirits. A warm wind blew in my face. I breathed it in deeply. How beautiful and simple my life could be if I were not drawn into other people's affairs, getting shot in the process!

My brother pointed to the rear view mirror and turned it slightly in my direction. Several meters back, a car appeared to be following us. Michael accelerated. The car did as well. Michael slowed down, and so did the car.

We turned into a side street. The car followed us. There was no doubt now. My carefree mood evaporated.

Michael picked up speed, taking the side streets to shake off our tail. He repeatedly leaned the motorcycle over to take a sharp curve. We hurtled into an intersection, crossing it just before a truck barreled in from the right. The driver braked hard. I looked into the rearview mirror again. The car was still on our tail but further back. Michael swerved abruptly to the right, immediately made a U-turn, headed back toward the intersection, and slowed to a stop.

"I can't shake him. Let's at least see who's chasing us," he said, turning his head a little so I could hear. My stomach was glad that the fast ride was over. Sitting in the back did not make me feel as secure as Michael must have felt. He was in control. I wasn't. We waited. Michael had chosen an intersection full of people, a security precaution to some extent. The car sped toward the intersection and turned right. The driver saw us waiting on the motorcycle, braked, and brought the car to a stop a few meters down the street.

"I know him," I said. "Wait."

The car backed up, stopping next to the bike. Kommissar

Erb sat in the passenger's seat. He let down the window and yelled, "Are you crazy? What makes you think you can race around neighborhoods like that?"

"Why are you guys stalking us?" I asked. I was really surprised to see the Kommissar. Yet I was also relieved. He surely wasn't going to shoot us as the burglars had shot me.

"We're not stalking you," responded Erb calmly. We're trying to protect you. But if you ride like that, there's not much we can do."

"Protect? Why on earth do you need to protect us?" I cried.

"Because as long as this thing isn't completely over, you could be in danger."

"What thing? What isn't over?"

Erb ignored the questions. "Daniel, you especially need to be careful. According to our intelligence, you are in danger or at least have been in danger. Maybe this whole thing has blown over. We're just not sure. It's true that, for several days now, we've not seen or heard anything new."

"Then we can go now?"

"Sure. But don't drive like before. If the traffic police catch you, you'll have to pay a fine. We'll stay close. Let us know if you notice anything."

***

When we arrived at the University, we separated. Michael went looking for a lecture hall so he could get back to his studies while I went to see Bucher. I announced myself, and his secretary took my name and request. She disappeared somewhere, eventually coming back to say Dr. Bucher would see me. She led me into the professor's study. To one side stood a heavy desk covered in stacks of paper. There was a telephone. A lamp on the wall lit his desk. A sitting area with leather-upholstered furniture was off to the side. Shelves filled with books and electronic devices covered the remaining walls.

"Herr von Arx," the secretary announced.

A man wearing a white lab coat stood up from the chair behind the desk, walked over to me, and held out his hand. Professor Bucher pointed to the sofa, and we sat down. "Nice of you to come," murmured the professor. "I'm a little ashamed. Should have visited you in the hospital. But time, time just got away from me...."

"I hope I'm not disturbing you," I replied. "Thank you for seeing me."

"Oh, heavens. You're more than welcome! How are you? You seem to have recovered."

"Yes, Professor."

"I'm very glad. For you and for me. When I think—you could have lost your life. And poor Roos. I still can hardly believe he was killed.

"Well, I'm okay now and trying to put the experience behind me."

"Thanks for not holding it against me."

"Against you? You couldn't have prevented it, Professor. If you had been working in your office, the criminals would surely have attacked you."

"Maybe."

"But I'm curious, Professor, very curious. What's this all about?"

"I can't imagine. I didn't even have anything useful to tell the police. I can only guess. I am working on something that could be groundbreaking, maybe even earth-shattering for some. Perhaps someone got wind of it and wanted to know what it was before I published."

"But why would someone kill for it?"

"Throughout the history of science, there have been cases of duplicate, simultaneous work. Perhaps other scientists are working on the same material and want to publish their work before I can. Sometimes people can get quite nasty about it."

"But who might these people be?"

Bucher spread his hands. "Anybody. The Chinese, Japanese, Americans, Europeans. As I said, it could be anybody. Based on the burglars' statements, I don't think anyone knows anything conclusive about the person pulling the strings."

"So you don't have any idea who was behind killing Roos and shooting me?" I asked.

"No, no idea. I just know the burglars were amateurs. They found nothing and are not likely to try again."

"Why not, Professor?"

"Because I've hidden the manuscript, such as it is at this point. The people trying to get at it are bound to know this, too. They won't find a thing, even if they try to break in again." He pointed to the stack of papers on his desk. "This is worthless. Just some seminar work from my students. No danger there."

"Does anyone know what you're working on, Professor?"

"There's been no publicity. Perhaps my students might know, but the details are secret. It's possible there was a leak. The first part of my findings has already gone to the publisher, and I suppose that someone with the publishing house might not have kept his mouth shut."

"So, what are you working on? May I ask?"

"It has to do with a unified theory of physics—'The Great Unified Theory,' as the Americans like to call it, or 'The Theory of Everything.' Apparently, someone has found out that I've put the final pieces together."

"How fascinating. But rest assured I'll keep my mouth shut."

Bucher made a dismissive gesture. "The break-in tells me that soon it'll be impossible to keep this a secret." He settled himself in more comfortably and asked, "Do you want to know what the unified theory of physics is?"

"Absolutely, if you don't mind."

"All right, I'll tell you. In science, we talk about matter, on the one hand, and force, on the other. Let's talk right now about force. Physicists speak of four kinds of force that act on matter—electromagnetic force, gravitational force, plus strong and weak nuclear forces. The first two forces act at greater distances than the nuclear forces do, thus creating force fields. They were discovered and researched first. Maxwell developed the model describing how electromagnetic force acts on matter. Before him, Newton gave us the model for gravitational force. Each of these two models, however, is only valid for its specific field. The two models are not compatible. It took Einstein's theory of relativity to show the effect of the two forces in a single model. Later, it was possible to incorporate the weak nuclear force into the model because, with the high energy and high velocity of particles, this force conflates with electromagnetic force. However, we still lacked a theory that incorporated all four forces. What I have done is to develop a model that does."

"My brother is studying physics," I interjected. "I've learned a bit from him. Are we talking about the contradiction between relativity and quantum theories?"

"Your brother is studying physics? I should know him then. Michael von Arx?"

"Yes, that's my brother."

"Fine. He studied with me and is fully capable of explaining the basics. You're guessing right. The theory of relativity and quantum theory are the two most important models offered by physicists in recent years. Einstein's theory of relativity explains events in the spatial domain, where they can be perceived by us directly through the senses. We call this the macrocosm. However, quantum theory, created by Niels Bohr and his staff, models events in the realm of the smallest particles, those we can't see, thus in the microcosm."

"I know a little about their work."

"Okay. So the theory of relativity applies to the macrocosm, quantum theory to the microcosm, and they contradict each other in certain respects. In particular, quantum theory does not agree with ordinary physical laws and fails to account for the effects of gravity. My unified theory links the two and creates a new model that is valid for the microcosm and the macrocosm."

"Hence the name 'unified theory'?"

"Yes. Einstein worked on it, tried to formulate it. Since then, numerous physicists have tried to design a unified theory, and many scientists have nursed the ambition to contribute to such a theory. So the discovery was fully expected."

"And you've now formulated the unified theory?"

"Yes. It's the last building block of physics. Now all known physical phenomena can be explained."

"All physical phenomena?" I was amazed. "Everything? From the beginning of time to the end?"

"From the beginning to the end. Perhaps not everything, but we can now explain the structure and operation of our solar system and the whole universe almost completely and also for the Earth and its development up until today."

"The universe since the Big Bang? Until today? You created this model?" My breath felt so short I could barely speak the words.

"Yes, I think so," Professor Bucher said modestly. "As I said, scientists have been researching it since Einstein, and my discovery is the logical consequence of scientific progress. With this model we can explain all physical processes since the birth of the universe up to the present, both for huge celestial bodies and for the smallest particles in atoms."

Question after question raced through my mind. I couldn't contain myself. "You mean, you can theoretically describe and explain the origins of the universe, the sun, the Earth, life on Earth, and everything that has happened up to present time?"

Dr. Bucher chuckled at my astonishment. "Yes, Herr von Arx."

"With this discovery, you've joined the greatest of all physicists—Euclid, Galileo, Newton, Gauss, Einstein, Planck," I said enthusiastically.

"That's something for history to decide," he said.

"I understand that you work alone, not with a team," I remarked. "I admire you."

"You know, Herr von Arx, there is a proverb that says,

'Everything great is simple.' My theory is simple. You just have to be open to simplicity, and that can be done alone." Professor Bucher paused, then added, "Many of my colleagues will be wringing their hands and thinking, 'Yes, of course, what Bucher found is really obvious. Why didn't I think of it myself?' "

"I have a question though. If the origins of the universe and its evolution up to present time and today's human beings can be explained in physical terms, is there any room for a supernatural power?"

"I understand your question," Bucher said. "Does such a model leave room for God?"

"Exactly. I know that many physicists and other scientists are atheists."

"Let me answer the question this way. Science has no reason to assume the existence of influences from unknown forces. There is simply no evidence. The universe and Earth developed according to the laws of physics."

"Is this true for all phenomena?"

"In a manner of speaking, I think so. Right back to the Big Bang. Only, what was before, no one can say. Still, there are some scientists already taking a look at the time before the Big Bang. We are constantly pushing the limits of science."

"Isn't that reaching a bit far? The other side of the Big Bang?"

"No. I'm simply expressing my convictions. But you know, between the Big Bang and human beings, there is still a lot of territory to explore, areas we don't know much about. Despite all the evidence and hard work, our knowledge is still fragmentary. Many questions remain unanswered. Just consider the mutations that occur randomly. Chance is part of the physical system. We can only collect data on chance statistically, but that doesn't always do us much good."

"I admire you, Professor," I repeated. "I am grateful that you've taken me into your confidence."

Bucher continued as if I had not interrupted. "Just because we see a gap in present knowledge doesn't mean that we have to fill the gap with a presumed intervention by a higher power. Such intervention has never been demonstrated."

"I understand." I paused. "Anyway, I didn't come to ask about higher powers." I smiled and took the two disks out of my pocket and handed them to the professor. "The burglars dropped these in my office."

"So they did take something! Many thanks." He took the disks and held them loosely in one hand.

"Didn't you miss the disks?"

"Well, I noticed they weren't there but didn't worry about it. I had other things on my mind."

"Do they contain your research paper or notes?"

The professor hesitated. "Did you load the disks into a computer?" he countered.

"Well, to be honest, I tried, but the computer wouldn't take them. It just flashed ERROR, ERROR until I gave up."

I had not intended lying to Dr. Bucher, yet I did. And I didn't know why. Maybe I sensed that something about Bucher seemed off. Or maybe I felt unsure or didn't want to insult the professor by intruding on his privacy. Bucher believed me. I could see it in his face. He knew that the high density of the disks would render them unreadable on any computer to which I might have access.

"No, the disks have nothing to do with my work," he said.

"Strange. Why would anyone steal them?"

"I have no idea," Bucher said and looked off into the distance.

I looked away from him in embarrassment. My eyes wandered to the bookshelves and fell on *Newton in the Thirty-First Millennium*. I got up, walked over to the shelf, and picked it up.

"What's this book about, if you don't mind my asking?" I said.

"It's a description of Newton's age."

"But the thirty-first millennium? Newton lived three centuries ago!"

"Of course, of course!" The professor laughed. "It's science fiction, nothing more. The author assumes that history repeats itself over and over again, and Newton will be back at work in the thirty-first millennium."

"So, just a fun read?"

"Indeed. A physicist can have a little fun with science fiction now and then, don't you think?" He smiled.

"Certainly." I put the book back. Next to it lay a device. It looked much like the machine the hunter carried in the video from the first disk. My mouth fell open. I looked at the professor and asked, "Would you tell me what this is? I've never seen anything like it."

"A timepiece."

"A timepiece?"

"Yes. A clock, if you will."

"Aha."

Professor Bucher grew suddenly distant and cold. It was time for me to go. I thanked him again for the conversation, said goodbye, and left his office.

***

Kommissar Erb walked into his office and sat down. He'd told the von Arx brothers of his qualms. The matter had indeed blown over and the danger had passed. So, why did he still have such a sinking feeling in his gut? He'd wanted to mitigate their fear, and he'd done so, taking the pressure off them. But he didn't completely believe what he'd said. It was true that the police had picked up the three burglars at the train station, but who could say whether other accomplices still lurked in the area or someone else would be sent in to finish the job?

The three prisoners had been taken to the Detention Center in the prefecture of Bern, where they underwent separate interrogations. The transcripts sat in front of Erb. He went through them again. After initially denying their involvement, all three had admitted to the burglary. DNA analysis of saliva residue on the rope placed them in Bucher's office and the office above it. The police had the weapon, the slugs, finger prints—everything. When confronted with the evidence, each had given a full confession. All three had claimed they were the only ones involved in the crime and there were no other accomplices. Why they had committed the burglary remained unclear. None of them seemed to have a motive. They said they had received an order and did not know from whom. Even what they had been looking for in Bucher's office remained unclear. All three said that they were supposed to photograph any loose manuscript, copy files from the computer's hard drive, and bring back any disks they saw lying around. They were also instructed to take whatever else they found of interest. But, since they were interrupted, they didn't finish the job. They hadn't taken or copied anything—not even disks. Kommissar Erb thought all this extraordinarily strange. Anyone who would hire burglars would surely give them specific orders and a clear mission. To steal whatever random things they found just didn't seem credible.

Still, their statements confirmed their guilt of breaking and entering, the murder of Heinz Roos, and the attempted murder of Daniel von Arx. They remained in custody, and the case had been technically cleared on the grounds that the criminals had been caught. Kommissar Erb, however, wasn't satisfied. He wanted to know what exactly they had been looking for in Bucher's office and who wanted them to take it. Further investigation and interrogations were in order. He was determined to find the answers to both questions.

Heinz Roos was dead because he had come into the office shortly before von Arx. Why he had gone there remained a mystery. Presumably, he had heard something and had gone upstairs to investigate. The murder had foreshortened the planned burglary. Wanting to escape undetected, the men were already in retreat when von Arx had entered the room and foiled their plan. So, why had they not killed von Arx as well? According to their statements, they had been ordered not to kill anyone. They had overreacted with Roos and did not want to make another mistake. Reading this part of the record, Kommissar Erb paused. Such behavior didn't fit with professional killers who committed crimes for money. Perhaps the three were not true professionals as originally thought.

He read through the background portion of the men's files again. All three belonged to the same religious sect in the United States. Strange, he thought. He wondered if that was the connection. He decided to make inquiries.

Pestalozzi

Looking back from where I am now, I can't really say how much time elapsed between the break-in and murder and what I'm about to narrate. Surely weeks had passed, perhaps a few months. Anyway, my wound had completely healed, and I had resumed my old life. At first the police had looked in on me often, checking to see if everything was all right. But eventually they stopped checking, and long periods would pass without the police watching me from afar. Although the events of the burglary greatly affected me, my life seemed to fall back into a routine.

    I remained a graduate assistant to a law professor at the University and had the same office as before. I finished my dissertation, which was accepted, and I graduated with the degree J.D., Juris Doctor. Shortly afterwards, I began to look for a position even though I had made few definitive decisions about my future. I considered joining a large law firm in the city. An offer from an industrial company also attracted me because the position would give me an opportunity to travel and negotiate contracts abroad. Finally, I considered a job with the federal government, which offered a high entry salary, something I found very attractive. I just couldn't decide. All I knew for sure was that it was time to get away from the University.

I still lived in the same small apartment. From time to time, I went out with different women, some were quite good-looking, and some of them even came home with me. I could have asked several of them to marry me. I am sure that one or two would have even said "Yes." But I could not imagine myself tied down for the rest of my life to one woman exclusively. Occasionally a woman would push me gently toward a closer relationship. For me that was always a signal that it was time to break up. But ending a relationship triggered unwanted scenes. An easy breakup for me involved a few tears and a farewell. It was more difficult when the woman still came around hoping to change my mind. Once the mother of a former girlfriend even came to tell me how thoughtlessly I had acted and how unhappy I had made her daughter. I was just not ready to make a commitment and wanted, first, to establish myself professionally. Except, well, even with the potential to establish myself, I made no progress on the domestic front. Maybe I simply didn't find the right woman—or that's what I told myself. Perhaps I was simply too immature.

As to the break-in, everything remained quiet. I had heard absolutely nothing except for occasional questions and conversations with friends, and those, of course, brought no new information. After the police stopped watching over me, I no longer felt threatened. However, I still had no explanation at all for the crime. I didn't know why those men burgled Professor Bucher's office or what they were looking for. Nor could I gain any reasonable perspective on why my colleague was killed and I was shot. I really would have liked to have known more.

To be sure, the perpetrators had been arrested, and their trial was scheduled. They would have to serve sentences of fifteen years or more. Even with good behavior, at least two-thirds of the time would be in prison. I had nothing more to fear from them. Also, Bucher's thoughts on the motive behind the crime were plausible. It was easy to imagine that unscrupulous people would want to steal his work and claim for it themselves. The mastermind behind the break-in might have hired professional burglars who knew nothing about science but were capable of murder if need be in order to carry out the mission. There were reasons for thinking along these lines. The burglars had found nothing and had no idea what they were looking for. Otherwise they would not have taken two disks randomly. Moreover, it was easy to explain the absence of further attempts at theft. Bucher had been warned and surely would have taken appropriate measures to keep his work secure.

I completely rejected the notion of any purposeful criminal action directed at me. The target was obviously Dr. Bucher, not me, even though my office had been part of the crime scene. The key resided with Bucher, a man ahead of his time, who sought to push human civilization forward. Progress depended on such people.

One evening after work, I went with friends to a small restaurant in the university district. Afterwards I walked alone back to my apartment. It would be a night of solitude, and I wondered if I should turn on the TV or go to bed. For some reason my thoughts were agitated. They turned to Michael's so-called mathematical proof of the existence of God. Michael had claimed that without a god, or at least some "ordering principle," the evolution of humans to their present stage would have taken much longer. He had used Newton as an example. He claimed that much more time should have passed for random mutations to produce such a man. Newton should not have lived in the seventeenth century but much later, say, in the thirtieth millennium.

I suddenly remembered the science fiction book on Bucher's bookshelf. Michael had intuitively named almost the same point in the future that appeared in the title, *Newton in the Thirty-First Millennium*. I was a little surprised at my mental leap and wondered whether the connection went back to my original thinking about God as an ordering principle. The question for me was how close to people this "ordering principle" was. Did it have direct access to human life? Did it control every individual's destiny, as the god of many religions was said to do? Was it always present like a god, knowing exactly what the faithful were doing? Could one call on the "ordering principle" for help, carry on a conversation with it, bless its name? Did it act on each person individually, or did it act only by establishing rules at the beginning of the universe, rules according to which evolution takes place?

The way people have imagined their gods has changed over the course of history. The gods of antiquity were immediately present and even had feelings. You could easily run into them on the street. This view evolved over time and became the monotheism of many of today's religions. Even in the Christian Middle Ages, there was, in fact, no consistent idea of just one god, although the church claimed the opposite. Along with God, there were Jesus and Mary and the archangels and other angels or saints, who were all in some way divine. They were all also accessible and could influence the fate of individual people. Only in modern times did we arrive at the idea of one God, who became more and more distant, becoming the "ordering principle" of the Enlightenment, no longer having influence on individual destinies.

In our brief conversation, Bucher had been of a different opinion. For him no ordering principle existed as a sort of minimalist version of God. He had clearly stated that the development of the universe since the Big Bang occurred in accordance with the laws of physics—rules that we understand to a great extent. In his view, God had absolutely no place.

I forced my thoughts back to Dr. Bucher. Something bothered me, and I couldn't let it go. Back then, however, I had not yet fully recognized my own unease. It had something to do with time. Yes, that was it. I kept going back to the videos on Bucher's disks. The characters did not fit the era in which the action took place. The hunter on the first disk was not an Alaker, but came from modern times. And Sumid? The story told of the divine introduction of writing to the Sumerians, about human progress in the broadest sense, the hub around which everything else revolved. But even in Amat's story, there was an out-of-sync character—Sumid, god of scribes. Then there was the book on Newton in Bucher's office and Bucher himself.

I got a beer from the fridge and sat down in front of the TV. I wasn't making any progress with my pondering today, so I decided to distract myself instead of dwelling on the problems. Nine-thirty was too early to go to bed. TV would provide distraction, and the beer, I hoped, would make me sleepy.

I hadn't looked at the television schedule and didn't know which of the many channels I should turn to. Usually I would just surf until some movie or show caught my interest.

I started with channel one, German Swiss Television, then clicked on further. Bloody thrillers and documentaries flashed across the screen, but I was looking for light fare, something without a plot. I surfed on to the French channels. The first and second channels showed advertising. France 3 was airing a program about development aid in Africa. Bored, I was about to move on when something caught my eye.

A figure on the screen looked vaguely familiar. The program was showcasing a supposedly very efficient agricultural program led by an international aid worker. He had helped the people in an arid region build an irrigation system and a school for agricultural workers. The school provided a backdrop for two black Africans discussing the program. Then the man came onto the screen again. He was head of the project and looked just like the hunter on Bucher's first disk. How could that be? He seemed to be wearing the same shirt, the same pants, the same shoes. The camera zoomed in for a close-up. I no longer heard what was being said. I just stared at the image.

No, it wasn't the hunter. But he was dressed the same way, and he carried the same device hanging from a strap over his shoulder. What had Bucher said it was? A timer, a clock?

I jumped up, grabbed the phone and called information to ask for the phone number of France 3. I wrote the number down and decided to call the next day. That night I enjoyed very little sleep.

The next morning in my office at the University, I could hardly wait to dial the France 3 number.

"Télévision France Trois," said a voice on the phone.

"Daniel von Arx here. Good morning. I would like some information about your 21:30 broadcast last night."

"Just a minute, please, while I connect you to someone who can help."

I waited while classical music played.

"Programming department. May I help you?"

"My name is Daniel von Arx. Good morning. I'd like some information about a broadcast aired last night."

"Which one?"

"Your 21:30 broadcast on . . . ."

"I'm sorry," interrupted the receptionist. "If you wish to discuss the program, perhaps you should speak with the director of 'Opposing View' or . . . ."

"I only want some information."

"Information? Fine. Just a moment while I connect you."

I waited again as the music played.

"France Trois, Editorial Department, Foreign Features. Good morning. How may I . . . ?"

"Good morning. Daniel von Arx speaking. I'm calling

from Switzerland." I hoped that mentioning I was calling long distance would speed things up. "I would like some information about the 21:30 program on development aid in Africa."

"Development aid in Africa? Just a moment, please, and I'll connect you with the department that deals with Africa."

Meanwhile the seconds clicked by, indicating a rapidly increasing phone bill.

Finally, I found out who had shot the film. An assistant also told me that the project was located northwest of Djibouti City in the former French colony. But if I wanted to learn more, I would have to talk to the film's producer. The administrator gave me a name and address. He did not have the telephone number. If I wanted to see the show again, however, they could send me a copy.

"Yes, please," I said. "I would like to order it now."

"Wait one moment, please, while I connect you."

After a while, someone in the Archives Department answered. Again, I said what I wanted. Of course, they would send me a copy.

"Can I pay by check?" I asked.

"No. But I can take your credit card by phone."

I agreed, especially since the price seemed reasonable. Then I called Michael and asked if he could quickly put his hands on the tape recording of Bucher's first disk. Although we had returned the disks themselves, we had kept the tapes. Michael said he could.

"When can I watch it again?"

"Whenever you like."

***

When the package arrived from Paris a week later, I was able to compare the two people on screen. My memory had been correct. They were actually dressed the same and had the same equipment. The aid worker was a man named Pestalozzi. He had been working in Africa for several years.

A monstrous suspicion arose in my mind. When I look back, I see that this was the moment I first caught a glimpse of what was going on. But before I confronted Dr. Bucher about it—not that the professor knew I had seen the films—I had to talk to this Pestalozzi. I had some vacation time coming and adequate savings, so I decided to go to Africa!

I made preparations quickly. I ordered a round-trip ticket at the university travel agency, a cooperative operated by students and usually very cheap, and went to the embassy in Bern to get a visa. Next I informed Michael and asked him to keep my trip a secret. That evening I cancelled a date with a girlfriend telling her that I had to be away for a few days. I couldn't imagine anyone worrying about me. As an unmarried loner, I bore no responsibility for anyone and did not want anyone to feel responsible for me. Young men bear responsibility for others only when they start a family. I know that now.

***

I flew from Zürich to Paris and changed there to get to Djibouti in East Africa. As I descended the portable staircase onto the tarmac of Ambouli International Airport, a burning wind punched me in the face and whipped at my clothes.

What a contrast to the cold and wet weather at home! I filled my lungs with the hot air. It felt strange to be so abruptly transplanted to Africa.

At the entrance of the single-story terminal stood two military guards. They wore khaki uniforms and the stiff white hats of the French Foreign Legion. On the tarmac, I could see a machine gun bunker beneath a camouflage net. Two legionnaires sat next to it. France maintained a strong presence in many of its former colonies and exerted a great deal of political and economic influence over them. Not everyone would agree, but I personally appreciated the sense of security and felt that France's continued presence contributed to the country's stability and order.

A native man stood inside the terminal but outside the customs barrier. He was wearing long pants, sandals, and a very colorful, short-sleeved shirt. He was even younger than I, or maybe about the same age. He held up a piece of cardboard with my name scrawled across it. I spoke to him in French. Yes, he would be my driver for the next two weeks and looked forward to the job. His said his name was Napoléon, after the French emperor. The vehicle waited outside, he said. I gave him my duffel and walked with him along the unpaved road to the car, a small, all-terrain Citroën, just as I had requested. The vehicle had no air-conditioning. I couldn't afford the extra expense. After a brief inspection, I wedged myself into the passenger seat. Napoléon took the wheel and asked me where I wanted to go.

I told him to take me to a supermarket. He had to think for a moment but drove me to a nearby settlement. I wanted to stock up on food and beverages. Who knew what would be available in the interior? I also wanted to get a propane camp stove and insect repellant for the plague of mosquitoes I expected. I had forgotten to buy repellant at home.

When I came out of the store, a crowd of youngsters shouting "cadeau, cadeau" immediately surrounded me. Most just wanted money, but some actually clutched at me. I found it annoying and felt unsafe, fearing they might get rough. On the other hand, I felt sorry for them. They had no choice but to hang around and beg. They had no work. Napoléon just laughed and dismissed the fellows with an imperious gesture. I could never have been so brusque. In developing countries, one is confronted with such brutal contrasts between the rich and the poor, I thought. Napoléon apparently belonged to the group that had a bit of money. He had a good job, even if, from a European perspective, he was only a driver and earned a pittance. Consequently, he behaved in an arrogant manner toward his compatriots, much more high-handed than I ever would. Although I felt a short-lived anger at his haughtiness, I had to concede that he had gotten rid of the annoying youngsters. Besides, how he dealt with his own people, really wasn't my concern.

We next secured two canisters of gasoline and set out. Although I did not know what lay ahead, I felt no apprehension. On the contrary, I was full of energy and eager to find out what I could as quickly as possible. This journey would bring me closer to solving the mysteries that had upset my life.

The journey to M'bene consumed three full days. The drive took us over bumpy dirt roads, sometimes no more than wide trails. It was tremendously hot. The car sucked in heat that increased under the metal roof. Rolling down the windows was out of the question because of the dust.

Occasionally, we drove through a village seemingly undisturbed by modern civilization. The villages looked poor and dirty. The houses were built of mud, a centuries-old practice. The people lived in family groups with their animals. Modern conveniences did not exist—no running water, no sewage system, and no electricity.

When our car appeared as we approached a village, children came out running and shouting. They pursued us until we disappeared from view at the other end of town. These children didn't go to school and lived as they might have long, long ago. They probably saw a car only every few days. Napoléon paid no particular attention to the children or other people or the animals in the road. He never reduced his speed but drove heedlessly straight toward anything blocking the road. People scrambled, pushing animals back and scooping up children, often diving out of the way at the last minute.

I was amazed we never had an accident. Apparently, people here always drove their cars with such reckless abandon. I couldn't stand it and asked Napoléon several times to drive more slowly through the villages. I was ashamed, not only because of the threat to others, but also because we left a huge wake of dust that enveloped everyone near the road. Napoléon promised to slow down but never did. Driving was his responsibility, and he was not in the mood to relinquish control.

I felt best when I shut my eyes and dozed. Sometimes my thoughts drifted toward my problems. I thought of my work at home or about the riddles swirling around Edward Bucher. Occasionally, my thoughts wandered toward the women I had been dating. In the heat of the car, behind the dirty windshield, I imagined going out with the long-haired brunette from the philosophy department or the red-headed law student I had recently met. Mentally I planned our dates, each ending in a night spent together. Time passed the most quickly during those drowsy fantasies. I admit that I began wondering if I was crazy to be traveling on the bumpy roads of hot Africa just to chase a foolish theory about the break-in.

Often my thoughts circled back to the upcoming task. I knew what I wanted to verify in M'bene, but I had only a vague idea of how I might go about doing it. I wanted to meet Pestalozzi and get to know him as well as I could in such a short time. I wanted to find out what kind of person he was, where he came from, and how he thought and acted. To achieve this, I had to spend as much time with him as possible. I wanted to visit the development project in his company and get to know all the locations the project would affect. My vacation would last fourteen days. Six days would be spent travelling to and from M'bene, so only about a week remained to spend with Pestalozzi. That should be enough to determine whether my suspicions made any sense.

I was at a loss, however, about what to do if they did make sense. Probably the best thing to do would be simply to go home to consider the matter thoroughly before taking any additional steps.

I wavered as I thought about how to present myself to Pestalozzi. I wanted an excuse to be near him as much as possible without arousing suspicion. I had a fleeting thought of saying I was a journalist like the one who had made the documentary for France 3. But this seemed too risky. I couldn't pull it off without an expensive camera and other equipment. If Pestalozzi was the person I thought he was, he had good insight and was superior to me in many ways. It was probably best to say I was interested in his work, tell him I wanted to learn about development aid and the problems in Africa. I was not at all confident that my plan would succeed.

How would Pestalozzi react? What would he do if he discovered the real purpose of my trip?

On the road, I spent two nights in a small tent I set up near the car. I didn't sleep much. Every noise woke me, and I would lie awake and listen for a long time, wondering what was going on outside the tent. Where Napoléon slept, I didn't know. Anyway, he was not in the car.

Toward evening on the third day, we finally came to M'bene. I had expected a village but saw only four houses. The largest had no walls, just a cement floor and a thatched roof that rested on slightly crooked wooden poles made of saplings. Under the roof stood a blackboard and wooden benches. A school, I thought. One of the three houses was a little larger than the other two. It had a sizable covered veranda. Napoléon stopped the car in front of it.

I crossed a patch of scorching, dusty ground to the veranda. On one side, under the thatched roof, stood a simple wooden table with some chairs. On the other, a man sat in one of two wooden recliners with leather cushions. In between, the door to the house was wide open. The man stood up and walked to the porch steps. He wore a wide-brimmed hat, an open short-sleeved shirt, Bermuda shorts, and leather shoes.

"Hello, welcome to M'bene," he said.

"Hello. I'm Daniel von Arx. I'm looking for the M'bene development aid station."

"You're in the right place then."

"I'm glad of that, to be on target I mean." I was tired. Perspiration dripped down my forehead. It was still brutally hot although the day was turning to evening. Stiff from the long drive, I stretched before climbing the two steps to the veranda.

"What brings you to such a desolate place?"

"I heard about this station and the work going on here. I'm interested in finding out more."

"And you made this long, arduous journey all the way here?" He cocked his head to one side and looked at me curiously. "But, please, have a seat." The man gestured to the empty chair. Napoléon remained in the car. When he saw me sit down, he started the engine and drove the car under the meager shade of a tree. He opened both doors in the hope that the slight breeze would dissipate the heat inside the vehicle. Then he lay down under the tree and closed his eyes.

"Was the trip okay?" the man asked.

"Yes, well, good enough."

"All the way from Djibouti City?"

"Yes."

"And no problems? How long were you on the road?"

"Absolutely no problems. We took three days to get here."

"So you drove right through." My host clapped his hands. A black man appeared from inside of the house and my host asked him to bring two glasses of lemonade.

"You must be tired and thirsty, I imagine."

"Yes, I am. Thank you."

"Why are you interested in our program here?" said the man.

"I saw a report on TV and thought to myself, 'you've got to go there.'"

"You're out here because of a television show?"

"Yes. The broadcast piqued my interest. Especially the part about the modern educational methods that have been so successful in Africa.

Besides, I had vacation time coming to me."

The man just looked at me in disbelief.

"What do you do? Teach?"

"No, I'm a lawyer." The houseman brought two glasses on a tray. I thanked him and took a long drink. The lemonade was just the right thing. The sour juice assuaged my thirst and gave me new strength.

"I ask because volunteers come to me for different reasons, sometimes political, and with a variety of different attitudes toward international aid. Sometimes people come because they have a strong need to help."

His voice betrayed a dislike for do-gooders with a naïve attitude.

"I don't belong to that crowd," I assured him. "I would simply like to become acquainted with Mr. Pestalozzi and his methods."

"Mr. Pestalozzi? You've got him."

I was amazed. "You're Pestalozzi?" I had imagined Pestalozzi quite differently. I expected the athletic, powerful man from the television documentary. Instead, I sat across from an intellectual who looked rather delicate.

"Yes, I'm Pestalozzi. May I ask why a lawyer is interested in international aid for development?"

After giving the question some thought, I replied, "Because I believe that all countries in the world should enjoy a reasonable standard of living and a similar level of wealth and that development aid will help us achieve this."

"I see. So you don't think that the northern hemisphere is guilty for inflicting poverty on the southern hemisphere and now must atone through foreign aid?"

The question made me uncomfortable.

"No, we are not to blame," I finally said.

"There are many who argue that industrialized nations exploit developing countries."

"I'm not one of them. I believe, rather, that the standard of living enjoyed by industrial countries doesn't depend on the exploitation of developing countries. Our standard of living wouldn't drop if we were cut off from resources in developing countries—apart, of course, from some initial difficulties in restructuring."

"I only ask because people with such ideas have come to me. A guilty conscience doesn't produce a good teacher or staff member. In most cases, the inner fire of such people burns out quickly, and then I have more problems with the aid workers than with the locals whom the workers are supposed to help."

"I understand."

"Do you belong to the Green Party?"

I laughed. "Is this some kind of entrance examination? No, I'm not a Green. I would just like to stay here for a few days to learn about your methods so I can get a better grasp on how I might participate in development projects."

Pestalozzi seemed relieved. "I can't use ideologues. Unfortunately, they're quite common in development aid."

"Have I passed the test?" I asked and grinned.

Instead of answering my question, Pestalozzi asked, "How long do you want to stay?"

"I only have five days."

"So you don't want to work with me?"

"No. I just want to look around and observe. May I?"

"Of course. Five days is not a problem."

"Thank you." I was relieved to have been accepted.

"Not a problem at all. You can stay in the guesthouse over there. It's empty right now." He pointed to one of the other two houses that stood about thirty meters away.

"Thanks. That's very kind."

"By the way, where are you from?"

"Switzerland."

Pestalozzi gazed into the distance. When he resumed, his voice had a dreamy quality. "Switzerland? I had a brother who used to work there. He was also an educator."

I stared at him in amazement. "Your brother is Johann Heinrich Pestalozzi?"

"Yes," my companion said absently.

"Your brother was one of the world's greatest teachers and educational philosophers. He reformed the educational system in Switzerland, and his reforms and theories remain valid and in place today. In fact, he practically invented the elementary school, an institution now found in countries all over the world."

"Yes." Pestalozzi spoke automatically, his thoughts far away.

"Wait a minute. That doesn't make sense. He lived in the latter part of the eighteenth and early nineteenth century."

"I don't know. I don't remember dates." Pestalozzi looked up sharply. His face regained its vitality. He'd come back. "No, no, of course not. I'm sorry. My brother is a teacher and works somewhere in Switzerland."

"What a coincidence! You could give me his address, and I could look him up and give him your greetings."

"That's kind of you but not necessary," he responded. "We're in touch."

Before I fell asleep that night, I thought back on the conversation. I shuddered at the audacity of the question I had put to Pestalozzi, "Your brother is Pestalozzi?" Even more disquieting was his talk of a brother who had lived two centuries earlier. Had he accidentally revealed himself to me? Had we seen through each other's covers?

***

I asked Napoléon to sleep in the hall of the guesthouse so that no one would walk in on me in the middle of the night. He refused. He would sleep outside next to the car, as was the custom. I insisted, and finally he gave in.

Around midnight I got up and quietly opened the door to the hall to see if he was actually there. He wasn't.

***

For the next few days, I followed Pestalozzi as he went about his work. We drove in a four-wheel-drive Land Cruiser to the different schools he had established in the area. All were run by local teachers whom Pestalozzi had trained. In addition to basic reading, writing, and math skills, they taught agricultural science. I saw that the schools were well organized and, in the fifteen years of their existence, had already contributed significantly to raising the standard of living in the area. Farmers not only produced enough food for everyone. They harvested surpluses to be sold in other areas. Communities had even committed to producing their own handcrafts. Pestalozzi placed great value on the schools but no less on ordinary maintenance and the expansion of the water and irrigation systems. Agricultural fields were irrigated, and every village had water, thanks to a high-yield well. Pestalozzi was tireless in his work. He was always on the go, giving instructions, teaching, and insuring efficient development throughout the area. He was, I noted, highly regarded and respected.

Whenever the opportunity arose, I tried to engage Pestalozzi in conversation to find out as much as possible about him as a person. I was interested in where he came from, how he thought, and what motivated him. In our conversations, I heard about the enormous problems he had encountered over the last two decades while he built up the aid program. He had to fight against prejudice, established traditions, laziness, and indifference. There was a time when the local witch doctors opposed him. A rumor spread that Pestalozzi was possessed. Evil and misfortune would befall anyone who worked with him. The village elders opposed him because he was undermining their authority with his commanding presence.

Again and again, he had to contend with those who disapproved of his agricultural methods in the fields, rejecting them as new-fangled. Pestalozzi remarked that many people had simply become too comfortable with the way they lived and feared any effort to introduce something new, even if the change made life easier. Such people rejected new ideas, new ways of working, and new technologies because they were too lazy to deal with them. Incidentally, he noted, people like this also existed in Europe. What he experienced here on a small scale, the western world experienced on a larger one, engaging in conflicts over nuclear power, stem-cell research, genetic engineering, and exploration of space.

Some opponents even vandalized Pestalozzi's work. Facilities were damaged and newly cultivated fields destroyed. Schools were burned down twice. It was incredible, Pestalozzi said, how emotional and blind people could be in their refusal to accept progress. They often preferred hunger over cultivating fields with modern techniques because they believed the rumor that products from these fields were poisonous. Eating grain from them, they thought, would cause abdominal pain and lead to a slow death.

But the biggest obstacles to his work were the claims and demands made by local tribal chiefs and potentates. Many of them wanted to share in Pestalozzi's success, demanding fees or percentages without doing anything to earn them. Corruption drove profit into unproductive hands. But Pestalozzi was determined to reward work and entrepreneurship—not greed. If he didn't, those who worked hard trying to build a business would lose all motivation and would eventually stop working. Then the prosperity of the region would decline. Pestalozzi said that eliminating corruption was a necessary condition for development aid to be effective. When he spoke of these problems, his voice rose and he made grand gestures with his hands, emphasizing each point.

Pestalozzi had, however, experienced many beautiful things, and as his first successes became evident, positive recognition followed. That gave him satisfaction. He could reap the fruits of his labor. But whenever I asked Pestalozzi about his past or where he came from originally, or when I asked him about what motivated him, he dodged the questions. It was as if his life began when his project in Africa commenced.

On the evening of the second day, Pestalozzi and I sat on the veranda of his house drinking beer. We enjoyed the relative cool of the evening and talked again about development aid.

"Why do you actually do all this?" I ventured to ask once more. "To help the people here? Or do you do it for love of humankind?"

"Both sort of. Mainly I want humanity to progress in its development in general."

"Is progress so necessary?" I asked.

"I think so."

"Why? Couldn't people be happy without our western notions of progress?"

"Maybe, if they had no basis for comparison with us. But modern communication creates needs. Why do you insist on knowing what motivates me?"

"I'm interested in why someone would tackle this kind of work with such spectacular energy."

"The reason I do this work is very personal. You couldn't understand—so, please just let it go." Pestalozzi had become cool and cautious. He took a sip from his glass.

"I beg your pardon. I didn't mean to pry."

Conversation stopped. It was awkward. I thought about how I might get him talking again. For just a moment, I was tempted to let the cat out of the bag and tell him why I was really there. I rejected the idea as quickly as it came. Do nothing rash, never act out of emotion, I thought. I changed the subject. Since I couldn't choose another personal topic, I decided to turn to the abstract and asked, "What do you think actually started humans on the road to progress?"

"Language. Without language, human beings could not evolve at all," replied Pestalozzi without hesitation. "And humans are still evolving."

"Human beings are subject to evolution and are still evolving, becoming more intelligent from age to age?"

"Yes, of course. Why should evolution suddenly stop?"

"Many claim that human beings were created by God, all in one act, perfectly complete, just as they are now."

"Pure nonsense. Humans have passed through a long evolutionary process, which always takes place in many small steps."

"And you think that one of those steps, even the first, was language?"

"Yes. But it didn't come about all at once. Primitive sounds came first, and these gradually evolved into the structures and vocabulary we have today. With language, people could share their knowledge. The next generation could build on that knowledge and didn't need to start all over again. So progress accelerated."

Again, silence settled between us. This time it was Pestalozzi who picked up the thread of the conversation.

"The next crucial step was writing," he said. "It provided a significant improvement in how knowledge was communicated. Writing allowed for the storage of knowledge in books and documents, thus making it accessible to others."

"So you encourage language and writing in your aid work?"

"Absolutely. Writing was an important step in evolution and is essential here. But equally important was the next developmental step, widespread teaching of writing. One of the great evils of early history is that literacy, and with it knowledge transmitted through writing, was accessible to only a select few—priests, scribes, and the aristocracy. They did everything in their power to keep common people ignorant because they didn't want to lose their position of power and privilege. Progress depends on the participation of as many people as possible applying their skills. Therefore, general education is required to achieve progress."

"I'm with you on that. As long as only the upper social classes are educated, humankind will struggle to move forward. Members of the upper social and economic classes will cement their power by preventing progress. The introduction of the elementary school led to a surge in development. And that occurred only two centuries ago thanks to your Swiss namesake, Johann Heinrich Pestalozzi."

"Exactly. But we still need a more liberating environment. Those who become educated must be free to explore, produce, act, and turn their crafts into business."

"How did humans attain those earlier stages of development and then continue to progress later? By chance? Or did someone help them? Maybe even a god?"

"I don't know," the aid worker said, cutting the conversation short.

The evening that conversation occurred, Pestalozzi was wearing the same clothes he'd worn in the television show. Initially, they had piqued my interest more than anything else. So I plucked up my courage and asked, "How did you come by these clothes?"

"Someone gave them to me before I set off for Africa."

"So you didn't get them here?"

"No, why do you ask?"

Pestalozzi grew cool again and unapproachable. He got up and went into the house as if to get something. But after a few minutes, he came back and said goodnight. He was tired and wanted to go to bed.

I knew that change and progress in industrialized countries occurred much faster than here in Africa. I also knew that this had not always been so. Only in modern times had progress accelerated faster with us than here in Africa. Instead of libraries, we had databases. Global communication fostered instant access and enabled each researcher to review previous findings and seamlessly expand upon them. Basic groundwork did not have to be tediously repeated because research was systematized as never before. In earlier times, centuries passed between major discoveries, moving us from one epoch to another, but the intervals had shrunk considerably. For example, the intervals between the major discoveries in physics were continuously shrinking—from Euclid to Newton to Einstein—and in modern times, the famous names fell in line one right after the other. As a result, new findings and technical innovations flooded humanity, the rate of change increasing rapidly. This was true not only for people and their environment, but also for social organizations. Political structures, companies, and even nations constantly changed, requiring repeated renewal and adaptation. This spiraling rate of change even held true for historical eras. For example, the agricultural age had lasted several millennia, while the industrial age lasted only a few centuries. The age of a service-based economy lasted just a few decades, and the era of communication had only just begun.

Where did this acceleration come from? Who or what caused it?

In a later conversation, Pestalozzi returned to the topic of change. His theory fascinated me. Pestalozzi claimed that many people felt comfortable only in the environment of their ancestors and in their present, well-established circumstances. They opposed any change, perceived it as stress to be avoided. Their resistance made change slow and laborious. He mentioned again the destroyed fields and burned-down schools, not only as part of a power struggle between him and the tribal leaders but also as an expression of resistance to change. He attributed the same cause to conflicts in industrialized countries, where any new technology, like those based on stem-cell research, would be fiercely opposed. Of course, new technology carried the risk of abuse. Even electricity, now a firmly established and trusted technology could be abused, as in the instance of the electric chair, used to kill the condemned. However, prohibiting a whole new technique because it might be abused was often merely a way of expressing resistance to change in general. People often claimed caution when they simply preferred the good old days because innovation overwhelmed them. The faster the pace of change, the greater the number of people who opposed it. They became obstructionists by turning against anything new.

"The larger their number," Pestalozzi said, "the slower the pace of development. The challenge of successful development is one of optimization. It is important to choose a speed that minimizes an increase of active obstructionists. In small numbers they can do nothing."

"Choose? Is it possible to choose a speed and thus optimize the rate of change?" I asked.

Pestalozzi hesitated. I could tell that he thought the question annoying. Finally he replied, "No, of course not." His answer wasn't honest. I didn't press the issue, although I had more questions. Confirming or contradicting my suspicions about Pestalozzi and Bucher lay in the answers to these questions: Why were the two of them, each in his own way, working so hard to foster human progress? Why did progress have to occur at a calculated optimum speed? Why were they forcing progress so robustly?

Instead, I asked, "You speak of active obstructionists. Are there others who get in the way?"

"No. But unfortunately there are people who can't come to terms with this world. They don't oppose development, but neither can they cope with change or adapt to it. They simply drop out. That's why we have drug addicts and other marginalized individuals. High rates of suicide are also indicative of a society being pushed to change too rapidly."

***

I had never entered Pestalozzi's study. He always kept me out on one pretext or another. But I had to see it and decided to try and sneak in on my last day. I had packed my things and stowed them in the little Citroën. Napoléon, who had spent five days doing nothing, was already at the wheel, eager to leave. As always, the dry air was burning hot. I skipped up the steps and walked across the veranda. The wooden boards creaked with each step. Pestalozzi undoubtedly heard me coming. I went into the house and up to the study, knocked, opened the door, and walked in.

"Hello," I said to Pestalozzi. "I'm about to leave and would like to say goodbye."

Pestalozzi glared at me. He rose hastily from his desk, stepped in front of me, thereby partially blocking my view. "You're leaving already?"

"Yes, unfortunately. I have to." I looked around. The only pieces of furniture were an ordinary desk, a chair, and a bookshelf constructed of raw wood. The desk was clean and tidy. On the bookshelf lay various electronic gadgets that were familiar to me. I had seen similar devices in Professor Bucher's office. On the floor nearby lay the device that I had supposed was a portable recorder. Above it on the shelf, I saw a disk just like the two I had returned to Bucher. I took a deep breath and stepped toward Pestalozzi, stopping next to the compact electronic device. I bent down and picked it up. On the front side, it had two digital displays. One showed the current year, the other, the number 3416.

"My goodness, what is this?" I asked.

"A timing device. Give it to me."

I did.

Pestalozzi turned and set it on his desk. Meanwhile, I took the disk and dropped it into my pocket. I asked in what I hoped was a guileless tone, "It's displaying the number of this year?"

"Yes."

"What's the other number?"

"I can't explain. It's too complicated."

"Is it a year, too?"

"I told you, it's too complicated," Pestalozzi snapped.

"I suspect that 3416 is also a year. The display allows a six-digit number. Was the number originally larger and has now dropped back to 3416?"

Pestalozzi's nose flared. "What makes you say that?" he rasped.

"Just a guess."

For a brief moment, we looked each other straight in the eye and felt both insight and mutual distrust. I turned to go. I stopped at the door and thanked him for allowing me to observe his aid work and for his hospitality. We shook hands and I rushed back across the veranda, got into the car, and motioned Napoléon to get moving. The engine roared, the car took off, and we left M'bene behind in an unfortunate cloud of dust. How glad I suddenly was for the ridiculous pace of Napoléon's driving style! Pestalozzi did not even come out onto the veranda to see me off.

***

"Hello, is this Professor Bucher's office?" Pestalozzi stood at his desk with a phone to his ear.

"Yes. Who's speaking, please?"

"This is Alfred Pestalozzi. Please connect me." He waited until the line crackled.

"Bucher."

"Edward? This is Alfred."

"Alfred? How on earth are you?"

"Very well, thanks. And you?"

"Also very good, thanks. Nice to hear from you."

"Yes, it's good to hear your voice. We haven't seen each other for a while."

"Yes."

"At least we have telephones in this world. Good that we finally have a satellite connection as well. I can reach across the globe from here."

"Just in time for us. Our efforts have amounted to something." Bucher laughed and asked, "How's your work going?"

"Okay, thanks. It's tedious with the Africans, but I'm moving forward. And you?"

"Me, too. Things are moving forward. The people here cooperate."

"Ha. You have it easier in Switzerland than I do here."

"Don't complain, Alfred. You had a choice. You wanted to be an educator."

"Absolutely right. Anyway, I'm not complaining. Not even because you're going down in history as a famous physicist while I remain an insignificant aid worker."

Bucher laughed again. "It's the nature of my profession. I will be mentioned over the next few centuries. But if everything works right, your contribution will be as honored as mine."

"Well, what a comfort! But seriously now," Pestalozzi continued, "do you know a guy named Daniel von Arx? He lives in Bern."

"Von Arx? Sure, I know him. If we're talking about the same man, his office is right above mine. Why?"

"He was here for five days and just left M'bene. I think he's on to us."

"Are you sure?"

"Pretty sure. He kept asking me very precise questions, as if he knew something. Today he managed to grab a look at the year-count indicator and interpreted it correctly. That's what gave him away."

"He was here with me a few months ago and seemed suspicious. He was interested in my year-count indicator as well."

"So, what now?"

"Once he gets back, I'll check him out thoroughly. If our suspicions are confirmed, I'll take him out of circulation."

"What if we can get him to play along?"

"No, I don't think that's a good idea. It would be too risky."

"Well, the ball's in your court. But don't try to fool him. I'm sure he knows everything. Better take him right out of circulation."

"Thank you, Alfred, for your call and the tip. I'll have to think things over. By the way, when are you coming back to Europe?"

"Not sure, but it won't be for a while. I'll let you know beforehand."

"Too bad. I would really like to see you again. There are only two of us here on Earth right now. Thanks again for the call."

"Goodbye, Edward."

The Third Disk

The hot and dusty return trip to Djibouti City and the flight home to Switzerland fortunately included no incidents, and I arrived safely in Zürich. As an expression of my gratitude, Napoléon had received my tent, two empty petrol canisters, and ten US dollars. I had plenty of time on my flight home to consider next steps and was eager to get started. Not stopping for coffee, I took the first available InterCity to Bern. I couldn't wait to drop off my luggage and wash the residual grime from my body. When I arrived at my apartment building, I checked on my car. It was just as I had left it. When I opened the mailbox, however, it was overflowing. I scooped out the contents and took it up to my apartment along with my bag. Everything seemed in order. No one had been there, and of course no one had watered my plants. They had all withered. I immediately got a watering can and filled the pots to the brim.

Next I began the tedious task of going through the mail. Most was junk mail and outdated copies of the *Bernerbär*, the free newspaper. I threw them away. I had bills from Energie Wasser Bern and VISA. The remainder of the mail had to do with my job. I found nothing out of the ordinary. After I showered and put on fresh clothes, I flew down the stairs, as always taking two steps at a time. I hurried to my car, opened the door, and sat behind the wheel. Releasing the brake and clutch, I put the car in second and let it roll forward. I had become used to this procedure and felt no need to repair the electric starter. I always parked the car so that I could use gravity to turn over the engine.

I drove to Michael's apartment building. I wanted to look at the digitized tapes of the two disks from Bucher's office and ask Michael to process the third disk that I had purloined from Pestalozzi.

Parking the car again so that I could let it roll forward, I ran up to the door and punched the bell. When the lock buzzed, I hurried in and made my way to Michael's studio.

"Ho, Michael!"

"Daniel. Back already?"

"I got back a couple hours ago."

"How was it?"

"Beautiful and interesting. Especially interesting."

I told him quickly about my trip.

"With all the sitting in cars and planes, I had some time to think. Mostly about Bucher's disks and what's on them. You still have the tapes, don't you?"

"Of course." Michael opened a dresser drawer and held out the two tapes. "Here you go."

"Can I watch them?"

"Sure, if you really want to. What's up?"

"Got an idea, and I want to check it out."

"What kind of an idea?"

I didn't answer. Instead, I pulled the third disk from my pocket and held it out to Michael.

"I have another disk. Think you could get it transferred to tape so we can see what's on it?"

"Is it like the others?"

"Yes, I think so."

"Of course," Michael agreed. Where did you get it?"

"In Africa." I grinned. "I found in Pestalozzi's study."

"Found it?" He smirked. "Pilfered, is more likely."

"Whatever. Anyway, how long will it take to transfer the contents to tape?"

"Not long."

"Could you get it done today?"

"You mean right now?" Michael looked at me in astonishment. "Gee, Daniel, I'll need equipment and help from the people at SoftBau."

"Okay. While you're working on that, do you think I might watch the first two tapes on your machine here? Would that be okay?"

"Is it really that important?"

"Yes, but I don't want to talk about it too much right now. First, I want to watch the other tapes again. Will you take this over to SoftBau now? Please."

Michael nodded and accepted my odd request without further ado. He left, and I made myself comfortable on the bed in front of the screen. Michael didn't care about the contents of the film. He had really only been interested in solving the technical issues and deciphering the disks.

I, on the other hand, watched the scenes unfold before me with fascination, paying close attention to the narrative about the Sumerians Amat and Posthup. I wanted to know exactly what was said about Sumid the Wise.

When the film ended, I just sat there, lost in thought. I created a line-up in my head, like those in police shows on television. I placed Alfred Pestalozzi, the hunter of the first disk, Sumid, and Bucher in a line next to each other against a white wall. I examined each one—his personality, actions, and motivations. Then, I compared them to each other. My thoughts jumped next to Isaac Newton. I added him to the lineup. I wondered if there were more people I should include, like the Hamilton couple. Maybe. There may even have been others of whom I was still not aware. Who knows? At least I knew what all these particular people had in common. They had each served as a catalyst for human progress, causing a leap forward that went far beyond what evolution could achieve solely through random mutations. These people had brought about such rapid progress for their respective generations that a backlash occurred and many of their contemporaries simply found it impossible to cope.

I reached a decision. I would call Bucher and tell him what I was thinking.

***

Michael returned just before midnight and laid the desired tape and the disk next to me on the bed.

"Thanks," I said. "It worked?"

"Yes, finally," Michael replied sullenly.

"Uh oh. You had some trouble."

Michael sighed. "You can say that again. Nobody was at SoftBau except the janitor. I had to reconstruct the dubbing unit all by myself."

"How about a drink?" I looked at Michael with concern.

"No. I'm fine." Michael sat down. "All I want is some rest."

"But you got it done fast. What a guy!" I really meant it. I wasn't just trying to make Michael feel better.

"It wasn't easy. When I played the movie, everything seemed to be working just fine until I realized there was far too much information on the disk."

"Too much data? What do you mean?"

"Don't you remember how ridiculously long it took to transfer the second disk? I wanted to avoid doing an all-nighter for the third disk."

"But you're here. What happened?"

"I got an idea. I decided to transfer the data on the disk to the tape at high speed. First, I had to calculate the speed of the two systems and then coordinate them with each other. Then once the transfer was made, I had to check it."

"And? Did it work?"

"I think so. Here's the tape." He tossed it to a spot beside me on the bed.

I put the tape in the playback machine. Michael had done me a huge favor, and I felt obliged to him. I sat back again on the bed. Michael crawled in beside me and curled up so he could fall asleep if he became bored. For a few seconds, the screen just flickered. Next came a humming sound. Finally, the picture of an elderly man with thin, gray hair and a thick, gray beard appeared on the screen. Despite the man's age, his eyes were alert. He wore a heavy, brown wool smock with two rows of horn buttons running down the front. The collar of an off-white linen shirt circled his neck underneath the smock. He matched the image I had always had of a medieval monk. The man looked directly into the camera and spoke.

Yes, dear friends, it's really me, Galileo Galilei, the same Galileo you've heard tell of since your youth. I've grown old and wrinkled, but some among you will recognize me. Some of you have even received my reports or have encountered me in earlier days at headquarters. Others of you will have forgotten me. No matter. I take this opportunity to greet you all, my dear friends, and describe at some length what has happened in my life now that it is possible to do so. However, before I show you where I live now, I will answer the question that must be uppermost in your mind. No, I will not return among you, especially not now, after undergoing the wrath of the Inquisition and such a difficult trial. My daughters have remained close-by. The elder visits me almost every day. I do not want to lose my children. But that's what would happen if I came back. And it would break my heart. Besides, I've grown accustomed to living here, and I should like to end my days in this place. You will surely understand. Most of you would do the same.

As long as my eyesight holds, I will be able to see the rolling hills of Toscana from here, almost down to Siena.

The man was seated on the porch of a stone farmhouse with a tiled roof. The camera panned out then swept across the surrounding countryside. The lush green of the fields was abundantly punctuated by the distinct red of poppies, indicating springtime. Only occasionally did a tree or a small cultivated area mark the landscape. Beyond the porch stood a cluster of houses on the slope of a hill. They too were of stone with tiled roofs, their walls overgrown with grape vines and ivy. The man continued.

I have been happy here in Arcetri, despite the maladies that come with age. True, gout has made it difficult for me to walk. I sleep badly, and my eyesight diminishes daily. But I have become accustomed to growing older, and it does have its advantages as well.

The camera cut back to a wooden table and chairs on the porch.

The Pope himself banished me here. That I cannot leave my residence would have upset me earlier in life, but now I have no desire to travel. This makes the papal ban trivial. My daughters live in the convent of San Matteo. Virginia has taken the name Sister Maria Celeste and brings me everything I need. She is now thirty-two and has suffered much more under the Inquisition than I have. I am grateful she was not at my trial but heard only fragments of what happened. She delights me every time I see her. Livia also comes to see me now and then. Only my son Vincenzio, who also lives nearby, does not come as often as I would wish. Not that discord exists between us. On the contrary, he has always stood by me and shows his affection by making sure I am comfortable. As happens with sons, he sometimes forgets me when he becomes focused on his work.

I don't mean to complain. I have found my peace. As you can see, I live in a big house and have everything I need. Exile bothers me, but only a little because I can't walk far. Anyway, I want to tell you what has happened over the course of my life while I still can. Take time to listen, my friends, and do not forget that both you and my life here have left their mark on me. Remember, I have spent much longer here in Toscana than I ever did with you.

I'll start with the events of the last few months because even friends with whom I regularly communicate don't know what has happened.

I was very fortunate. After the terrible trial by the Inquisition in Roma, I received permission from the Pope himself to be transferred from the Inquisition's prison to Trinità dei Monti, a palace in Roma belonging to my friend, the Grand Duke of Tuscana. This occurred on June 23, 1633, the day after my judgment was pronounced. I had no physical strength and was distressed. A great relief washed over me when finally I could leave the hostile prison. I much appreciated how well my friends received me and how steadfastly they stood by me. I began to recover somewhat over the following week. Then, on June 30, the Pope allowed me to leave Roma. He would not permit me to return to Firenze, my adopted home, but did grant me permission to stay in Toscana, specifically in Siena. I was overjoyed and set out immediately.

The trip in the summer heat was almost as arduous as the journey the previous winter. Of course uncertainty no longer *plagued me as it had on the journey to Roma. The trial was over, but it had weakened me badly. I arrived in Siena on July 9. There, Archbishop Ascanio Piccolomini received me graciously. He seemed ashamed of the proceedings in Roma and did everything he could to help me recover. His example proved that not all Church leaders agreed with the suppression of scientific truths.*

The man calling himself Galileo paused for a moment, wrestling with his emotions. Only with great effort did he manage to continue. His face was lined with weariness, yet his eyes showed the determination of a warrior.

Only later did I learn why I was not allowed to return to Firenze. The Pope had instructed local officers of the Inquisition to summon all scholars in Firenze to an assembly in order to read them the Church's decree against me. At this meeting, they announced not only my conviction and exile but also my recantation under threat of torture. I was not even able to defend myself and naturally became discredited.

Fortunately, my friends did not abandon me. Piccolomini, especially, stayed by my side, helping me a great deal—help for which I am very grateful. No one would ever have expected an archbishop to receive and take care of someone whom the Pope had exiled. Yet, for six months, I stayed with him as his guest. Then the Grand Duke of Tuscana convinced the Pope that I should move here to Arcetri, near my beloved city of Firenze. Once, to my great pleasure, the Grand Duke even visited me. Through him I learned that the seeds of my teachings had landed on fertile ground and had taken root. In spite of their power, the Church and Inquisition could not hold back scientific truth, proving once again that truth will always win out over intolerance and willful ignorance.

The screen flickered and filled with white static. I sat up and stretched. I didn't know what to think. I needed time to process the story. I wondered whether Galileo's life corresponded at all to what I had just watched.

Then it returned, that nagging suspicion I always carried with me, the one that had prompted me to go to Africa. But right then I felt too tired to indulge in it for very long. I decided to go to sleep instead. Just as I was about to turn off the tape machine, the flickering stopped, and Galileo appeared again. He now sat at the wooden table on the porch, a jug of wine before him. He held a clay cup in his hand. He extended the cup toward the camera as if to toast the health of his audience, then brought it to his lips and took a sip. He set the cup down and began to speak.

Yesterday, I gave you the bare facts about the events surrounding the Inquisition trial. Today, I would like to tell you about the events leading up to the trial. We have beautiful spring weather now, as you see, and it has given me strength.

As you may know, on August 5, 1580, at the age of sixteen, I began my studies at the Università di Pisa. However, medicine bored me, and it wasn't taking me anywhere. You will find this hard to believe, but in that era, dominated as it was by the Church, the view of the world that applied to theology also applied to medicine. Only two authorities existed, and they alone were permitted to explain things. For matters pertaining to the supernatural, of course not accessible to the human mind, only divine revelation mattered, and it was articulated exclusively by the Church. For the observable world, accessible to the human mind, the Greek philosopher Aristotle and some of his commentators reigned as the sole authority. Can you even imagine the severe limitations this placed on people who wished to think for themselves? We students received neither education in natural history nor instruction about the human body, which would have been really good for a physician.

Galileo smiled and winked.

At the Università, we only heard what Aristotle and a few other thinkers of antiquity had written. Just imagine—Aristotle lived in the fourth century BCE!
But I already had an inquiring mind. I tried, a bit hesitantly, to bring into our discussions some elements I thought were scientific. For example, I told them how, in the Duomo di Santa Maria Assunta in Pisa, I had noted that the oscillations of the chandelier took the same amount of time even when the length of the arc decreased. I had measured the intervals with my heartbeat. At any rate, my efforts attracted little attention, and no one took my pendulum laws seriously then. Years passed before the principle of the pendulum was applied to measure time.
The amateurish and archaic teachings of medicine soon became unbearable for me. That's why, after five years, I left the Università without a degree. I knew at that point how human society worked and understood the system of patronage. I would only be taken seriously if I could find a high-ranking patron

who recognized my work. My pendulum laws would have attracted attention immediately if some well-known person had commented on them.

So I left Pisa and went to Firenze, the capital city of the regional princes. Many highly placed lords and ladies lived there, and I hoped, with skill and some luck, to make useful connections. To earn my living I taught private lessons, giving preference to the children of nobility so that I could get to know their parents. For four long years, I got by this way in Firenze.

Then one evening, at a meeting of a scientific society, I met the Marquis Guidobaldo dal Monte of Pesaro. He was researching mathematics. Carefully and humbly, I asked if I could give him some of my mathematical work for his review. He agreed. Thus, I managed to attract his attention and eventually earn his friendship. We exchanged views on math problems. When a position in mathematics became vacant in Pisa in the summer of 1589, we knew each other well enough for me to ask him for a recommendation. The recommendation helped, and I go the post. My detour through Firenze had been worthwhile, and I returned to Pisa at the age of twenty-five as a lecturer.

Now I was able to tackle scientific questions with more authority and show my students that some physical problems could be solved only with the help of mathematics. I taught that one must measure what was measurable and make measurable what was not. For example, Aristotle claimed that objects fall faster the heavier they are. On the contrary! I showed that the speed of a falling body is independent of its weight, but the acceleration of the falling body is critical to the duration of the fall. My students and I confirmed this with an experiment at the leaning tower. We recorded the results in mathematical terms. I *also described the curve of a projectile as a parabola and, in my book* De motu, *addressed issues of dynamics. It was a wonderful, carefree time that brought me much attention because I had demonstrated that, despite the power of the Church, progressive scientific teaching was possible if one did not question the authorities but accepted their support.*

The screen flickered again and the image disappeared. I got up and turned off the tape machine even though I knew that the story wasn't over. I went to the bookshelf and pulled out the volume of Michael's *Lexikon* covering "G." I looked up "Galileo" and began to read about his life and work. I wondered if the recorded story was historically accurate or poetically embellished. The narrative on the tape was consistent with the information in the article as far as I could tell. However, the version I had just watched contained far more detail than an encyclopedia would have anyway. I decided I needed to acquire a detailed biography of Galileo in the next few days and compare the information there with the story I had just watched. Mostly I wanted to know whether a historically accurate narrative would strengthen my suspicions.

Satisfied with this decision, I went back to the video playback machine and turned it on. Michael had fallen sound asleep, and, although I was very tired, I wanted to see another segment. The image appeared again. I sat on the bed and concentrated on the story. Galileo sat at the table on his porch, dressed as he was before.

In 1592 a messenger arrived with a sealed letter. I opened it and read with joy that I had been appointed by the doges of

Venezia to the Università di Padova. Although located in the hinterland, Padova was ruled by those who governed Venezia, one of the most prosperous trade cities of my time. Located on the Adriatico, it maintained solid relationships with Constantinople and Asia Minor, thus giving merchants access to the Orient. The fact that the city's merchants had to deal with Muslims instead of Christians didn't matter. In fact, many a Venetian had even reached the Han in China via the Silk Road.

Thus, a call from the doges of Venezia was quite an honor. I accepted the call and went to Padova. I felt elated to be teaching at one of the oldest universities in the West and one that far surpassed the reputation of the provincial Università di Pisa. The proximity of the cosmopolitan city of Venezia, which was very open and liberal thanks to its port, tended to attract an international student body, especially since Venezia was strong enough to defy the Pope himself. I had students from Germany, Poland, and the Netherlands. The local population of Padova tolerated them well, and the students maintained their local customs. There were even a few dozen Protestants, something that contributed to the open spirit of the city. In Roma, the Counter-Reformation Inquisition publicly burned such heretics.

The free spirit of the city and my newfound recognition bolstered my spirits. Although completely engrossed by my work, I managed to meet and fall in love with Marina Gamba, a lovely Venetian who persuaded me to live with her. She gave me my daughters Virginia and Livia, who, as you know, are now nuns. Marina also gave me Vincenzio. Marina and I never married, and when she left me—she did not wish to follow me to Firenze when I returned there later—I didn't pine for her. Nonetheless, I am grateful for the children, who all came and stayed with me.

I wondered if Galileo had suddenly realized how personal his narrative had become. He looked down, lifted his cup, and drank.

I must now turn to something that moves me more than my private life because it has to do with my work—the telescope. As you know, I did not invent the telescope. It came from Holland. When I heard about it, however, I copied and improved it. I then demonstrated it to a select group of noblemen on the Campanile di San Marco. The Council of Nobles of Venezia, the Signoria, immediately recognized its utility, especially in war, for it would enable early sightings of the enemy on land and water. The Signoria was extremely interested in obtaining it. Negotiating through an intermediary, I gave the city the telescope. As a token of appreciation, I received an appointment for life to the chair of mathematics at Padova. The city also doubled my annual salary to 1,000 guilders. In one fell swoop, I became a made man. With this honor came the attention of many envious people—and how could it be otherwise? Because the Dutch telescopes arrived somewhat later, the envious vipers claimed that I had appropriated and taken advantage of the Dutch invention. I asked myself if I should make a deal with such people. What for? I chose not to respond and devoted myself to my work—probably a mistake. I have learned that one should expose envious people before they can do their dirty work behind one's back.

As I said, I ignored them. The telescope opened up many opportunities. I immediately set to work and used it to study heavenly bodies. I could see and interpret much of the firmament that, up to that point, had been hidden from humanity. The telescope led me to important discoveries that I published in various journals. These writings increased my fame. However, they drew more envious people into collusion and brought about my confrontation with the Church, finally culminating in the Inquisition's charges against me.

I summarized my first discoveries in Siderius nuncius. I was the first person to describe the surface of the moon, which resembles that of Earth, not soft and smooth, but covered with bulges and deep hollows. I was also the first to discuss Jupiter's four satellites orbiting around the planet as the moon does around Earth. That particular document also included the most important idea of my life, one that had evolved gradually until it became at last a certainty. I began with this question: How can the planets circle around the sun, as Copernicus recognized, and the moon around Earth if the Earth is not moving? All of you have known for a long time that Earth is not the center even of our galaxy. Rather, it revolves around the sun, which is merely the center of our particular solar system.

Galileo paused and stroked his beard. After a swallow of wine, he picked up the thread of his story.

Although I had a very comfortable life in Padova, full of amenities, I suffered greatly from the hostility of my envious colleagues, who became more and more oppressive, constantly throwing my ideas into question. Perhaps that is the reason Marina and I grew further apart. I was always occupied with my work and fending off attacks, leaving her utterly alone. In her dissatisfaction, she nagged me about little things, and this drove me out of the house even more. Our relationship became a burden to us both. I eventually decided to give into a long-held yearning and return home to Firenze. I knew she would not follow me.

Before I had received my life-time appointment in Padova, I had written to a young Florentine prince and former student of mine for an appointment at the Università di Firenze. Then, when the call actually came some seven months later, I accepted it with pleasure. In retrospect, I must say that I was probably unwise to give up my permanent position in Padua. Perhaps I would never have been brought to trial in Roma. Venezia protected its citizens from the Inquisition, and the long arm of the Pope did not reach Padova. At the time I didn't consider these things. I was at the peak of my fame and used it to engineer my return. In the fall of 1610, seven months after the introduction of the telescope in Venezia, I left Marina Gamba and moved to the city of my heart. Later I learned that Marina was living with a wealthy merchant, and I hope that she has found in him the happiness that I could not give her. One thing is certain—the children were not happy in Padova. Over time, they all migrated to be near me.

Galileo's voice took on strength. He seemed proud and confident.

In Firenze, I became court mathematician to the princes. I devoted myself—as I have already told you, my dear young friends—to further research and teaching. I continued to write about the planets, for example, how Venus underwent changes like the moon. That is, it waxes and wanes, depending on the planet's position in relationship to the sun.

Nevertheless, mostly, I focused attention on past knowledge, trying to gain recognition for earlier scientific findings. This had become more important to me than discovering something new. I introduced a Copernican worldview, according to which the Earth revolves around the sun and the sun, not Earth, is the center of what was then perceived to be the universe. I reiterated my ideas about the phases of Venus again and again. I lashed out at those who stubbornly refused even to look objectively at the planets or the sun or moon, much less through a telescope. With ancient writings in hand, they argued that Earth was the center of the universe, just as Ptolemy had claimed. Repeatedly, I asserted that one must seek scientific truth about the universe with the telescope, not by consulting biblical and ancient Greek texts.

In the spring of 1611, I traveled to Roma to persuade the guardians of religious orthodoxy. Thanks to the interventions of Florentine envoys, I was even able to present my arguments to the Pope. Every evening I participated in discussion circles at various palaces, where I submitted my ideas. I had enjoyable conversations with highly placed personalities of the Inquisition, like Cardinale Bellarmine. Many seemed to agree, or so I thought. I returned to Firenze very much satisfied. I thought I had swayed them.

Now the voice fell, and Galileo's shoulders slumped.

What I couldn't predict did, in fact, happen after my departure.

The opponents of Copernicus united in their cowardly fashion behind my back, rejecting all scientific truth revealed through study of the stars. Their only concern was whether the "theory" of the Earth's motion aligned with biblical scripture. What an erroneous approach! A very dangerous one in my mind. The Council of Trent had already decided to take a stand against the heretic Martin Luther. No one could voice personal opinions on matters of faith. Interpretation of scripture in any way contrary to the teachings of the Catholic Church was forbidden, and so, if the Copernican worldview contradicted scripture, anyone who advocated the view would be a heretic. I was threatened with denunciation. That's why I wrote my rebuttal, stating that there could not be a biblical and a contrary scientific truth. There could only be one truth. Thus, I argued, it was the task of the interpreters of scripture to find meaning consistent with science. Would God, who endowed us with senses, reason, and judgment, forbid us to apply those gifts?

Galileo looked out thoughtfully from the porch into the distance. His experiences had left deep, clearly visible traces on his face. After a while, he continued,

The Church assembled a panel of eleven ecclesiastics to take up the question of whether the Earth revolves around the sun. They planned to rely only on their interpretations of the Bible in their deliberations and did not plan to use any of the knowledge gathered by my friends and me.

The panel held its first meeting in the spring of 1615. When I finally found out about this event in the fall, I immediately traveled to Roma to make a case for my ideas. Unfortunately, I

arrived too late. The Holy Office condemned Copernicanism on February 24, 1616, and declared what they considered the only truth, a theological position—that Earth was the immovable center of the universe. The Pope stated in his instructions to Cardinale Bellarmine that I was to abide by the judgment of the Congregational Index. What could I do other than to assure him that I would?

***

I yawned and stretched. I had watched the video much longer than originally planned. I got up and turned off the playback machine. I didn't know how much longer the film would go on but had seen enough for tonight. I had enjoyed learning the many details of Galileo's life and wondered if they were in fact true. Although I couldn't yet tell, I would find out. I had no idea who the performer was or why the film was made. If I consulted a biography before continuing the movie, I should have enough information to determine how much of the film was accurate. Secretly I hoped that everything in the movie was true. That would confirm my suspicions, and I would be one step closer to proving my theory.

I wrote Michael a note telling him to leave the playback machine as it was. I would come back tomorrow to finish watching the film. Then I sneaked out, leaving him asleep. I let my car roll down the street in my normal way and drove off. Taking the curve onto the Autobahn, I looked in the rearview mirror and noticed a car. I had seen it earlier as I left Michael's. On the Autobahn, it stayed a couple of car lengths behind me even when I changed my pace. Was it coincidence, or was someone following me? Now slightly worried, I kept an eye on the car.

I drove slowly and glanced at the rear-view mirror every few minutes. The car matched my speed. When I exited the Autobahn, no car followed. I was alone. Maybe it was just a coincidence. My thoughts turned back to Galileo. Once home, I opened the mailbox as usual, tucked its contents under my arm, climbed the stairs, and entered my apartment.

I suddenly felt again as if someone had followed me. I didn't turn on the lights but went straight to the living room window and looked out onto the road. A car maneuvered into a parking space in front of my building. I watched as it came to a halt and the headlights went out. No door opened, and no one got out. I waited a while and thought about what to do. Finally, I went through every room in the apartment. Everything was in order.

I took a bottle of beer out of the fridge, opened it, and went back to the window. The car was still there. I couldn't tell if anyone was in it. I stood there in the dark and drank my beer. Nothing outside moved. Had the driver gotten out while I was in the kitchen? Again, I wondered what to do. I didn't much like the idea of going down to look. My imagination was probably just working overtime. Blaming my fatigue, I decided my mind had played tricks on me and went to bed.

Persuasion

The next morning I slept so late that the sun shining in my face woke me. I blinked and turned over in bed. The sun warmed my back. A few minutes later I got up, stumbled to the bathroom, and turned on the shower. As the warm water flowed down my body, my mind wandered back through the events of yesterday. Now, in bright sunlight, my anxiety about being followed seemed unfounded, and I was a little ashamed. After I toweled off, I walked naked through the room to the window. I couldn't resist looking to see whether the car was still in the parking lot. Peeking from the side of the window, I saw the empty parking place. Reassured, I turned away and got dressed.

I walked to a bookstore near my house and found three books on Galileo Galilei. The longest was a novel and would embellish the facts. The second didn't appeal because Galileo's life was not the focus. The author concentrated instead on the history of the era. The last was a seventy-page booklet, part of a series of monographs on famous scientists. It seemed more like what I was looking for. I bought the booklet and returned to my apartment.

On the way, I walked by a parked car occupied by two men. As I passed, they turned their heads away from me. I didn't pay them much attention.

Back home, I made a pot of espresso in my Italian coffee pot, filled a bowl with muesli, and added milk. I read while eating breakfast.

After a couple hours, I had finished the booklet. It confirmed the story on the third disk, up to the point of Galileo's return to Florence. I would check the rest that evening. I studied the photograph of Galileo's portrait on the cover more closely. There was indeed a resemblance between the painting and the man on the tape. I then scanned the table of contents and re-read the chapters pertaining to the part of Galileo's life that I had not yet seen on screen. I wanted to impress the details in my memory so I could detect even the slightest deviation.

The muesli hadn't really satisfied my hunger, so I set out to find a cheap restaurant in the university district. I thought briefly of inviting one of my girlfriends. I hated dining alone in a restaurant and usually went out to eat with friends or a girlfriend, preferring the advantages offered by the latter. Today, however, I dismissed the thought. The meal needed to be quick, and I had already made plans for the day. I studied the menu posted outside the entrance to a favorite haunt. It featured three set meals, a plate of organic vegetables with salad for vegetarians, a macaroni cheese casserole, and a plate of meat and rice. Entering the restaurant, I selected a table in a corner. I ordered a green salad as a starter, followed by the macaroni cheese casserole. Again I went over the events of the past few days.

A few minutes later, an elegant, average-sized man entered the restaurant. He was remarkably well dressed and did not fit in with the relaxed atmosphere of the place. I had the feeling he had not come here by chance. To my amazement, he headed straight for my table and sat down opposite me without so much as asking if the seat was vacant. The waiter brought my salad, and I began to eat. My table companion ordered coffee with a cognac. I felt an inner edginess but tried not to let it show. Fortunately, the food service was prompt. The casserole came quickly, and I attacked it with relish. I carefully avoided showing any interest in the man but watched him secretly out of the corner of my eye. As I ordered coffee, he took his last sip of cognac. Looking me straight in the eye, he spoke in a remarkably quiet tone, "May I ask you something?"

I returned the glance, tenser than before. I replied in as steady a voice as possible, "Of course."

"You will probably not be surprised if I ask whether you know Professor Bucher."

"Why should I know him?"

"Since your misfortune, you've been looking into his affairs."

"What makes you say that?"

"You secured a recording of a French television program. You traveled to Africa, and you've tried to decipher some disks."

I held my tongue but with difficulty.

The stranger cleared his throat and asked, "Did you manage to decipher the disks?"

"What makes you think I have any disks I might or might not have deciphered?"

The man said nothing, just looked me squarely in the eye. I decided to take the offensive and asked, "What do you want?"

He didn't respond. I looked around the room. It was now filled with customers, mostly students. Nobody paid attention to me or the man at my table. The crowd of people did give me a sense of security, however. I turned my attention back to my table companion and asked again, "What is it you want?"

This time I received a reply.

"I'm also interested in Bucher's work and would like to propose that we work together."

"How so?"

"You tell me what you know, and I'll tell you what we know. That way we both benefit."

"I see." I pondered. I had to stall. What did he mean by "we," and what did "they" expect to get? "I'd like to think about it."

"Of course, but don't take too long."

"How can I get in touch with you?"

"No need. I'll contact you again."

"Who are you? I have to know with whom I'd be working."

"We're a group of people interested in Bucher's work."

"That's not good enough. I want to know exactly who you are."

"You'll find out as soon as you've made your decision."

"I can't decide until I know who wants to make a deal with me."

"Think it over. I'll get back to you in a few days."

The man put some francs on the table, stood up, and disappeared through the door.

***

Back in front of my brother's monitor, I reflected on the meeting with the well-dressed stranger. Others were interested in Bucher and his mysterious work, and they wanted to find out how much I knew. No surprise there. My interest was relatively recent. It began only after the break-in. These people must have been following Bucher for much longer than I. They had to know more. But then maybe I had learned something in Africa from Pestalozzi and from the disks that they didn't know. I felt excited but wary. I was ready for adventure, but this whole thing could turn dangerous. I decided to delay for now and quietly pursue my own investigation.

I turned on the playback, waiting expectantly for Galileo to appear. He did and peered out anxiously at his audience.

I hope you understand, dear friends. You gave me a mission, and I never forgot it. I had to fight for the truth of science. Yes, I enjoyed high prestige thanks to the support of those at court in Firenze and scholars from near and far. This is what allowed me to stand up for my beliefs. I never gave up even though the intolerant Church made every effort to suppress scientific truth. You see, the Inquisition had spies and informers everywhere and enforced its rule through bloodshed and torture. I needed to proceed with caution and, for a while, wage battle from under cover.

Next, I wrote Il Saggiatore, a work about the phenomenon of sunspots. *I showed that sunspots could occur only because the sun rotated. I also mentioned in passing that the Earth revolved around the sun. The Inquisition granted permission to print the work with no further ado. Amazingly, it even expressed some praise for the work. Did I dare to hope that the Church had changed its view? I decided to go to Roma and try to persuade the Pope to lift the ban on Copernicanism.*

The journey proved arduous, but the Pope immediately granted me an audience. In Roman society I enjoyed great respect as a scientist. However, I did not attain my goal. On the contrary, the Church leaders exhorted me again to renounce my delusions.

Disappointed, I returned to Firenze and remained quiet for a few years. I pursued my work, attempting to publish non-provocative ideas, careful not to upset the Church. Over time, my conscience began demanding that I defend myself. Nevertheless, I held my tongue. The Inquisition was too vigilant, too powerful.

The older I got, the more my impatience turned to anger. I could not bear that people who had never looked through a telescope were making claims about what one could see through it. They based their statements solely on scripture. These people had the power to impose their interpretation as the only truth possible. Finally, after ten years, I wrote Dialogo sopra i due massimi sistemi del mondo to give voice to my ideas. The work is a conversation among three men. It takes place over a period of four days. One of the men argues for the modern scientific worldview of Copernicus. Another asks piercing and intelligent questions. He contributes significantly to the understanding of the problems presented. The third man, whom I called

Simplicius, advocates the Ptolemaic worldview of the Church. After some quibbling over the title and prologue, I received an ecclesiastical imprimatur. The work appeared in 1632.

Received enthusiastically in professional circles, the work was rejected by the Collegium Romanum and the Jesuits. The Pope felt personally insulted. He thought he recognized as his own some of the remarks coming out of Simplicius' mouth. As if I would dare to have Simplicius voice what his Holiness had actually said! I vehemently denied such allegations. However, the Church accused me of violating the decree of 1616. They accused me of heresy! I had promulgated an interpretation of reality that contradicted the Bible. Six months after the book's publication, the printer in Firenze received an order to print no more copies.

At that point, I began my most difficult battle for truth based on science. I took it on with confidence despite my seventy years. I felt certain that I would not be tortured, given my high-ranking friends and previous dealings with powerful people. I would simply have to behave pragmatically. I could manage such behavior because my books spoke for themselves. Their message was unstoppable.

On orders from the Pope, the Inquisitor of Firenze asked me to appear before the Inquisition in Roma to explain myself. I secured three medical certificates that stated I should not travel in winter because of my age and my present health. The trip was postponed. However, the Pope proclaimed that such excuses would not be tolerated. He ordered a doctor of the Inquisition to make a ruling. The physician confirmed my ability to travel. Toward the end of January 1633, I made the trip under guard to Roma.

I received permission to live under house arrest at the residence of the Florentine Envoy. The Inquisition began the task of investigating the theological implications of my writings. Finally, on April 12, they took me in for interrogation. I learned that the theologians responsible for my prosecution had argued to the court that, with the writing of my book, I had violated the Pope's admonishments and the decree of the Congregational Index. In their indictment, they expressed the suspicion that I still followed Copernicus. They threatened me with torture if I did not admit the truth immediately. From that moment until the end of the trial, I was imprisoned in the quarters of the Inquisition, something that frightened me and left me uncertain about my fate.

Galileo paused. His eyes fell to the table. The moment stretched awkwardly.

I ask for your understanding and forgiveness because I could not abide the prospect of physical pain administered by Church torturers. I remained convinced that the truth would prevail even if I preserved my body and yielded to the power and terror of the Church. So I testified that I had vacillated before the decree and held both the doctrines of Copernicus and Ptolemy acceptable, although only one of them could actually be true. Hearing the Church leaders' wise words had led me to make a firm decision. I was no longer uncertain and would accept their judgment. The Inquisition received this statement with some relief and was glad to avoid torture.

On June 22, 1633, judgment was rendered. The Cardinals and officials of the Inquisition, wearing their clerical vestments, gathered in the hall of the Dominican Convent of Santa Maria sopra Minerva. I stepped forward in my obligatory hair shirt and bowed before them. They looked sternly upon me from above, some looking as if they despised me. Others, however, behaved with a certain deference. The ruling stated that my book Il Dialogo contradicted the teachings of the Church and should remain prohibited. Then, the verdict stated, "You are suspected of having held and believed to be true that the sun is the center of the universe and that it does not move in the heavens from east to west, that the Earth moves and is consequently not the center of our universe. You must therefore accept the penalties prescribed by ecclesiastical law." The verdict also stated that the penalties could be somewhat abrogated if I recanted with all my heart the errors and heresies I had committed.

So I recanted and swore that I now believed, had always believed, and would always believe, with God's help, in all that the holy Catholic Church preached, taught, and held to be true. I admitted that I had toyed with the erroneous view that the sun was the center of the universe and that I would report to the Holy Office anyone I suspected of harboring such heresy.

Consequently, I was sentenced only to lifelong house arrest. I also had to recite the seven penitential psalms once a week for three years. I can add, with some satisfaction, that the judgment was not unanimous. Of the ten cardinals who officiated as judges, only seven signed their names to the verdict. I do not think my retraction made me a failure as some hotheads claimed. It saved my life. Many heretics had been burned alive in Roma, and burnings still occurred.

There's one more matter I need to set straight. Some people have said that after the trial I mumbled the phrase, "And yet it moves." This is not true. I never would have dared to say such a thing and certainly not immediately following the trial. But I've always thought that. For Earth does indeed revolve around the sun, and I can state with satisfaction that even today some cardinals of the Inquisition vacillate in their opinion. However, they did not express their doubts aloud. Thus I have growing hope that religious fundamentalism will not survive. Fundamentalists, as you know, check every scientific truth to see if it accords with scripture as interpreted by Church authorities.

Dear friends, this is my story. I have contributed to our common work as much as I could. I'm now going to spend my last years here in Arcetri, and I hope Church authorities will leave me in peace. A visit from the Prince of Firenze gives me hope. I know that, among the many who have dedicated themselves to the same mission, I did not experience the best fate, but neither was it the worst. I wish you all a life as fruitful as mine and hope that you come to understand my decision.

The screen began to flicker. I sat up and whispered to myself, "Galileo Galilei." Was that really Galileo Galilei or was it just some actor playing him? Recording equipment certainly didn't exist in his day. I went through the possibilities in my mind. Could it really be? I would go to Bucher and confront him with my suspicions.

***

Just as I was about to get up and turn off the equipment, the screen flickered again. Surprised, I looked up. The picture showed a kitchen in a nineteenth-century house. There was a deep sink with running water. On a wood stove, a kettle steamed. Dozens of test tubes, small round containers, and antique chemistry equipment sat on a table. A middle-aged woman walked into the picture. She had short hair and deep, intelligent eyes. She looked into the camera and spoke.

Thank you, Alfred, for your messages and greetings. I am always glad to hear from old comrades. You are in Africa! In our era, few have traveled to Africa, only a handful of adventurers, and we cannot imagine this "terra incognita." Do you recognize me after so long? Do I look like the same Marie Sklodowska with whom you spent your youth?

I've nearly accomplished my mission and have told people here everything essential about radioactivity. I am happy and can now enjoy life. I've met a wonderful man who loves me and whom I love. His name is Pierre Curie. I've taken his name and am known as Marie Curie. I've guided him toward making some important discoveries that he has published.

Marie laughed, glanced down for a moment, looked up with a smile, and continued.

He's now as famous as I am. I've settled in well, marrying a smart man who understands me and helps me in my work. Consequently, like most of us, I'll remain in this time and not return. How're you getting on? I heard from headquarters that your mission is quite challenging and you have to work very hard. Please let me hear from you again. All the best, dear Albert!

I sat thoughtfully as the image faded. What now? I pulled

out Michael's *Lexikon* again and looked up "Marie Curie." The entry read, "Professor of Physics at the Sorbonne University in Paris, born in 1867, died in 1934; discovered the radioactive elements polonium and radium and authored various publications on radioactivity. Nobel Prize in physics in 1903, with her husband and another researcher; Nobel Prize for chemistry in 1911." I sighed. Was this really possible? Could it really be that these people from different centuries all knew each other?

The Vatican

From his luxurious office in the administrative center of the Gospel Church of True Christians, Alco Sci stared out at the eight-lane arterial road that gave access to the center. There was little traffic. Now and then a car drove by. Sci studied the various reports his administrative assistant had arranged on his desk. Yesterday's Sunday service at the Cathedral—broadcast on his own channel, Certain Truth—had brought fantastically high ratings. In general over a quarter of all households in the Bible Belt had tuned in, and in some areas almost half of the households had. His ratings were comparable to those of the most popular entertainment shows on mainstream channels. Mel Court had transported everyone in the room to another plane with his preaching. He had done a superb job, and Sci would most certainly praise him at the next Board meeting.

Despite this success, Sci planned to invite a talented young preacher to deliver next Sunday's sermon. Sci had noticed him at one of the congregation branches. Court needed some competition, and it would not do if he became too strong. Sci doubted that Court would ever figure out his ulterior motive and would probably even be grateful for a break. Sci believed in the principle of "checks and balances"—dispersal of power—favored by the founding fathers of the United States, a principle they had built into the Constitution. He had enormous respect for these great men, even though most of them could not truthfully be called religious. Some had even been secret atheists or deists—almost the same. He also admired Caesar and the other great Roman commanders of ancient times who applied the principle of *divide et impera*—divide and rule. In fact, Sci probably thought more of Caesar than he did the founding fathers of the United States.

He picked up and perused a statistical study. According to the latest surveys, 53% of all Americans believed in the biblical creation story and thus were creationists. Three states even required their schools to teach this doctrine as equivalent in authenticity to the Darwinian theory of evolution. Sci's church and other churches had been successful in their efforts. Not that he cared how the world was actually created. He did love statistics. They measured success, including that of the GCTC and its religious teachings. This latest batch showed that he and his evangelical compeers were gaining influence. Sci reveled in that fact.

One detail in particular struck him today. Those who adhered most to the teachings in the Bible tended to be among the lesser educated populations. The better the level of education, the lower the number of creationists, with only around ten percent of all college graduates being creationists. He resolved to tackle the problem of academics more robustly later. Today he had no time. That the number of creationists in Europe was miniscule disturbed him as well. Why was there so little support for religious movements in Europe?

He sifted through his papers for the interim report from his three men in Europe. As an immediate measure shortly after his return from the conference in Bern, he had sent over three more troop members. This time they would not dress in dark suits but remain unobtrusive. Their only task was to gather information. So far they had reported that Bucher was behaving very discreetly and seemed to be working hard because he rarely left his office before late at night. Daniel von Arx had gone to Africa but had stayed only two weeks. The report contained little else. Sci did not quite know how to proceed. He considered various options and decided to talk it over with Pete Donnor, the young economist he had recruited two years earlier to supervise his business and perhaps become his deputy one day. Maybe talking to Donnor would stimulate ideas. In any case, it would give Sci an opportunity to put the young man to the test and determine whether he thought along the same lines in such matters. Mel Court was definitely not an option for such a conversation. He was a good preacher, but he did not have the intellectual depth to deal with tactical questions.

Sci also decided to make a call to Switzerland and order his three men to collect information more aggressively. In particular, they should approach von Arx and try to gain voluntary cooperation from him. Perhaps they might also encourage him to collaborate by applying their more forceful, tried-and-true methods.

***

Pete Donnor marveled at the stack of resumes his boss' secretary handed him. They were the same ones an old man had given to Alco Sci years ago. They had remained in the archives since then. Now, they arrived with all the reports of Sci's people in Switzerland. Donnor had not even known that there were such people in the service of their church. He immediately began to study the documents in preparation for his meeting with the boss.

Since he did not know quite where Switzerland was, he consulted the Internet. It was not in Scandinavia as he had thought at first. It was a small country with some seven million inhabitants in the middle of Europe. He had heard of Geneva, where the reformer, John Calvin, so often mentioned in church histories, had worked. Wow, he hadn't realized Geneva was in Switzerland. And wasn't the UN in Geneva, or at least some part of it? What else was there? Yes, of course, CERN, the world's largest particle accelerator. CERN attracted eminent physicists from all over the world. Then there was Zürich. It was also in Switzerland. He'd heard of Zürich—something about banking—but had forgotten the exact context. But Bern? On the Internet, he discovered that Bern was the capital. He had never heard of Bern. Strange, the Church had sent three members of the troops to this little country several months ago. Even the boss had gone at the beginning of this mysterious mission. Something big must be going on.

Donnor did not want to embarrass himself in front of the boss. He searched the Internet for more information about the people whose resumes he had received. All were scientists—physicists—and the commentary pointed out something in each resume that did not quite make sense. And this Edward Bucher? Was he also a physicist?

After prepping thoroughly, he phoned Sci's secretary and asked for an appointment. He got one the next morning.

Sci received him cordially. "Sit down, Pete. Would you like coffee or water?"

"I'd love a cup of coffee if it's not too much trouble."

The secretary brought in coffee. While she served, they talked about the weather. When she closed the door behind her, Sci came right to the point. "What do you think about the documents?"

"An interesting and highly explosive set of stories."

"Yes, you could sure say that."

"They bring up a lot of questions."

"I'm listening. Fire away."

"The first question I have is this. Do we have enough information to draw definitive conclusions? Or is this whole thing just a matter of conjecture?"

"It may be just conjecture."

"But even if it is just conjecture, we should still do some research to get some hard information." He paused. "I think we should learn more before taking any action."

"Of course," said Sci. "We need to learn more. Only how

do you think we should proceed? How and from whom are we going to get more information? I can't help but wonder if we're out of our league."

"I can't say, and I don't really know what all our options are. But I do want to mention something else."

"What?"

"Increasing our knowledge could be only the first step. We might need to act."

Sci nodded.

Donnor thought about it and asked, "What should we do if this conjecture turns out to be true? Wouldn't we have to launch a massive campaign? I mean, if we are in a position to undertake such an action and actually be effective. Or would it be beyond our capabilities? We should only proceed if we are willing and able to follow through."

"You mean that it makes no sense to pursue this conjecture if we can't act on our findings—assuming we actually have findings?"

"Right. Some sort of power play on our part could backfire and threaten our very existence, even if we were well prepared. This raises another question. Suppose that our suspicions are true. How would this impact the GCTC?"

Sci replied without hesitation, "We and all other churches would become superfluous, meaningless. We would disappear."

"How long would we have?"

"Until it goes public, until everybody knows."

"When might that happen?"

"Hard to say. Certainly not before Bucher publishes his work. Maybe much later, perhaps years or even decades later."

"So our church could hang on until then?"

"Yes."

"So maybe what we want to do is just wait but stay on guard. Maybe we wouldn't be affected, just our successors."

"Also a possibility. But doesn't that seem a bit spineless?"

Donnor paused and thought. Then he suggested, "Let's start again from the beginning. We are too small. Given our resources, we can neither research this conjecture thoroughly nor do anything effective if it's confirmed. Could we join forces with others? This problem, if it really is a problem, will strike at the heart of all churches."

"So you're thinking of an association of churches with the sole purpose of dealing with this thing. You think that might work?"

"Maybe."

"That's going to be hard. We are all competitors. Nobody trusts anybody. Every denomination has some theological peculiarity that makes it 'unique and better' than the others. It'll never work out."

Donnor agreed. "Getting cooperation would be a huge undertaking anyway. By the time we convinced everybody to cooperate, our time would be up. Better if we had the power to do something just ourselves."

"I think so too."

"But we are too small. We know that already."

"That's true, unfortunately," Sci affirmed.

"What if, instead of going to all the other churches, we approached only a few, or just one? If we could convince the leader of a powerful denomination, wouldn't he do something?"

"Who would that be?" Sci was enjoying Donnor's enthusiasm.

"That'd be the Pope in Rome. The Roman Catholic Church."

"The Catholics would have the power to act alone. But I have to say, I'd have a hard time collaborating with those people," said Sci bitterly.

"I understand. The Catholic Church is our main competitor, the Whore of Babylon."

"Exactly. We struggle against their dominance everywhere and all the time. So you think we should take them into our confidence?"

"It's our very existence we're talking about—ours and theirs."

Sci laughed. "Actually, you're right, Pete. You've convinced me. Besides, the Catholics are not as strong as they once were. When you consider that they've had two thousand years to set up their organization and we've had only a few decades. Thinking about it that way, we're actually more successful than they are."

"All right. Let's take a deep breath and try to start a conversation with them. How do you suggest we do that?"

"I'm sure we won't get anywhere with their cardinals here in the U.S. And that would be repugnant. I really despise those guys."

"We could go straight to Rome," offered Pete.

"That appeals to me, and an audience with the papal pimp would give this whole thing a lot more weight."

Once the decision was made to go to Rome, they discussed how to prepare for the trip, exactly whom they should approach, and when they wanted to go. Donnor took it upon himself to call the Vatican and request a meeting. He acted cautiously and did not reveal too much over the phone. He did drop a few hints, however, so that they would at least gain a hearing.

During the conversation, Donnor came to realize that Rome did not take the Gospel Church of True Christians very seriously. The request for an audience with the Pope was rejected outright. His Holiness would receive no American cult leader, revealing himself more than a little arrogant. The chairman of the Congregatio de Seminariis atque Studiorum Institutis (whatever that was), a cardinal, would not receive them either. The Secretary of the Congregatio, however, a Monsignor Bellini—an ordinary priest—was obliging and would see them if they wanted to take the trouble to come to Rome. The date was set. Sci's secretary booked a first-class flight for Sci and Donnor on Delta and made all their travel arrangements for the trip.

***

Sci and Donnor emerged from their plane in Fiumicino. Before their flight from Atlanta, they'd had a couple of bloody marys, so they were in good spirits when they boarded the plane. After settling into their roomy recliners, they enjoyed glasses of champagne, followed by a tasty meal, red wine, and cognac to top it all off. Not surprisingly they slept well and felt rested if a little dehydrated when they landed. They avoided the suburban railway, which would have led them from the airport to I Termini, preferring an hour-long trip in a chauffeur-driven limousine through midmorning traffic. The driver took them to their four-star hotel on the hill above the Scalinata della Trinità dei Monti, better known as the Spanish Steps, where they repaired to their separate suites.

Sci tipped the porter and turned to open one of the tall windows. Rome spread out before him—a magnificent view. In the distance, he could see the Piazza Venezia and the giant white Monument to Victor Emmanuel II. The ancient Roman Forum and Coliseum were close by although he couldn't make them out. He could also see the dome of the Basilica di San Pietro at the Vatican. According to legend, reiterated in the colorful brochure prominent on the desk of his sitting room, the city was founded about 750 BC, making it over 2700 years old, about 2500 years older than Petersburg, Kentucky. Over the millennia, Rome had experienced much and withstood severe trials, so the city would hardly be shocked by any news that might arrive from Kentucky. In any case, Sci's problems seemed for a brief moment small and insignificant against such historical background.

He closed the window and unpacked his suitcase before catching the elevator to the roof terrace of the hotel, where he enjoyed the same wonderful views. Donnor joined him. They sat down at a table and again rehearsed what they would say during their afternoon appointment at the Vatican.

When the time came, they had a taxi summoned and directed the driver the take them to the Sant'Anna entrance of the Vatican. The taxi crossed a bridge over the Tiber and bore right along the Lungotevere to approach the Basilica, the largest church in the world, from the north side.

Pulling to the side of the busy Via di Porta Angelica near the main entrance to the Vatican, the driver stopped, pointed to a modest archway, and dropped his two guests off. To either side, within the shelter of the arch, stood Swiss guards holding halberds. A uniformed papal policeman emerged from a kiosk and asked their business and names. Checking his clipboard, he nodded and led them inside the walls and into a narrow lane branching off to the right. Within a few steps, the policeman gestured toward a substantial wooden door. Sci and Donnor found no bell but an old-fashioned iron knocker. After some hesitation, they let it slam against a metal plate. The blow rang through the house. A man in a blue smock soon opened the door. He looked them over, listened politely, and, saying nothing, led them into an anteroom.

Everything was very clean but old. Antique pictures hung on the wall. A precious old carpet with religious motifs lay on the floor. Heavy walnut furniture from centuries long past adorned the room. A side door creaked open and a handsome young man appeared. He could have been mistaken for a fashion model were it not for the black cassock he wore. His somber attire suited him.

"Bellini," the priest introduced myself and beckoned for them to follow. They sat down on leather-upholstered chairs in the next room. The man who had let them in brought three glasses of mineral water and closed the door as he departed.

"How may I serve you?" The priest said with a light Italian accent. After Sci introduced himself and Donnor and mentioned the Gospel Church of True Christians, Donnor took over. He described the information they had run across and the irregularities in the lives of various important people throughout history. To make his case he provided detailed accounts of the lives of two individuals widely separated in time—Archimedes and Nicola Tesla. Then he told Bellini about Dr. Bucher and the words Bucher had exchanged with Alco Sci.

"We believe that we should confirm or allay our suspicions, suspicions that, if proved true, will require all churches to react. Ultimately, this is a question concerning the relevance of religion and the existence of churches, all churches, even the Catholic Church."

Monsignor Bellini listened attentively. When Donnor had finished, he asked, "Why do you come to me? What do you expect from us?"

"The Catholic Church is huge and powerful. You have more options available to you than we do. We want to entrust the matter to you and acknowledge your leadership." Donnor had spoken without consulting Sci. A glance at him, however, showed that Sci agreed with the tactic.

Bellini looked at them sharply. He replied, "I'll think this over, consult with my superiors, and let you know. I will also obtain some documents from our archives that might interest you. I suggest that we meet here again tomorrow at the same time."

Sci and Donnor sat back in their chairs, stunned that their audience had come to such an abrupt conclusion. They had expected a discussion about advantages and disadvantages of different approaches to the issue. But Bellini stood. He ushered the two to the door, thanked them for coming and speaking so openly, and confirmed the appointment for tomorrow.

***

The next day, Monsignor Bellini, Sci, and Donnor sat again in the same room. Bellini placed a hand on a stack of papers in front of him and took control of the conversation.

"You've spoken of irregularities or, more precisely, inexplicable events and sequences, in the lives of several famous people. The Church has known about this for a long time. Throughout our history for some two thousand years, we've observed these irregularities repeatedly and have kept an eye on these people. No one here was surprised by the reason for your request to confer with us."

He paused a moment and looked at the two men. "Yesterday, despite the fact that we already knew much about you and have maintained a file on you for some time, I wanted to find out exactly what you were seeking and how much you knew before I responded. In any case, I was surprised that your organization had taken up the matter and was pursuing it in a way that I find quite intemperate. I'll come back to that, however."

Sci cleared his throat. His face burned with anger, but he controlled himself and said nothing. Donnor remained outwardly unmoved and just listened.

Bellini shuffled through the papers, took one out, and continued. "Yesterday you mentioned two great physicists, Archimedes and Tesla. I would like to bring up a third case, namely that of Galileo Galilei. His trial is often used as an example of the conflict that exists between faith and science and as an example of a colossal blunder by the Church. His trial is unusually well documented in our archive. We still have all the transcripts of his interrogation, all written commentary and considerations, as well as a detailed description of the circumstances at the time. Above all, we have a transcript that the Church has kept in strict secret. It is here before me. You will not be able to read it yourself. It is written in Church Latin. However, I will summarize some of the contents. Should you reveal my summary, we will take measures to insure that no one believes you."

Bellini began to translate fragments from the paper in his hands. Galileo was not tortured, although torture was the usual method of questioning at that time. The examining magistrate who would have supervised the interrogation under torture had expressed the suspicion that Galileo Galilei was of supernatural birth. He arrived at this conclusion for various reasons, specifically that Galileo had in his possession a strange object that his jailors had discovered when searching his clothes. The object in question could not have been made in Italy—a clock, which ran "of itself."

Bellini looked up from the paper and stared at Sci and Donnor, who leaned forward in their seats. "It's still in our archives, and Galileo probably didn't even realize where he'd lost it. The clock is a quartz timepiece, powered by a solar cell and designed to last dozens of years, presumably for the entire lifetime of the wearer."

Sci opened his mouth to say something but thought better of it. Bellini answered his unspoken question. "It would probably still run if it hadn't been stored in a dark vault. Galileo also had other knowledge that the interrogators felt could hardly have come from his own studies."

Bellini looked Sci straight in the eye. "So, you see, we

have a solar quartz clock from the seventeenth century in our archives." He smiled. "And that is just one of the many curiosities."

The two Americans said nothing. Bellini looked down at the document again and continued. "The panel of judges was satisfied that Galileo had recanted—if only half-heartedly." Bellini laid the document back on the stack of papers.

Sci and Donnor both knew the name Galileo Galilei. They knew that he had lived during the Middle Ages or the Renaissance, which Bellini had just confirmed. However, they had no clue exactly why he was famous. Was it because he and what he knew were "not of this world"? Both clearly understood that the Catholic Church claimed knowledge about beings of supernatural origin.

Alco Sci broke the silence. "So what you are saying is that supernatural beings do exist. How has the Church responded to them?"

"We haven't. We simply recognize and document such phenomena."

"Why haven't you done anything about them?"

"Well, gentlemen, we have a term for such beings. We call them angels, and we adore them."

"Our church doesn't believe in angels," Sci replied. "I've always thought that they were mythical creatures from some earlier time, maybe something from the past history of the Catholic Church, but without real significance in modern times."

"You obviously don't know what angels are—creatures of supernatural origin. We recognize, for example, three archangels, Michael, Gabriel, and Raphael. In addition to the archangels, we recognize other types of angels. The best known are probably guardian angels. According to tradition, angels were created from light, thus their supernatural origin. Often they are asexual, represented with wings and dressed in white. But we also know that angels often appear in our world looking just like humans. No one can tell them apart from mortals. There have always been such angels, but because we can't recognize them, we don't know how many there actually are."

"Angels. Hmm. I've honestly never given angels much thought," Sci admitted. Donnor remained silent.

"Angels are not only part of the Christian faith. Jews and Muslims believe in them, too. In the Jewish tradition, and sometimes in the Christian tradition, there is even a fourth archangel, Ariel. There has also been occasional talk of seven archangels."

"So the scientists we've described could be angels?"

"It's possible. We've known about angels for millennia and have documented many occurrences of their existence. If you could go through our archives, you would learn a great deal about these beings who have come to spend time among us on Earth. We've even dedicated a church to them here in Rome, the Basilica di *Santa* Maria degli Angeli. It's worth a visit. You should go there. So in answer to your question, yes, I believe the entities and events you've described are angelic phenomena."

"Why hasn't the Catholic Church reacted, spoken out, or done something about them?"

"Come now, gentlemen. What should we 'do' about divine beings? On precisely this point, I must say that I don't care for your attitude or the presumptuous request you've made of us."

Alco Sci hesitated. He had not expected Bellini's reaction. "So angels are divine beings in human form," he said. "I wouldn't have thought of that. But Bucher and people like him? Are they angels?"

"I don't know. We'd have to gather and document the facts."

"But if he were an angel, wouldn't we need to take action?"

"Take action? Why?"

"Because what he's doing undermines our churches. Because he's advancing anti-religious theories."

"Listen, that would be his business. We're not about to rebuke a divine being, assuming that is what he is. What's more," continued Bellini, "the Church leaders here at the Vatican are not naïve. We have never renounced the idea that angels are divine beings created from light. We have, however, gone back and combed through our records to gain a better understanding of certain pieces of information. For example, how a solar-powered quartz clock might appear in the seventeenth century and who could have made it."

"Did you find out?"

"As I said, we are investigating. But we will certainly not share our findings. At any rate, whatever we know, or find out, will not justify any action against the people we still call angels, even if they do have characteristics and origins that are different from those we have previously known."

"But aren't you going to do *something*? You have to save your church!"

Bellini paused. Then he said, "His Holiness has already led the Curia through several discussions on the subject. The

Curia's conclusions will remain secret, and I'll not reveal them to you, but since you already know so much, the Pope agreed yesterday to my giving you a bit of information."

"Thank you. We appreciate that."

"Our Church assumes that people have a spiritual need, whatever the truth about God. As representatives of an independent church, you should know that. You certainly exploit the need ruthlessly."

"We do no such thing!" Sci's voice rose in frustration and anger.

"You can't even admit what you're doing. Partly for that reason, we abhor any contact with you. We will never cooperate with you, especially since we can deal with the issue without any assistance."

Sci realized he may have gone too far and mumbled, "I apologize for interrupting, Monsignor."

Bellini seemed to relax a bit. "So spiritual need is always there. Even with all the progress brought by science, some things will always remain inexplicable. Science explains many things, but it also generates new puzzles. At present, science can explain much that has happened since the Big Bang. But what about before the Big Bang?"

"You're very up to date here in Rome."

"We certainly don't find it necessary to deny proven scientific knowledge just to assuage our traditional religious assumptions. For example, if you fight against the theory of evolution and claim the biblical story of creation is literally true, your argument becomes simply absurd. In the long run, you make the teachings of your church unbelievable because scientific truth will always win out. We've known this at least since the trial of Galileo Galilei—since the seventeenth century. The Catholic Church has committed enough errors over the years. We can't do anything about past mistakes, but we will do everything possible not to lose our credibility in modern society. Over time, your church's approach will drive people away because they will realize that you aren't preaching the truth."

"But you will destroy yourselves by acknowledging evolution!"

"We don't think so. There will always be a need to explain the mysterious. So there'll always be a need for a higher power and the Church to explain that power. In our deliberations, we have decided to accept a gradual transformation in the image of God. We will allow the image to become a more distant higher power. In the Church, we will depict God as we perceive he depicts himself at this particular time."

"That's very brave—or foolhardy," said Sci.

"Not at all. The Church must survive. It's your irrational chatter about the creation story—what you call Creationism—that endangers your survival. You should know that such nonsense can't endure."

"So you won't help us in the fight against Bucher and his kind?"

"Of course not. We'll go our own way. Now, gentlemen, this conversation is over."

On the way back to the hotel, Sci said, "Well, at least he didn't beat around the bush. Looks like we'll be on our own in Switzerland."

***

Several weeks earlier Kommissar Erb had received notification from the border police that three more members of the Gospel Church of True Christians from the United States had entered the country. He secured their photos and personal data and immediately questioned the detainees in jail about the new "tourists." He decided to have the three new men watched for now. They, it turned out, were watching Edward Bucher and Daniel von Arx. That noted, they had kept a low profile and had not contacted either man. A search of their bags and clothes at the border and, later, a discrete inspection of their hotel room revealed that they had no weapons. There was no pressing reason to intervene, and Erb had no legal basis to arrest or expel them from the country. He decided to suspend continuous surveillance and only renew it periodically and very discreetly. He arranged for the hotel manager and the border police to notify him immediately if the three disappeared for more than a day or appeared ready to leave.

He had, however, just received an alarming message. The border police had reported that two heads of the Gospel Church of True Christians had entered Switzerland at Chiasso. Erb immediately sought information about their lodgings in Bern, for he was sure they were headed to the city. The search was easy. They had booked two rooms at the Bellevue Palace, a splendid five-star hotel. He asked the manager to give them rooms 4 and 5, which the police carefully prepared. These were junior suites with balconies facing south toward the majestic Alps. The two would be very pleased with their accommodations.

Professor Bucher

Edward Bucher locked the door of his office at 4:00 p.m. and headed down the stairs to the parking lot. He passed a couple students and a lab assistant in the stairwell. All greeted him respectfully, but he hardly noticed. He got into his car and drove through the neighborhood along Länggassstrasse toward Neufeld stadium on the outskirts of Bern, carefully keeping under the speed limit. In Neufeld he turned onto Autobahn E27 and accelerated. At the Wankdorf intersection, he struck out in the direction of Thun-Interlaken. Reaching the third exit, he left the Autobahn and dropped back to a quiet pace. He drove his car along a winding road in the alpine foothills, enjoying the sunshine through an open window and the sweet air on his skin. He breathed in the fields, some dotted with cattle. He turned onto a dirt road that led into a small, isolated valley. No one saw him. The trees quickly thickened into a forest where nature reigned supreme.

In a clearing toward the end of the valley, a lone building stood surrounded by a high wire fence. One might have thought it a military ammunition depot, as one often sees in the foothills of Switzerland, if it had not been marked with the sign "Physikalisches Institut, Universität Bern." Bucher opened the gate, drove through, and closed the gate behind him. He parked his car in a shed behind the building and entered. The room was dark. Bucher flipped a switch in an electrical control box next to the entry. Lights flashed on as he closed the door. He looked around. The vast room had a dome ceiling like an observatory. At the center, three rails arranged in a triangle led up to the dome. In the middle of the triangle, stood a round, tapered object that looked much like a plastic rocket balanced on three fins. Bucher opened a wall panel, revealing several electrical switches. Attached to the inside of the panel door was a small card that read "Function Control." He put on his glasses and read carefully. Then he flipped a switch. Silently, the dome in the ceiling opened. He flipped a second switch. With a soft hum, the three rails, along with the rocket-like object, shifted, much as a telescope in an observatory might be directed toward different stars in the night sky. Bucher nodded and looked up to the dome. The mechanism worked.

He sat down at a console in front of the triangle, pressed open a spring-loaded drawer, and pulled out a leather-bound notebook. He opened to the second page and booted up the computer. Next, he began to enter positions and directions. He tested all the settings and functions for nearly two hours, checking his work repeatedly against the instructions in the notebook. After a final check, he was satisfied. Everything worked perfectly, as it had the last time.

He got up from the console and walked over to a cabinet on the other side of the room. Retrieving a ring of keys from his pocket, he found the special key he needed, unlocked the cabinet, and pulled out the top drawer. Several metal tubes rolled to the front. Each had an opening on one end. He searched the corner of the drawer and pulled out a metal pellet about a millimeter in diameter. He inserted the pellet into one of the tubes, aimed at the opposite wall, and squeezed. Once he heard the pellet strike the wall, he searched the floor and retrieved it. He then loaded the next tube. After making sure that all the tubes worked, he loaded three of them with pellets containing an anesthetic. He laid the three tubes on the console, turned everything off, locked up, and headed back to the car. The sun had just set in the sky, and Bucher was ready to go home.

***

Returning home from Michael's studio around midnight, I opened the mailbox and found two letters. I pocketed them both.

When I let myself into my apartment, I had the feeling that someone was there. So I did not turn on the light. I closed the door softly behind me and let my eyes become accustomed to the darkness. I tiptoed from room to room. Finding no one, I walked back to the door and locked it. Then I parted the curtain and looked through the living room window onto the street. Nothing unusual. Only after I was quite sure that no one was in the apartment and no one was outside, did I turn on the light. Why did I feel that someone was watching me?

I sat down at the table and opened the first letter. It contained a note from Kommissar Erb. He wanted to see me in person and suggested a meeting tomorrow at 9:00 a.m. in a nearby sidewalk café. If that were not possible, I should call him. He had included his phone number. The note contained no hint regarding why he wanted to see me.

I opened the second letter. Professor Bucher's business card fell out. I unfolded the paper with it and read. Bucher wanted me to stop by sometime for a visit. He would like to know how I was doing. "Right," I said out loud. He already knew how I was. I wondered what he really wanted. Okay, Professor, I thought. I'll go and visit you tomorrow. It will be a day full of visits.

I went into the bathroom, showered, and brushed my teeth. In bed I turned out the light, but I couldn't sleep. The events of the last few days whirled around in my head. One thought tumbled after another, and I tried to put it all together, make sense of all the different participants' behaviors. There was also the issue of what else I should do.

The church bell rang twice, signaling 2:00 a.m. I wanted to be alert tomorrow. But still I could not sleep. I got up and peeked once again out the window onto the street. Nothing moved or seemed suspicious. I puttered over to the fridge and poured myself a glass of milk. Back in bed. I must have fallen asleep right away because, the next thing I knew, sunlight was streaming through the window. The clock showed 8:00 a.m.

I quickly got dressed and strolled to the café. I wanted to

read the newspaper and have a cup of coffee in peace before meeting with the Kommissar, but it didn't work out that way. Cornelia entered the café shortly after I did. We had gone out a couple of times, but I had kept my distance because I felt she wanted more than an occasional nice night together. Of course she came over and sat down. She ignored the fact that I was reading the newspaper and began to chat. No one else was in the café. The waiter came, and we ordered coffee and rolls. I unfolded the paper and handed her a section. She waved it away and chattered on. Giving up on reading, I folded the two sections back together and set the paper on the table next to me.

After twenty minutes, Cornelia put her hand on my arm and said, "I have to go now."

"Already?"

"Yes, unfortunately. When can we see each other again?" she said.

"I'll call you."

"Soon?"

"Yeah, sure, we'll see."

She hurried away to work.

Just as I was about to pick up the paper again, Kommissar Erb sat down. "That's a pretty lady. I hope she didn't leave on account of me," he joked.

"No, not on your account, but you're a fairly poor replacement." I smiled so he wouldn't take it the wrong way.

"Ha! I'll concede that! Only I'm not here entirely on a voluntary basis as the lady was."

"Okay. What's driving you to seek my company?"

"I wanted to re-establish a connection. You'll be seeing a lot more of me soon."

"Really?"

"Yes. We have information that the people who threatened Professor Bucher have resumed their activities."

"What does that have to do with me?"

"We don't know, Herr von Arx. But we think it prudent to check on you occasionally. In order to protect you, we may even need to shadow you again, depending on the situation."

"I see. You're a bit late. Someone has already bothered me."

"Bothered you? How so?"

"Yes. I suppose I should bring you up to date." I told him how a man had approached me demanding that I cooperate in some sort of investigation of Dr. Bucher. Kommissar Erb insisted that I describe the man in detail.

When I had finished, he closed his notepad and said, "My assumption was correct. You are, in fact, a target of these suspicious activities. Remember that the police will be nearby. Don't be startled by their presence."

"Thanks for letting me know."

"Here's my card again. If you notice anything unusual or if someone approaches you again, don't hesitate to call me. We're here to help you."

Kommissar Erb left, and I finally read the newspaper. Afterwards I walked to the university and just sat in my office for a while.

Around noon, I returned to my apartment. The mailbox was empty. Contrary to habit, I went up the stairs slowly. To my surprise, the door was wide-open. I knew I'd shut it. I felt nauseous. I didn't move but waited, listening from the hallway.

Inside, nothing stirred. Should I go in or get help? I pushed the door open with the tips of my fingers. Still not a sound. I entered on tiptoe. All doors stood open. The living room was a hopeless mess—cabinet doors ajar and drawers pulled out, their contents scattered on the floor. The furniture had been overturned, the pillows torn, and the carpet ripped back.

I stood looking at the wreckage around me, wondering where to begin. The phone rang. I picked it up and said, "Von Arx."

"Have you thought over our offer?" asked a voice I didn't recognize.

"What offer?" I stalled.

"To work together."

"What are you referring to?"

"Don't play dumb. You know exactly what I'm talking about—exchanging information about Bucher."

"I see. But haven't you already tried to procure this information yourself? At least, it seems that way."

"What do you mean?"

"You tore up my apartment looking for it. You've resorted to violence and theft to get what you want. In other words, you are not exactly a reliable partner."

There was a pause. Then the voice shouted, "You have no choice. Cooperate or we will force you to."

"Right, what a lovely prospect," I sneered, undaunted. "Maybe I'll cooperate if you tell me who you are and what you're after—or maybe not."

"Don't try to set conditions!"

"As I said before, I won't partner with anyone I don't know."

"Then we'll make you. We have ways. Think hard about what you're going to do."

"I've done that already. Basically, you don't want me as a partner. You want information from me without telling me who you are, why you need the information, or what I get in return. That's unacceptable."

"Your final word?" the voice threatened.

"My final word."

"You'll regret this." The connection clicked and went dead.

I hung up and wondered what to do. I wasn't up to dealing with criminals. That much I knew. I needed to talk to Professor Bucher again—and the police.

***

Dr. Bucher's secretary led me into his spacious office and announced loudly, "Doktor von Arx." I was startled, still not used to the new title preceding my name.

I looked at her, smiled, a little embarrassed, and said awkwardly, "You certainly keep up with university promotions."

She smiled back much more boldly. Bucher came to meet me. We shook hands. He pointed to the sofa in the sitting area, and we sat down across from each other. I looked around. The desk and bookshelves remained unchanged. The various electronic devices were still in place as if I had just left.

"Nice of you to come so quickly," Bucher said. "I assume you got my letter."

"Yes, thank you for the invitation."

"How are you? No distressing sequelae?"

"I'm fine. May I ask you a question, Professor, perhaps a presumptuous one?"

"Yes, of course."

"Did you invite me here just to inquire after my health?"

"Not at all. But I am glad that you're well. It didn't seem right that you suffered because of me. Grant me that."

"Thank you." I paused and picked up the conversation. "But on that topic, Professor, have you learned anything about who was behind the burglary and murder."

"No, unfortunately not. I have reached no other conclusion than it had something to do with economic espionage."

"You've had no trouble since then?"

"Not the slightest. Those involved have probably realized that I'm keeping my powder dry. I've been fair warned!"

"Of course."

Bucher paused and looked directly at me. "Herr von Arx, you have been keeping tabs on me."

"Does that upset you, Professor?"

"I'd rather remain undisturbed."

"I can understand that."

Again, a pause. Bucher rubbed his forehead with his thumb and index finger. "You went to see Alfred Pestalozzi in M'bene?"

"Yes. Do you know him?"

"You already know the answer to that question, don't you?"

I nodded. "Yes."

"What else do you know?"

"Very little compared to you, Professor."

"Don't be so modest."

Then I asked him straight out. "When was the last time you saw Alfred Pestalozzi?"

"Maybe a year or two ago. He always visits me when he comes to Europe."

"How long have you known him?"

"Since our youth."

"Where did you spend your youth? In another world?"

Bucher stopped rubbing his forehead and met my gaze. "Oh, come now. Do you really believe that?"

"No. Still, I suppose you do come from a different world, so to speak."

"Pestalozzi called and warned me about you."

"So, I'm right," I pushed.

"You are close to the truth."

"Would that be bad, I mean, for me to know the truth?"

"Hard to say," Bucher admitted. "We've never dealt with this kind of problem before."

"May I ask you a question about your work, Professor?"

"I suppose. Go ahead."

"Your field is theoretical physics. What did you do before you came here? Where did you acquire all your knowledge?"

"That's not a question about my work." He looked at me a long time. "But I will answer it anyway. Might as well, given what you know." The muscles in his face fell, almost as if he'd given up. "I acquired my knowledge as a very young child and worked with children before I came here, supporting their education."

"Wait a minute. Where you come from, children already know what you're teaching university students here?"

"Could we change the subject, please?"

"As you wish." I shook my head in disbelief and decided I had nothing to lose. "Professor, if you will allow me just one more question." He sighed and nodded. "Given our current knowledge of physics, is it possible for a person to travel through time?"

Bucher looked at me thoughtfully. "Do you mean does the technology exist to create a time machine? Something like what you might find in a science-fiction novel?"

"Yes."

"Theoretically it's possible. It's just not practical, at least not with the technology we have today."

"How would it work in theory?"

"Do you really want to know? I would have to outline various theories for you to understand."

"If it's not too much trouble, Professor, please."

"Very well then."

At that point, I experienced an awe-inspiring lecture on physics, an explanation of the nature of relationships and processes in the world. Bucher explained these theories simply and in understandable terms. He spoke slowly and emphatically.

"Imagine three-dimensional space. Take for example, our universe. Now add a fourth dimension—time. At each moment the perceived position of any star shifts as the Earth rotates. This means that space looks a little different at each point in time. In a manner of speaking, space unwinds in time, just as visible objects in a movie shift as a film unwinds. Do you understand?"

"Yes. I'm with you so far."

"Good. This four-dimensional space, which occurs in time

and in which objects move, we call spacetime. In spacetime, a point is not only determined by the three planes of the old Cartesian coordinate system. It also has a precise date, an axis of time. This means that a certain point can no longer be referred to as a 'point.' Instead, it is called an 'event.' The event is thus determined both spatially and temporally. Are you still with me?"

"Somewhat. Each point in spacetime carries a precise time stamp. It cannot be described simply as a point in space, but as an event specified by space and time."

"Good summary. You're following this very well." Bucher called out to his secretary for bottled water. "Would you like a glass?" he asked. I gladly accepted the offer. Then he continued. "Between one designated event and another event, there is a shortest distance, which we physicists call an 'interval.' The interval between two events in spacetime can be calculated using methods analogous to the methods used to calculate the distance between two points in three-dimensional space."

The secretary brought in a liter bottle of mineral water. I used the interruption to ask a question. "Please back up a little and remind me how distance is measured in three dimensions."

"The method used is similar to the one based on the Pythagorean Theorem," replied Bucher. "Pythagoras was a Greek philosopher who lived in the sixth century B.C.E. and developed a theory to calculate the distance between two points." Bucher pulled over a pencil and a notepad sitting on the table and opened it up to a blank page. He drew two points on the page. "Here are the two points, x and y. Imagine that we want to find the distance between them." Bucher drew a line between the two points.

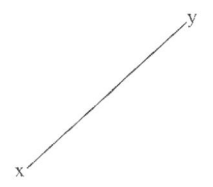

"You start by drawing a line through points x and y in such a way that they intersect to create a right angle at a third definable point z."

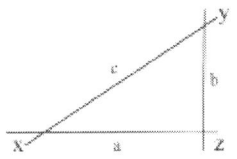

"Since you know the distance of the line xz and of line yz, you can calculate the distance of line xy by using the Pythagorean formula $a^2 + b^2 = c^2$. Remember?"

Bucher put the pencil down and looked at me expectantly. I nodded. All this geometry was familiar, even if I hadn't used it in years.

"This formula for the right triangle in two-dimensional space is easily expanded to include a component for three-dimensional space or, adding yet another component, for four-dimensional space. Thus it's not difficult at all to calculate the shortest distance in spacetime."

"This makes sense," I said.

"Good. I'm trying to keep this simple. Imagine an event in spacetime and the same designated event an hour later but unmoved in space. The interval, that is, the distance between the two events would measure only in time since no spatial displacement would have taken place. The interval is temporal.

On the other hand, simultaneous events at different spatial points would have an interval purely spatial. Should I give you an example?"

I nodded.

"The spot on Earth where we both sit has shifted in space and time over the course of the past hour. It has shifted because the Earth rotates and revolves around the sun, and the sun, in turn, revolves around a point in the Milky Way. Our spot has thus followed a spiral path. In other words, we haven't traveled the shortest route between events but rather in a curve. We've made a temporal and spatial detour."

That seemed pretty clear to me. Viewed against a fixed background, Earth would appear to reel through space, and a point on its surface would not follow the shortest route from one event to the next.

Bucher studied me. He decided that I was not lost and continued, "Now, however, we can theoretically calculate the interval between two events on the Earth's surface—that is, the shortest route. We can also calculate a path between two events that would take the shortest time, thus defining an interval in spatial terms. If we send a spacecraft on this shorter route, it will arrive at the second event before the Earth gets there. On Earth, we take an hour to move through space. The spacecraft needs less time. It arrives at an older or future world. It flies into the future. Does this make sense to you?"

"Barely," I replied. "It goes beyond what I can envision."

"You just have to imagine a space that is unwinding in time, in spacetime, so to speak, from event to event, that is, from point to point in spacetime, following the shortest line. This line is the interval. A spaceship can trace the interval, whereas the Earth with its reeling detour would arrive later."

"Really?"

"In theory, yes."

Bucher leaned back. He searched my face and spoke firmly, "Up to this point, my lecture is still to some extent understandable. Now, however, comes the difficult part."

"I'll try to follow," I promised.

"Very well. Here it comes. Einstein showed that the speed of light is absolute, independent of the observer's location or relative movement. Two points, connected to each other by the speed of light, therefore constitute a single event since the beam of light and the two points can be seen simultaneously. If I travel at the speed of light from one point to another, this is also a single event. An interval, that is, a distance in spacetime, can only be between two events. In the case of two points connected with the speed of light, the interval is therefore zero. The two points are connected to each other without a temporal difference. On arrival, I'm the same age as at the start."

"Can that be true? This means, then, that for an object traveling at light speed, no time passes?"

"Yes, exactly."

"But we do speak of light years. Doesn't light need time when it moves through space?"

"Only from a point of observation. If we were sitting on the beam, no time would pass. Time passes in relationship to the observer. Since the light beam is an event in time and space, no time passes."

"Wow. So, if you are traveling at light speed, you don't age?"

"Right. Only we humans can't travel at the speed of light. This is impossible because our cell structure would be destroyed. However, we can get close to a cruising speed of light. The closer we get, the less time passes. So between two events, we could choose the route with the shortest time axis. As a result, the spatial axes grow longer the closer we approach the speed of light."

"So I could," I asked thoughtfully, "select a point on Earth today and calculate its location in space a hundred years from now and then define the interval—the shortest path between the two events? I can also determine the path from one event to another and calculate a trajectory so that the journey takes very little time. This path would not follow the shortest route, that is, the interval, but two legs of a triangle, which could be selected to make the time axis as short as possible. And because of a velocity near the speed of light, an extended displacement along the spatial axis would result. I could go from one event to the next almost without aging?"

"Exactly," Bucher said. "You've got the picture."

"Then what's stopping us from flying into the future?"

"Only technology. We've had the theoretical knowledge since Einstein. But we aren't yet able to build spaceships that can travel fast enough or at a distance of several light years."

"Do you think we ever will?"

"Sure. You're going to experience it for yourself," said Bucher, rising to show me that my time with him was up.

On the way out, I turned the conversation back to the break-in. "You said you didn't know who committed the burglary?"

"That's right."

"Did you know that some guys are still sniffing around here in Bern?"

"No, I didn't. How'd you know that?"

"First, the police told me, and then a man I didn't know, but who mentioned you, approached me."

"Mentioned me?"

"He wanted me to tell him what I know about you."

"Did you?"

"No. But yesterday someone broke into my apartment and ransacked it."

"What? Another break-in?"

"Yes indeed. I suspect they were looking for any information I might have had on you."

"Did you have such information for them to find?"

"No."

"Good. But watch out for yourself!"

The door closed behind me, and I stood alone in the corridor. I knew our business together was not over.

I would experience "it" for myself?

Theories of Time

Alfred Pestalozzi sat on the porch of his house in M'bene drinking a beer and smoking a pipe. He felt relaxed. Darkness had fallen and the night sky was clear. A half-moon cast shadows over the landscape. He looked off into the distance. The thatched roof of the school and the trees and bushes around it looked like felt cutouts against the soft undulating hills behind them. The night air was still and hot. Pestalozzi had long since become accustomed to the quiet of the bush at night, only occasionally interrupted by the distant sound of a lion or hyena. His mind floated from one thought to the next. Never before had anyone come as close to discovering his true identity as von Arx had. Not that it worried him particularly. In his opinion, humankind was simply not prepared to face the truth. If von Arx made known his suspicions, he doubted that anyone would give them credence. But, if they did, it would jeopardize his work and that of his colleagues. It might even destroy their work. Therefore, he concluded, von Arx had to be stopped from talking about anything he'd learned. Pestalozzi had already suffered enough setbacks in his efforts to promote progress for humanity. He could not afford another because his work had been revealed prematurely. He had alerted Edward Bucher. Von Arx lived in Bern and was now Bucher's responsibility. He made a mental note to call him tomorrow and emphasize again the urgency of the matter.

Pestalozzi clapped his hands and immediately his houseman appeared. He asked the gaunt man to bring him another beer and the ashtray on his desk. His man disappeared into the house.

What if von Arx wasn't the only one who knew their secret? How would they keep the information from spreading? Long ago, it was much easier to go undetected. The Sumerians never caught on. Today, however, advances in technology made many ideas and notions more plausible. Even ordinary people might believe in their possibility. For someone like von Arx, he and Bucher had left behind too many clues, hadn't covered their tracks well enough, so to speak. If they had, von Arx never would have reached the conclusions he did.

The houseman brought a bottle of beer and put a disk on the table. "Thanks," Pestalozzi said, "but I wanted an ashtray, not this disk."

The man picked up the disk, which resembled Bucher's and carried the same inscription, PK, and read "double-sided, ultra-high density."

"What's it for?" he asked.

"You store data on it."

The man looked confused.

"Words and images are stored on it."

"Words and images? Why?"

"This disk is a keepsake. Oh, never mind. You wouldn't understand."

"A sort of souvenir? What does it remind you of?" The houseman was not simple-minded.

"It helps me remember my childhood friends. Now, please go and get the ashtray."

The houseman went inside shaking his head.

***

I presented myself again at the professor's office the next day. This time the secretary, unsolicited, brought two cups of coffee and placed them on the table next to the mineral water. I used the moment to organize my thoughts. I certainly didn't measure up to the professor. It made no sense to try and outsmart him. My only chance was to have an open and honest conversation with him and hope that he would treat me fairly.

With no preamble, he asked, "You came back. Why?"

"To warn you."

"Warn me?"

"Yes. I told you that someone had broken into my apartment."

"Yes, of course. I remember."

"Well, he called and threatened me as well."

"Threatened you?"

"Yes. He demanded information about you and threatened me if I didn't cooperate."

"And? Did the threat make you cooperate?"

"No, but this is hard."

"I understand."

"You're in danger, too. This is all ultimately about you."

Bucher understood the danger to himself. But these people needed him, so they wouldn't harm him. He had grown accustomed to such situations.

"How can I help?" he asked.

"No idea. Maybe by telling me the truth, so at least I know why they are after me—after you."

He paused. "You know I can't."

I considered what to say next. Finally I asked, "May I go back to our earlier conversation? The one when you explained space and time. It seems relevant to your situation, so I guess it's relevant to mine."

"The theory interests you?"

"Very much."

"All right. What else do you want to know?"

Thus began my second, highly interesting lesson about topics few people knew anything about. Bucher described a world governed by physical laws and in which everything had a scientific explanation. He was a genius. I knew I would never understand all of his explanations. Still, I wanted to make an effort. It was the only way to reach my goal.

I took a deep breath. "As you've explained, Professor, according to the theory of relativity, if an astronaut traveled into space and back to Earth again at near the speed of light, the astronaut would barely age during the trip while Earth would grow decades older. This means that the astronaut would come back to a time in the future. You say that such a journey doesn't violate any physical laws we know about. Right?"

"Yes, you've understood correctly."

"So my next question is how would it work in reverse? What about a trip into the past? Is this possible, too?"

"Good question," Bucher said. "I'm pleasantly surprised that you didn't try to solve the problem mentally by just changing the positive values to negative. It is indeed a new problem that must be solved with new ideas. You obviously think very logically, Doktor von Arx. Yes, a journey into the past is also possible without violating physical laws. However, the theoretical foundations haven't been worked out yet. The knowledge required to travel back into the past is different from that required to travel into the future. This knowledge is only just emerging at a very rudimentary level. Also, the technology for a trip into the past has yet to be created. It doesn't even exist in rudimentary form. Traveling into the future is technically much simpler than going back into the past."

"Can you still tell me about it?"

"I can try." Bucher took a sip of coffee, sat back, and began.

"Space is made up, as I said, of spatial points. Four-dimensional spacetime is also made of points that include the additional dimension of time. We call these points 'events.' Remember? We refer to the path of an object through spacetime as the 'world line.' It's not to be confused with the shortest connection between two events, which we call an interval. The world line is the actual path of an object in spacetime. The world line of a person is, in a sense, a sinuous line, like the path of a meandering worm in spacetime. It begins at birth and ends with death. We didn't get quite this far in our earlier discussion."

"Yes. And so far I've understood the theory fairly well," I said.

"Good. The world line of an object, its path through spacetime, hardly ever goes straight. Rather, it is curved in various places and forms a kind of worm, so we do sometimes call it a 'worm line.' Now we add something new to the equation. Just as a two-dimensional plane can be curved, four-dimensional spacetime can also be curved. The curvature of space—we can hardly imagine it—is mathematically predictable. Maybe I can illustrate it."

He thought for a second, and continued, "A ball resting on a two-dimensional plane gets a shove. It rolls straight because it received a push in one direction. It will continue to do so until the effect of the push dissipates. From our three-dimensional point of view, however, we see that the plane on which the ball rolls is actually like corrugated iron. It bends in repeated waves. The ball doesn't really roll straight. An invisible force caused by the curvature in the plane, a force we call gravity, compels the ball to follow the curve. A viewer limited to two-dimensions can't see these curvatures. For such a viewer, the ball rolls in a straight line. The same now applies to four-dimensional space. An object we perceive as flying straight is, in reality, following the curvatures of space."

Bucher watched my face to see if I was following him. Then he continued, "Einstein defined gravity as the force created by the curvature of space. This curvature compels a moving body to follow its curves. The object doesn't fly straight. Gravitational force, or in other words, the curvature of space, directs the object along its path."

"Where does this curvature of space come from?"

"Again, Einstein already had the answer. Every object curves the space around it, forcing other objects to follow certain paths. We perceive the curvature as gravity. For massive bodies like stars and black holes, the curvature of spacetime is particularly strong and thus bends the world lines of bodies in their vicinity. Those stellar masses bend space itself."

"I am not sure that I understand. Maybe you could explain it all in different words?"

"Sure. Gravity forces an object to follow the curvatures of space. An object that supposedly flies straight is compelled by gravity into a curved path. For example, the path of a light beam curves slightly as it passes close to a star. It moves in a worm line, even though the light beam seems straight to a three-dimensional observer. The degree of curvature varies from place to place. The world line of Earth, for example, curves around the sun as does that of the moon around the Earth."

"How do you know that?" I asked.

"You can prove it mathematically. The evidence is complicated however. It comes from the field equations of the theory of relativity."

"But it's clear in your view that the curvature of spacetime causes gravitational force?"

"Absolutely."

At the time I couldn't understand Bucher. But it did seem clear that only mathematical formulas could provide an in-depth explanation, and that level of math was beyond me. So I went back to the original topic and asked, "How do we go back to the past?"

Bucher cleared his throat. "Imagine a two-dimensional plane so strongly curved that the beginning and the end meet to form a circular tube. A ball rolling on this plane would return to its starting point. In the same way, four-dimensional spacetime could be curved so that an object we perceived as flying straight would actually follow the sharp curvature and return to its starting point. Its world line would form a circle and return to where it had started. This circuit could be temporally determined and end at a time in the past."

Bucher paused. "Such a world or curve line in spacetime is not only theoretically possible, but we can also determine the physical properties of spacetime at any point on the world line and thus form a corridor back into the past. If we followed such a corridor, we would inevitably encounter our past."

I said nothing. Bucher looked at me and knew that I had not understood. After another pause, he continued. "World lines that lead into the past already have a name in physics. We call them "closed timelike curves" or CTCs.

The secretary cautiously opened the door and said, "A call for you, Herr Professor."

"I don't want to be disturbed right now."

"It's a long distance call from Africa. The caller says it's urgent."

"Is it Alfred Pestalozzi?"

"Yes, Professor."

"Please put it through then." Bucher stood up and walked to the desk. He looked at me and said, "I'll play my cards face up. You can listen in."

My mouth fell open.

Bucher picked up the phone. "Alfred? Is everything okay? Why are you calling again so soon?" He listened a long time and eventually said, "He's right here. Should I say hello for you?" Turning to me, he whispered, "Alfred Pestalozzi says hello." He chuckled.

"Thanks, and I return the greeting," I muttered.

Bucher listened again. Once in a while, he threw in a "Yes" or "I understand" or "I agree." Finally he said, "All right. I've decided what to do, and it's undoubtedly what you have in mind. Goodbye, Alfred."

I was so busy trying to absorb Bucher's explanation of time travel that, as the call went on, I lost focus on it. When he hung up and returned to the sofa, he apologized for the interruption, but I pressed on. "What you said about the world line that extends into the past, Professor, was purely theoretical, but is a closed timelike curve, what you called a CTC, following the curvature of spacetime, would that really be possible?"

Bucher smiled and seemed eager to continue. "Yes, of course. There are situations, in particular with black holes, that make that sort of a curvature possible. Exploiting such a situation requires very precise and advanced technology. We still have a long way to go before we'll possess such technology."

"I think I need some background on black holes. I must admit, I can't imagine one."

"The best way to explain it is like this: if you throw a stone up into the air, it falls back to Earth. But what if you throw it so hard it disappears into space, that is, so hard it overcomes the gravitational force of the Earth?

"We call this speed the escape velocity. For Earth, it's about ten kilometers per second. For a beam of light, the gravitational force of the Earth doesn't even matter. Particles of light can escape it. Light can also escape from our sun, which is much denser and where the escape velocity is fourteen times greater than that of Earth. But there are masses so concentrated that their gravitational force is extremely strong. For example, there's the 'white dwarf,' a stellar remnant with a diameter of a few thousand kilometers and a density of several hundred tons per cubic centimeter.

"Neutron stars constitute an even denser sort of mass. They are only a few kilometers in diameter, but their density is several million tons per cubic centimeter.

"Then we have black holes. Their mass is so concentrated that everything is pulled toward it by gravity. Not even light particles at absolute speed—that is, the speed of light—can escape them. Light simply falls back into the mass. So only darkness exists in black holes."

I interrupted. "I once read that a black hole is a collapsed star that keeps all its mass in a small space, resulting in incredible density. Is that right?"

"Yes."

"Where are these things? How do we know about them?"

"Einstein at first doubted their existence, but his equations pointed to them and actually proved their existence mathematically. Now astronomers have found them. For example, there is a black hole at the center of our Milky Way Galaxy. It's called Sagittarius A*. The stars of the Milky Way orbit around it."

"Hmm. Then the enormous gravity of a black hole could warp space so severely that it would create a closed loop into the past, a CTC."

"Yes! Excellent! Imagine an object, let's say a comet, approaching a black hole. The black hole's gravitational force would affect it but perhaps not draw it in. Within certain parameters, it would loop around the black hole and disappear into space. But the comet would attain such momentum from the gravitational force that it would follow a closed loop into the past. There are other ways to create a CTC, but I would rather not go into it right now. Too complicated."

"Yes, I understand. But might I ask one more question, Professor."

"All right. Go ahead. The more you understand, the better for all of us."

"When someone returns to the past, can the person influence and change the future?"

"You ask the question that many science fiction novels address, namely, if anyone can, for example, visit his or her grandmother in order to influence her in the past so that she doesn't marry the grandfather. Then the grandchild, who returned to the past, would never be born—a classic paradox."

I had to laugh.

"Laugh if you will. Such a thing sounds ridiculous. But in scientific terms, the question is very interesting."

"You certainly have my interest. Please, Professor, tell me about it."

"All right. I think you deserve an answer, but the explanation is mind-boggling. Classical physics says that there is only one narrative or world line for humanity. That narrative is immutable. We shouldn't scoff! In some ways, classical physics achieved an excellent approximation of the truth. But with the closed timelike curve, the CTC, classical physics falls short. Here, quantum theory must come into play.

"Quantum theory describes all the theoretical results of an observation and calculates the probability of their occurrence. A neutron, for example, can be anywhere in space according to quantum theory, but all we know is the probability that it is located at a particular point. Only when we actually observe the neutron—that is, with each observation—is the location fixed for that specific observation. In fact, the neutron can be located with some level of probability at any point in space, and each of these spatial points is accurate for a possible observer— but only for that particular observer. Thus the neutron has multiple locations and, as follows, several narratives or world lines, of which only one, depending on the perception of the observer, is true. Another narrative, and thus a different 'truth,' is revealed to a different observer.

"The same applies to space itself. In reality, there are many spaces, one for each possible location of the neutron. And for every moment in which the neutron might decay, there is a universe where it actually does decay and one where it does not. So, we humans exist in multiple copies, one for each universe."

"Um Gottes Willen! Excuse me. Wow!" I said. "Now we've gone philosophical."

"That's true only if you don't understand the physics behind it. Philosophers try to understand and explain what humans have not yet grasped in scientific terms. A model based on the best science available, however, is the most accurate approximation to reality. And these approximations become more and more precise, especially as they include the model of multiple universes."

"So, according to physics, there are different ways in which our narrative unfolds?"

"Right, Doktor von Arx. The principle of randomness allows us to calculate the probability of a particle's location. When we locate the particle in a particular place, we determine our reality. But the other realities, with their other points of observation, also exist. It's just that we don't experience these other narratives. So there is not just a history of the universe but also a whole collection of possible histories. Each one is real. We live in our world today, because it is true for us."

"What? How is it true just for us? Why is the world what it is?" I could hear myself sputtering, but the concepts were overwhelming.

"I can only answer with the so-called anthropic principle. Of the various possible developments that the Earth could have followed since its formation, most would not have provided the conditions necessary to give rise to complex organisms like human life. Only in a world with parameters like ours would this be possible. Therefore, we live in this world. Only *we* can ask why the universe is as we see it. The answer to your question is this: If Earth were different, there would be no one to ask the question."

I struggled with the idea and asked again, "There are actually several narratives for our Earth?"

"According to physics, yes."

"A bizarre idea."

"Just a consequence of quantum theory. One can find all these narratives, that is, capture all these different processes in time mathematically and, in a way, add them together. This leads to the sum of all the narratives in an imaginary time. Our brains can't grasp such a thing. It might best be compared to a superhighway with millions of parallel lanes, all of which run at the same time, kind of like the Internet. The lanes—or worlds—lying closest to us are almost the same as ours. The more we move sideways in time, the more radically they differ."

"So does a CTC lead to the possibility of influencing the future?"

"That depends on which universe the world line leads back to. If it leads back to the same universe from which it originated, influencing the future is possible. Otherwise it is not. However, the probability that the world line goes back into the same universe is very low. Some physicists even exclude the possibility as illogical."

Consequences

Looking back, I can still see myself sitting in Bucher's office. Unfortunately, he gave me no time to process our conversation or review all the new ideas swimming in my head. As I sit now writing this book, I have almost unlimited leisure time to learn and think. If I need something explained to me, I have only to ask. This has allowed me to gain a general understanding of that which had so puzzled me before. In fact, the only reason I am able to summarize that conversation with Bucher on these pages is that I have this newfound perspective. Back then, I had to work hard just to recognize the theories and their applications. I simply did not have the pre-requisite knowledge to follow Bucher's train of thought.

However, one thing was clear. Time travel was possible, not only into the future but also into the past. Even though I didn't fully understand how one traveled through time, I did know with certainty that it could be done. "If you want to know more, I'll have to take you to my research center," I remember Bucher saying.

"A center? For time travel?"

"Yes. It's located in the foothills of the Alps."

I didn't even know there was a research center there, and the location seemed a bit odd to me.

"Why in the foothills?" I asked.

"Because I can work there undisturbed. I'll gladly show you."

Somehow, the suggestion made me uncomfortable. On the other hand, I felt intrigued. Could I trust Bucher? Once again, I decided to keep an open mind because, after all, I was dealing with a man of enormous capability and unquestionable integrity. So I just asked, "You're not thinking of kidnapping me, are you?"

"Certainly not. I'm not the criminal type."

"Or maybe kill me?"

"Ha. Even less likely. That would be crossing way over the line." Bucher paused for effect. "You do know too much, and we have to deal with the situation. But we will do so while abiding by the laws of humanity. You can rest assured that behavior has become more civilized and decent over the centuries. My peers and I adhere to a strict moral standard that isn't uniformly respected in this era."

His words reassured me. I told Bucher that I would report in a few days, ready to drive to the research center in the foothills. I said goodbye and left.

***

Alco Sci and Pete Donnor had settled in at the Hotel Bellevue in Bern. They summoned the three members of their Troops for the True Faith, the TTF, to render a direct report. The meeting took place in Donnor's suite because they wanted no one to see them together in public. The three men reported on Bucher's daily habits—when he arrived at his office and when he left, how much time he spent at home, which friends he met, and where he exercised regularly.

The information was similar to what they had collected on von Arx. Since they were unaware of the purpose of their surveillance, they did not include more specific information.

One of the men did most of the talking. When he'd received the phone call a few days ago from headquarters, he had immediately approached von Arx and made an offer. The trooper had been very careful and formal and had exerted very little pressure—or so he said. However, since he didn't know what the central administration of the Gospel Church of True Christians was really looking for, he hadn't known in concrete terms what he needed.

Von Arx had rejected the offer, and a subsequent telephone conversation raising the threat level had resulted in nothing. So the three troopers broke into his apartment and wrecked it. They had intended to soften up von Arx up for the next level of coercion. The trooper finished his report, stating that they would have to use more force and apply extreme methods if they wanted results from von Arx.

Sci asked if anyone had seen or followed them. They replied that they didn't think so but could not say for sure. Why would anyone tail respected members of a church anyway?

"Well," said Sci finally, "we'll kick it up a notch and make life a little harder for Daniel von Arx." Little did he know the police were listening in.

***

I believed I was close to a full understanding. In retrospect, I know that I actually had it. At the time, however, my knowledge triggered anxiety. The conclusion I had painstakingly reached seemed too far-fetched. I had no idea what to do. Should I divulge what I had learned? Write a newspaper article and inform the public? Turn to the police? Would anyone even believe me?

After leaving Bucher, I had gone to the restaurant on the corner to get something to drink and calm down. I pressed my way past the outer tables and sat down in a back corner. The place was packed. People came and went, making a lot of noise. A waitress finally appeared and I absent-mindedly ordered a glass of red wine. My thoughts drifted back to Professor Bucher. Should I go to the research center with him? Would I learn more there? I wondered again if I should take someone into my confidence or at least write down what I suspected and leave it somewhere safe.

The minutes passed, and then someone I knew strolled in. I came back to my senses and looked toward the door. A former classmate made his way through the tables, looking for vacant seats. Marianne followed him. Yes, the same Marianne who had visited me in the hospital a few months ago. Now she was with my classmate. I had no idea that the two knew each other. I leaned back so they wouldn't see me.

They sat next to each other with their backs toward me. Most of the clients sat facing the street so they could watch the passersby. Marianne did as well. Occasionally, she turned her head and laughed. The two apparently knew each other well. I wondered when it had all happened. I had gone to Africa alone, and I had been so preoccupied with my problems that I had neglected my girlfriends. These two obviously enjoyed each other, and I could not deny that Marianne was flirting with her companion.

Why hadn't she told me about him? I felt no jealousy—really. I just wondered about the situation. While I was chasing after outlandish ideas and turning over problems in my head, others were out enjoying life. Shouldn't I pay more attention to my girlfriends than to my obsessions? Look what I was losing! I took a long pull from my glass of wine and decided that, after my remaining questions had been answered, I would turn back to life and forget about Bucher.

***

Kommissar Erb's phone rang. The secretary announced, "Professor Bucher wants to speak with you, Herr Kommissar. I'll connect you."

Erb barely had time to wrestle his thoughts away from the case that currently engaged him before he heard, "Guten Morgen, Herr Kommissar. Bucher here."

Erb refocused quickly and said, "Hello, Herr Professor."

He had not spoken directly to the physicist for a long time.

However, he knew that something was brewing, so Bucher's call did not take him by surprise. "What can I do for you?" he asked.

"I've been threatened," was the terse reply.

"Really? What happened?"

Erb listened patiently to Bucher's report. Now and then he made a note or asked a question. Bucher proved very precise in the details, so the conversation did not last long. After it finished, Erb put away the file he had been reviewing. A new task claimed him now. He picked up the phone and gave some instructions. Then he left his office.

***

I left the restaurant and wandered home. I didn't hurry because my thoughts still preoccupied me, and the fresh air did me good. I felt somehow that this thing was moving rapidly toward a climax, although I didn't realize just how fast the climax would come.

I couldn't get over seeing Marianne in the restaurant. Hadn't she visited me in the hospital, showing such concern and affection? Now she was with another man. No, my sojourn had been months ago. Actually, she was right to look for another man. I hadn't wanted her as a steady partner, and I still didn't. I shouldn't feel insulted because she had moved on. Did it hurt my male ego? Perhaps. With all the other things happening around me, why was this bothering me now? No. I didn't want my thoughts to go in that direction. Besides, I was quite happy alone and not responsible for anyone. I could devote myself to my own issues and didn't have to look out for anyone. Tonight, or maybe tomorrow, I would call Cornelia and invite her out for a drink. It would be nice to see her.

I thought again about Bucher. Over time, I had arrived at the alarming certainty that I knew his secret. My brain repeated this fact repeatedly. What did this mean for me? And above all, what did it mean for him? How would he react? Was I in danger? Should I get away and hide? Impossible. For me, a life in hiding would be unbearable, and he would find me anyway. So running away was definitely not an option.

I stopped and gazed between two buildings at the distant mountains in the early afternoon sun. Because of unusually dry air, they seemed almost within reach. The familiar sight gave me a sense of security. Every time I could see the mountains clearly, I felt strong and unassailable. I reached a firm decision. I would take the offense. I decided to go with Bucher to the research center in the foothills, whatever his intentions toward me.

I opened the door, stepped inside, and turned to close it. Hearing a muffled noise in the hallway behind me, I started to turn and received a hard blow to the back of my head. My knees gave way, and I lost consciousness.

***

After speaking with Kommissar Erb, Bucher put the phone down carefully. He sat back in his chair and thought for a second. He went to the bookshelf and pulled out *History to the Twenty-First Century*. He turned quickly to the chapter "Special Events," took a disk from between the pages, and removed its envelope. He put it in the CD drive of his computer and turned on the screen. He scanned through several keywords until he came to "Daniel von Arx," clicked on the name, and very carefully read the text that popped up. He closed the file, ejected the CD, and put it back in its sleeve. Finally, he turned off the computer and placed the CD between the same pages of the book.

"I have just one more day," he muttered to himself. He picked up the phone and dialed von Arx's number. No one answered. Disappointed, he hung up and wrote a note to his secretary to cancel all appointments for the next day. He cleared his desk and left the office. In the corridor of the building, passing students greeted him, as always, respectfully. And as usual he was so preoccupied with his thoughts that he did not return the greetings. In the parking lot, he got in his car and drove off.

He had trouble finding Daniel's one-way street. Twice he saw the street sign but could not turn in the desired direction. Finally, when he did manage to find the way, he had to drive past Daniel's house before he found a parking space. Just as he was about to get out of the car, he spotted a familiar face. The police. What on earth were they doing there? He ducked lower behind the wheel of the car.

***

I regained consciousness strapped to a chair in my own living room. My head ached, and my hair and shirt were wet. Two men sat opposite me. They had poured water over my head to wake me up. The older, stocky man sported a crew cut of short silver-gray hair and looked uncompromising in his round, wire-rimmed glasses. The other was young and didn't seem particularly intelligent. He looked to the older man. They had drawn the curtains, and the room was dark. I tried to move, but duct tape bound my arms to the chair. I became keenly aware of my helplessness.

The older man was Alco Sci.

"Daniel von Arx," Sci said, speaking directly to me. "My people warned you. Unfortunately, you refused to cooperate with us."

I looked up at him silently. I had a headache and trouble focusing, but I couldn't let him draw me into a discussion.

"Now we'll bring you around. I hope you're reasonable. We'd like you to tell us everything you know."

I remained silent.

"We have reason to believe you know plenty about Bucher, so start now."

Sci gave a sign to his younger companion, who stood up, walked slowly towards me, punched me hard in the stomach, and returned just as slowly back to his place. I slumped forward against my bonds, gagging and trying to breathe. I was not able to think clearly. I only knew that I could not give in to them.

"So what's going on with Bucher?"

"I don't know," I gasped.

"Stop stalling."

"I said I don't know."

"I know very well that you've met with Bucher and have learned a lot about him."

"But I've found out nothing special. I really don't know anything."

"Don't test my patience, young man. We'll work on you until you tell us everything. It would be easier if you'd just start talking now."

"How can I tell you what I don't know?"

The younger man lit a cigarette with great deliberation and snapped the burning matchstick towards me with his thumb and index finger. It went out in the air.

"Do you like cigarettes?"

I stared at the burning cigarette. His threat was clear. I was afraid but stiffened my back. Sci noted my fear and my resolve. He laughed.

"You're headstrong. That won't last long. In just a few minutes, you'll be glad to talk—if you're still able." Despite the evident brutality, his manner remained formal. "For the last time, please tell us about Bucher."

When I didn't answer, he signaled his companion. The man walked slowly towards me. I froze and watched in disbelief as he began to extinguish the burning cigarette on the back of my hand. The pain came swiftly. A cry escaped my lips.

My cry had scarcely died away when I heard a tremendous crash. The door splintered and thudded against the wall. Three men stormed into the room. The first had a pistol in his hand and was dressed in civilian clothes. The other two wore uniforms and carried automatic pistols at the ready. "Police! Don't move," commanded the man dressed as a civilian. The officers directed their weapons at the two criminals while the lead man searched them. He found no arms and handcuffed them.

Only then did they cut away the duct tape. I recognized Kommissar Erb and said slowly, "Thank you, Herr Kommissar. You came just in time."

"Looks that way," he replied. "But a few moments earlier would have been a little better. I'm sorry about the apartment door. It took some punishment as well. You'll need to replace it."

"Don't worry about that. The main thing is you rescued me."

"We're going to haul these two off now. For you, Herr von Arx, there's no more danger. We have the accomplices of these two under guard. None of them remains free."

"Many thanks, Herr Kommissar."

"How do you feel? Perhaps we should have you checked by a doctor." Erb frowned.

"I don't think that's necessary. I'm okay. Really," I answered.

"What about that hand?"

"No really, I can take care of it. I don't need a doctor."

"All right then. If you're sure. Please come to the police station as soon as you can. We need your statement."

"Of course. I'll be there as soon as I've taken care of this burn."

***

The two police officers led Alco Sci and his henchman off in handcuffs down the stairway to the street. I went to the bathroom and ran cold water over the cigarette burn. Taking a wad of cotton from the medicine cabinet, I pressed it on the burn before returning to the living room to look out the window. On the street I saw one of the police officers direct Sci into a waiting patrol car. As Sci ducked to climb in, he suddenly went limp and collapsed onto the sidewalk. The officer immediately knelt beside him. The other officer held Sci's henchman back and looked around as if trying to spot an attacker. I myself hadn't seen anyone or heard anything.

My gaze shifted to Erb, who had kept his distance and was intensely scanning the street. He reached for his mobile phone and spoke into it. After a few minutes, I heard sirens in the distance. An ambulance appeared with two more police cars. They must have been stationed nearby. The additional officers immediately swarmed the area, cordoned off a large space, and searched the surroundings.

After the police seemed to have the situation under control, I hurried down the stairs to see what was going on. On the way, I loosened the cotton gently from the wound on my hand to let it breathe. A bandage could wait if necessary, and the wound would heal by itself without treatment. When I reached the street, the medical personnel were examining Sci.

"Dead," said one, and the others nodded.

Hearing the pronouncement, Erb walked over and asked the medics about the cause of death. They carefully turned Sci over and looked at his back, where they found the entrance wound of a bullet. "He was shot," one said.

"Um hum," said Erb so calmly that he must have known already, "but I didn't see or hear anything. Did you?"

"Not a thing. The shot must have come from a silenced sniper rifle."

"A professional killer," Erb said, more to himself than to the medics.

***

Bucher had remained slouched down as Erb and the two uniformed officers went into Daniel's building. He was convinced that the police would gain the upper hand, which of course happened. So he waited. When the police came out with two men in handcuffs, he peered over the dashboard. The police car concealed the men from view, but Bucher still managed to recognize Alco Sci.

So Sci was the back in town, Bucher thought. The police car partially blocked what happened next. Only when the ambulance drove up did Bucher realize that Sci lay on the ground. He decided that he had better go over and make himself known. Driving off would look suspicious. He opened the car door and strode over to Kommissar Erb.

"I was coming to talk with Doktor von Arx about possible threats," he said. "But I'm probably involved in all of this somehow, so I wanted you to know I'm here. Is there anything I can do to help?"

"Not yet," replied Erb. "I have to work out the basics first. Forensics is mobilized and will perform an autopsy. Once I have the initial results, I'll get back to you. "Is that your car over there?"

"Yes."

"Please stay here until we have a look inside."

"Certainly."

From the other side of the road, a Catholic priest approached. He walked up to Erb and asked, "Dead?"

Erb looked him carefully in the face. "Why do you ask?"

The priest hesitated. "Mmm. I wanted to ask if I could help, of course."

"Did you see what happened?"

"I was standing over there, a few doors down, and saw everything."

Erb looked at the priest in astonishment. "Of course, we would like any information you can give us," he said. "Could you please start with who you are." Erb nodded, and the two police officers approached and stood to the right and left of the priest.

"I'm Police Lieutenant Fumagalli from the Vatican."

"Then you're a colleague?"

"Yes. Rome sent me to watch Alco Sci. I was planning to make contact with you tomorrow."

"So you know who the dead man is?"

"I do. And don't worry. I didn't intend to meddle in your jurisdiction. I know international protocol very well."

"I hope so. Now, please understand. We must search you."

"Of course, that is your duty."

Erb turned to the officers on either side of the priest and said curtly. "Frisk him."

The priest did not resist. He raised his hands above his head and let them pat him down. He even opened his cassock in order to facilitate the work. They found nothing but Fumagalli's credentials. Erb inspected them slowly and gave them back.

"Thank you," said Erb. "Could you come down to the police station to make a statement? I'd like to understand your job better and why Rome sent you to watch Sci."

"Of course. Will tomorrow morning suit you?"

Erb confirmed the time and said, "One more question,

colleague to colleague. I am not clear why exactly you are here, right now, at this place. You wouldn't happen to be mixed up in this mess, would you?"

"But, my dear colleague, how could you ask such a question?"

Lieutenant Fumagalli looked Erb boldly in the face. The Kommissar knew then where he stood. Erb continued, "You can see that we've cordoned off a large area and are looking for the shooter. Do you think he's still nearby?"

"No, assuredly not."

"You're quite sure?"

"Quite sure."

"Thank you. Please leave your local address with the officer." The Vatican lieutenant did and walked away. Erb told his men to break off the search. They wouldn't find anyone.

***

An interview with the Vatican police officer on the following day did not produce much. Alco Sci was a ruthless cult leader from the USA. The Vatican routinely watched such people, especially men like Sci, who apparently were up to no good. Why else would Fumagalli have traveled to Switzerland?

Since Sci could no longer carry out his plan—whatever it was—his death alleviated some police work. Whatever Fumagalli's involvement, it would prove difficult finding evidence to support it. Probably just a shootout between two religious denominations, Erb thought, and let it go.

***

After the police removed the barriers and left, Bucher walked up to me and asked, "May I come in for a moment?"

I was surprised but could not refuse him. I accompanied him up the steps, opened the smashed door as best I could, and said, "Please, come right in, even though the state of things is not exactly inviting. Crime scene, you know."

Bucher almost smiled but then noticed my injured hand. "Those bastards! Let me look at that."

I fetched disinfectant from the bathroom, and he cleaned and bandaged the wound expertly. "It's not too bad. Second degree, almost third. The wound will heal in a few days."

"Good. The police got here just in time."

"Fortunately. Once again, I'm sorry that you've had to endure such unpleasantness because of me."

"I got off lightly today." I forced a small laugh. The burn still hurt. "What brings you here, Herr Professor?"

"I wanted to warn you. I was threatened, and I worried that you might become a victim of extortion again. Unfortunately, I arrived too late. But I also have another reason for seeing you."

"Yes, and that is?"

We sat down across from each other. I tried to think about how I should behave. Despite the events of the last hour, I forced myself to focus on Bucher.

"I would like for us to go to the institute today."

"Today?"

"Yes. It fits my schedule, and it will give you a chance to witness an experiment that will surely interest you."

"What kind of an experiment?"

"I'll tell you about it later."
"All right. Let's go."

***

I sat in the passenger seat of Bucher's car as he drove toward the Alps. When we stopped in front of a wire fence at the end of a winding country road, Bucher opened a gate and drove through. He parked the car in a shed hidden behind a nondescript building. We walked back around and entered. Bucher closed the door and threw an electrical switch. A dome above us slid open.

This is no research center, I thought, growing cautious. The isolated, fenced-in building in the woods made me uneasy, and I wondered how I might escape. Impossible. I had no car, and I was locked inside a fenced-in building.

"Let's make this short," I heard Bucher say. He came up to me with a peculiar expression on his face and some sort of tube in his hand. My brain caught fire. I had let myself be deceived. I turned around and looked for a way out. How could I have been so naive?

"Don't worry. No harm will come to you. I always keep my word," Bucher said calmly.

Nevertheless, panic seized me. I heard a soft "click" and felt a slight sting in my thigh. My hand gripped my leg reflexively. I staggered, and my body went limp. A pleasant, relaxed feeling came over me. Everything went black.

***

Bucher stepped forward and gently lowered Daniel to the floor. He gave a sigh of relief and opened a hatch in the rocket-shaped object poised in the middle of three rails under the dome. A recliner appeared. Technical equipment surrounded it. He lifted Daniel's body carefully onto the chair, strapped him in, put an oxygen mask over his face, and sealed the hatch.

Bucher walked to the control panel, where he meticulously calculated and programmed the system. A faint whistling sound filled the room. Everything began to shake as if seized by a great force. The whistle reached an unbearable decibel level, and Bucher placed headphones over his ears to protect his hearing. The rocket-shaped object in which Daniel lay unconscious trembled. The shaking grew more violent, and the object rose slowly. Then it accelerated sharply, following the rails up to the dome and, like a cannonball, shot up into the sky and disappeared. The vehicle had left Earth.

Bucher closed down the building and drove home.

***

Two days later, Michael reported me missing. The police initially did nothing. When I had still not appeared after three days, the police began an active search. Cornelia told them that she had not seen me for several days, but that was not unusual. Marianne claimed she no longer had a relationship with me, so she knew nothing about my whereabouts. Among the mail on my desk, the police found Bucher's note. They knew that Bucher had come to my apartment on the day of Sci's murder and the arrest of Sci's accomplices. Bucher himself testified that he had gone to my apartment to warn me of threats but had unfortunately arrived too late, as Kommissar Erb well knew. Supposedly, I had asked Bucher to give me a lift, and he dropped me off at an intersection just outside Old Town. There was no reason not to believe the famous scientist, and he was the last person to see me. A university friend of mine confirmed that he had seen me get into Bucher's car, which was parked down the street from my apartment.

Ultimately, no criminal charges were filed against Sci's strong-arm assistant. I, the victim, was missing. Kommissar Erb initially believed that someone had done away with me to prevent my testifying against members of the Gospel Church of True Christians. But he soon abandoned that suspicion. Sci was dead and his strongman was in police custody when I disappeared. The other two church henchmen and Pete Donnor remained under close watch, but their behavior revealed nothing. When questioned, they stubbornly claimed to have nothing to do with my disappearance. Eventually, Erb allowed them to return to the United States.

Erb spoke again, in some detail, with Lieutenant Fumagalli from the Vatican. Erb knew he would never get any official or verifiable information, but he hoped at least for something off the record. However, the churchman assured him that he was not involved in my disappearance and his protestations were believable. The Vatican officer had made one enigmatic remark that left Erb confused. "Von Arx got too close to an angel, and the angel didn't want to reveal himself." Erb did not pursue the remark. Church people often had rather peculiar notions.

So the search for me met a dead end. I had simply disappeared.

After the autopsy, Alco Sci's body was transported back to the United States. Administrators of the Gospel Church of True Christians were forbidden entry into Switzerland, and the church had not a single True Christian in the country.

This Side of Then

All I have left now to report is what's happened to me since my journey through time. Years have passed; however, I won't recount each one. So no full biography. I'll limit myself to telling you how, a few days after my arrival, I found God.

Up to this point in my narrative, I have made references to God or gods over the course of history. Although some readers may already be familiar with these references, most will not have guessed where or how God actually appeared. People tend to accept as true only what they can perceive through the senses. They do not strive to understand the reality hidden beneath the surface of their perceptions. In general, they don't care about the wider context. In those rare cases when people investigate context and their investigations lead to conclusions that do not fit neatly into their previous worldview, they reject the conclusions outright. A breakthrough in which new knowledge, and thus a new truth, gains credibility occurs only occasionally.

That said, I would like to show you now a new truth so that you may better understand your world from now on. I've already spent more than half my life in the new era. Although my purpose does not include describing this time, you should know that I feel comfortable here and will not return to the past.

I now understand all those individuals who traveled to your time or earlier periods and then didn't want to leave, like Galileo Galilei. I am not unlike Galileo. In fact, I think most people wish to stay in the era where they spent most of their later life, in a place where everything is familiar. My dear wife is here, my children and grandchildren, too. I treasure them. Why would I want to leave?

My apartment is just a few hundred meters from the place where I once lived as a student. I wasn't always here, however. After I settled in this world, I was drawn to different places and once even lived overseas. But I came back and took an apartment in this building. It towers over the city and has a large terrace facing south. I am sitting here now at a patio table and finishing this book. Not a single cloud drifts across the sky. It is hot, much warmer than in your time, but I enjoy the climate. I don't have to travel to the Mediterranean for it as you would. When I look up, I can see the Gurten, the Berner Hausberg, the Alpine foothills extending out behind it, and then the mountains themselves. How fond I am of the familiar contours of this land, the same as in my youth. True, the foothills are now protected and the peaks are not as white with snow as before. Nevertheless, their majesty never fails to take my breath away and give me a warm feeling of home. Perhaps that's why I returned here, to the place where I spent my youth.

I hear my wife Nancy moving around in the apartment behind me. She's bringing me coffee.

Falling in love floods one with happiness. I believe it's good to fall in love again and again, but I don't miss my time of "Sturm und Drang," my youthful exuberance, when I fell in love with a new woman every six months. I continued embarking on such adventures for several years after I arrived in this world and time. But then I longed for a lasting relationship, and that eventually led to children. Infatuation gave way to comfortable intimacy and familiarity and to the common task of child rearing and professional collaboration. Nancy and I complement each other well. I always know, almost without thinking, how she will react and what she will do in any given situation. And if the relationship threatens to become routine, I try to fall in love again—but always with the same woman, Nancy. Of course I do not consistently succeed. Yet, happiness always returns, and I'm very satisfied with this happiness born of familiarity. We've been together for decades, and I have never regretted our marriage.

This is my life. I'm fine and well. Now I'd like to return to my arrival in this world and describe my first days here.

***

"Hello. Did you sleep well?"

The words came from a distance. I gradually awoke from the anesthesia that Bucher had given me. I tried to remember.

"My name is Tom Knox," I heard the voice say.

I looked around. The room seemed familiar. Bucher had brought me here. Yet the room seemed different, brighter. I was lying on a sort of recliner in the rocket-like vehicle, which was open on one side. I turned my head in the direction of the voice and saw the control console. A man sat there, the person who had introduced himself as Tom Knox.

"Have I been asleep? Where's Professor Bucher?" I asked, dazed.

"You've slept a long time in one sense, for an entire journey, but a short time in another sense. Bucher isn't here. He stayed behind."

I tried to sit up but discovered that I was bound to the recliner. I attempted to loosen the straps, my hands moving mechanically. The man calling himself Tom Knox walked over to me. I feared he would prevent my releasing the straps, but instead he helped me unbuckle them. Once freed, I stood up. A bit wobbly at first, I managed to find my balance and look around.

"What journey?"

"You flew here," said Knox, "in this machine." He pointed to the vehicle. "You traveled far out into space and then arrived back here at the same place where you started—about an hour later."

"Oh," I said, not quite allowing myself to accept the statement. What did he mean by flying "far out into space"?

The question was on the tip of my tongue when I suddenly recognized a familiar object on the console. I walked over to it on unsteady legs.

Yes, I had seen this electronic gadget on more than one occasion. "Some sort of timer?" I asked.

Knox nodded. I reached for the device to examine it more closely, but Knox picked it up first. I did notice that it had two digital displays, both showing the number 3416.

"The year," Knox said.

"This year? Right now?"

"Yes."

"So I ended up in the year 3416?"

"Bravo!"

"Why does the same number appear twice?"

"On the right, we have the year in which we live," he pointed to the digital display on the right. "The left displays the year in which the instrument is temporally located, that is, the year in which the intervener lives."

"The intervener?" But I should have known.

"For example, Edward Bucher."

"Oh." The network of interrelationships was becoming clear. I remembered my long conversations with Bucher about time travel, and everything began to fall into place. "So Bucher's device would now be showing, on the left side, the year I just came from."

"That's right."

"Alfred Pestalozzi's device, too?"

"Right again."

Now I saw why the room seemed different. The equipment and lighting was from 3416 A.D.

"I see. I've made a long journey at near the speed of light and landed in the same place where my journey began, right? For me personally, almost no time passed. You said an hour, didn't you? Meanwhile, much time has passed on Earth. It's now the year 3416?"

"That's right."

"Why in the same place and in the same building?"

"It's technically easier for us this way. We created this building at the beginning of history. Initially, it was a temple, then a church. In one century, we disguised it as an academic department in a university. By always keeping it in the same place, we had only to calculate the Earth's path and determine the length of the trip when we sent people from one era to another. Programming is easier and more convenient, as is construction, since we don't have to build multiple buildings with sophisticated technology."

"I see."

I opened the door and stepped outside. Knox followed me. I blinked in the blinding light. I felt nature's presence with an intensity I had only previously experienced when in remote, pristine areas. My eyes swept over the surroundings. A wire fence cordoned off the area just as before, but no road led in or out. I saw only a lush thicket of shrubs and trees, almost like a jungle.

"Protected zone," said Knox. "Any area outside the cities is designated a protected zone. This one we call the Alpine Protected Zone. Nothing can ever be built here. Roads are all underground."

"It's beautiful."

"Yes. We keep it this way to counterbalance the urban zones."

"Who comes here?" I asked. I thought of the green belt, laboriously created in my time. People had hardly used it.

"Everybody. You can hike all through it. You just have to take a protector."

"A what?"

"It's an ultrasound device, about three centimeters long. It emits electronic waves that redirect animals so you can hike safely."

"It protects from animals? Are there dangerous predators?"

"Yes, the protected zones are nature reserves. They provide a haven to animals that have lived on Earth since its beginnings."

"Like lions, tigers, and other such creatures?"

"Not only mammals. We also have large birds of prey, dangerous lizards, and dinosaurs."

"Dinosaurs?"

"Yes, they are amazing creatures. We recreated them from genetic material and brought them and many other extinct animals back to live in the protected zone."

"How can they possibly get along with each other?"

"I see the anesthetic didn't knock all the sense out of your head," joked Knox. "You're right. They don't all get along, but we created separation belts and other mechanisms to provide for them. You'll get the details later."

"Interesting. Can anyone, I mean, can I hike through there?"

"Of course! With a protector you'd be perfectly safe. But we can talk about all that later. We have plenty of time. First we need to transport into the city. You can go hiking later."

We returned to the building. Knox walked up to a door

that had not been there previously. It opened automatically revealing a clear plastic cube with two bucket seats. Knox sat in one and motioned for me to sit in the other. The door closed and the vehicle, which seemed part of a big pneumatic tube system, shot into motion. We went from the light into a tunnel of darkness.

I began peppering Knox with questions. "Why did you bring me here? What's happening to me? What's your role in all of this?"

Knox urged me to calm down and explained, "I'm responsible for training interveners."

"What sort of training?"

"First and foremost, the language of the century in which they'll work."

"But you already speak my language."

"Yes, we can communicate. That's the main reason I got the job of picking you up. Language changes over the course of time. You can't imagine how costly and time-consuming reconstructing previous languages can be."

"I assume the interveners must learn an ancient language?"

"Learning languages is far less demanding than reconstructing them. We treat the brain like a computer. You'll see."

I didn't understand his comment and changed the subject. "What else happens in the training?"

"Well, language is the main thing."

I nodded.

"It's also my job to make sure they have the knowledge they must bring into the century in which they're intervening."

"Why do you do all this?"

"You'd better ask Heinz Fricke, the Division Head for History. You'll soon get to know him, and he can explain it better than I."

The vehicle slowed down at the end of the tube, a station on the surface. With a gentle jolt, the cube came to a halt in bright sunlight. The trip had lasted only a few minutes.

"You're about to be amazed at how your hometown looks," Knox said smiling.

The door opened, and we stepped outside. Yes, I was amazed. We stood in the middle of a gleaming, bustling city with tall buildings made of what looked like plastic. A multitude of small, transparent passenger vehicles were rushing by. I looked around and breathed in air as pure as that found in the protected zone, no trace of pollution. Even the walls were spotlessly clean. Despite the dense population—I saw only skyscrapers—plants and trees lined the streets and filled the terraces of buildings. A cloud of swallows swooped through the air above the main street and whirled into a side street. I followed them with my eyes. Not even in the countryside had I ever seen such a flock of birds.

Knox grabbed my arm, interrupting my diversion, and pulled me toward the door of the building behind us. It opened as we approached. He pointed to the southwest and said, "Down there's Old Town. It's been completely preserved as it used to look. I recommend a visit when you get a chance."

We stepped into a large hall with a snack bar at one end. People hustled and bustled around us. They spoke loudly to one another, sometimes even shouting. I listened carefully but understood not a word.

The kaleidoscope of movement and sound overwhelmed me. Knox pulled me back by the sleeve. "Come on. You'd first better learn our language."

He led me to a vehicle similar to the one we were in before. Only this time we moved through a transparent tube that apparently connected the floors of the building. We must have soared forty floors before we got out, and Knox announced, "This is where I work."

He led me into a small room. In the middle stood what looked like a dentist's chair. Knox motioned for me sit in it, which I obediently did.

"Now what?"

"You're about to learn our language."

"In this chair?"

"That's right." Knox set to work. He produced suction cups and used them to attach electrodes to my forehead and the back of my head.

"Don't worry. This'll take just a few minutes."

I sat bolt upright. I felt anxious and said, "Hang on there. First tell me what you're about to do to me."

"Oh, sure." I'm going to download our language into your brain."

"What?"

"Yes. It'll be saved in your brain just as information used to be saved on computers in your former time."

"Does it hurt?"

"Not at all. Everyone obtains knowledge by downloading it."

I leaned back and let the process go on. I felt a strange confidence. Bucher had assured me that ethical standards had increased over the centuries. This seemed credible, especially since it coincided with my worldview. Besides, here I was, handily delivered to these people.

Knox secured six electrodes to my head. I remember the exact number because I counted them. Then he activated some control buttons on the wall. I watched him out of the corner of my eye. Although I tried to relax, I waited uneasily for an electric shock or pain. But nothing happened. When Knox turned back to me after a couple of minutes, I figured he would explain the upcoming download. Instead, he detached the electrodes from my head and said, "Okay. All done. You can get up."

I stood obediently.

He grinned. "You see? I just spoke to you in the language of this time, and you understood."

"What about my own language?"

"I deleted it. Don't want to strain your brain too much. But it's archived. If you want it back later and have available capacity, I can reload the old language any time. For the time being, however, it's better to have plenty of empty space between your ears." He stifled a laugh at his own joke.

I said nothing. Then the matter began to intrigue me, and I asked, "Didn't you say that you load all sorts of knowledge as well as languages this way?"

"Yes. Any knowledge that the individual wishes to have." He was still gleeful at my curiosity—or perhaps at my discomfort.

"Don't tell me that everybody wants the same knowledge."

"No, of course not. There is far too much information for us to load everything into every single person. We download only what an individual needs."

"Individually tailored knowledge?"

"Exactly. Individuals decide what they want or need. They can also modify or supplement the knowledge throughout their lives."

"Where does the information come from?"

"There's a central memory bank. Everyone can access it directly."

"Then you don't need schools."

"Right. Completely unnecessary. Young people receive a standard package. They can add to it later on an individual basis. This has huge advantages."

"Like what?"

"Eliminating the need for compulsory education frees a young person to focus on personal development, and not having a school system saves national resources—no teachers and no school buildings to pay for. Another advantage is that the standard package children and young people receive doesn't contain the mistakes so common in the past. Since access to knowledge is universal and everybody enjoys the same opportunities in life, we no longer have juvenile delinquency."

"Interesting," was all I could say.

"I know this because I train interveners and thus have to deal with earlier eras. The people in this time have no idea what a school or juvenile delinquency is."

"Okay, so why do I remember them?"

"To avoid confusion, I left your previous knowledge intact except for your earlier language. With the language pack, I also downloaded part of a basic package for our time, so you can at least fit in. But there'll be plenty to learn and experience in the old-fashioned way."

***

The next day, I woke up later than was my habit. Having slept well and deeply, I lay for a while in bed. My hand reached for the bedside lamp but found nothing there. I sat bolt upright. Where was I? With difficulty, I tried to remember and gradually recalled what had befallen me. Not only was I not in my own bed, I was not even in my own time. Tom Knox, my contact. Yes, of course. He had told me he would put me temporarily in a hotel room.

The light came on. A sensor must have determined that I was awake, I thought. My basic package works. How practical the technology of 3416 is! I threw back the covers. The blinds opened, and, as daylight penetrated the room, the artificial light dimmed.

"The technology even realized I wanted to get up," I muttered to myself. In the bathroom, I found a shower, which I enjoyed for a long time. I was glad people still bathed in the same manner. I thought about what I should do. My room sat high above the city, and I could see far into the distance. I recognized the shapes of mountains to the south. They had not changed. I found peace of mind in the fact that I was at home—even if in a different time.

Knox had told me I had a day of leisure. He would pick me up tomorrow morning. I looked forward to having time to look around. But first, breakfast.

When I went down to eat, I found my way around with no trouble. I seemed to know the local customs, even though I still remembered what to do in a hotel back in my time. I served myself with utensils that seemed similar to what I knew from before and enjoyed my first meal in the new era. Fortunately food still tasted much the same.

After breakfast I decided to go to Old Town. I asked a passerby for directions. He was quite willing to help, assuring me that it was only ten minutes away on foot. I noted that in the thirty-fifth century people still walked to get around, and I set out.

Today, like yesterday, the weather reminded me of spring—warm and sunny. Soon I came across signs pointing the way to Old Town. Apparently "learning" the language included becoming literate in it. Finally I came to a high wall. The street led to a covered portico that served as an entrance. I read the instructions posted there and went in. I stopped abruptly. Can this be possible? My heart began to pound. Everything had been preserved just as it was. I couldn't believe it! I knew the houses, the streets, the arcades. I walked along the Spitalgasse. There to the right was the Bundesplatz with the Parliament Building, to the left, the main police station. I went through a side alley back to the entrance and picked up a printed city guide.

"The addresses are in the old language," I read. I couldn't decipher them. All the people walking around seemed to be tourists. No one actually lived here anymore, I realized somewhat sadly. I walked into the store where I had shopped a few days ago. It had become a museum and no longer contained any merchandise. Everything looked sterile and dead. What a shame. But all in all, I was pleased they had preserved a part of my native city, even if preservation meant that no one could live there.

Suddenly I understood the dilemma posed in maintaining monuments to the past. In order to keep a historical area alive, the people living there must incorporate modern comforts into its infrastructure. Over the course of generations, modifications would cause buildings, parks, and streets to evolve beyond recognition. The only way to keep the place the same would be for people to move away, but then the area would die, as had happened here.

In the department store, a guide was telling a group of tourists about Old Town. I joined them.

"The residents used a vehicle called a streetcar to get around. It ran on the rails you saw outside as we came in," he said, pointing through the open door. "It moved rather slowly, stopping at designated points for people to board and exit. The residents purchased clothing and other items for daily living here in this store and in other shops in the vicinity."

I already knew that. I turned away and left. I wandered up the Marktgasse and gratefully immersed myself in the past. I still found it hard to believe. For me "the past" was only a couple of days ago. I stopped in front of a preserved restaurant. It was here I had breakfasted on rolls and coffee with Cornelia. How was she? Had she even noticed I was gone?

The people I had spoken with just a few days ago were all long dead. The idea saddened me. How had their lives played out? Would that information be stored somewhere? I shook off these thoughts and forced myself out of my musing. I couldn't change anything. I had to come to terms with my present situation.

I walked back down the road and stood in front of the exit. My wistfulness remained, and again a faint sadness came over me. Was I just a museum piece in this world myself? Would I ever fit in? Could I make friends here? Could I perhaps even return later to my world? Could I become an intervener and go back? At that moment, I felt very alone.

On the way back to the hotel, I noticed three huge cylinders in the distance. They towered over everything. Each one had a diameter of a medium-sized office building. The cylinders seemed to expel a gas. The air around them was hazy and agitated. I asked a passerby what they were.

"That's the APS," the man replied in astonishment.

"Oh, yes." There must have been a bug in my knowledge package because I had no idea what he meant. Not wanting to embarrass myself, I didn't ask him to clarify but continued on my way.

When I later queried Knox, I learned the answer. "The APS is our Air Purification System that every urban area must build. Each person pays an APS tax, for himself or herself as well as for each pet in the household. In other words, the tax is levied on anything that consumes air."

"What's the tax rate per person?"

"It's levied on a point system. A person is ten points, a dog seven points, and so on."

What he said next amazed me even more. He explained that a central administration regulated and provided financial support for all the APS installations on Earth. The system measured emissions into the atmosphere and thus controlled the greenhouse effect and kept the climate constant.

Previously, periodic ice ages would have occurred due to fluctuations in the tilt of the Earth's axis. A significant ice age would typically follow four small ice ages. The last ice age, which occurred several centuries after my departure, produced glaciers descending from the North Pole all the way south to the Swiss Plateau. Now, however, everything was controlled. By regulating APS output, the Earth's inhabitants could maintain a constant climate. Periodic ice ages as well as solar flares could be anticipated and neutralized.

"What about global warming caused by humans?" I asked.

"That was a problem in your former time. Now it's well under control."

"But it seems warmer now than it did in my time."

"We had an international conference. After a lot of haggling and compromise to balance interests among various regions, representatives agreed on a set of coordinated temperatures. Since then it's remained constant, and I find it quite pleasant. Don't you?"

***

Over the next few days, I became more familiar with the new world and learned to use my brain's basic package. One morning I powered up the communication device in my hotel room. A friendly voice answered. I asked for the Archive of the National Bureau of Vital Records. After a short while, the voice said, "Bureau of Vital Records, how may I help you?" At first, I was surprised to hear the same voice. Then I realized I wasn't talking to a person but to a computer.

"Go to the twenty-first century," I said.

"Next," said the voice.

"Give me data from ...."

First, I asked about Michael—first name, last name, date

of birth. The information came promptly. According to the Bureau, he had married a woman named Ada Schwartz at age 28. I didn't know her. He had three children and died at 95. No other information was available.

I hesitated. I wanted to know the fate of so many people I had known. The first names that popped into my head were those of my girlfriends. Then I wondered if it was right to delve into their lives. I finally told myself that it was a long time ago and I couldn't change anything. I mustered my courage.

"Bureau of Vital Records," I said again, "go to the twenty-first century and give me information regarding Marianne...."

Again, the response came quickly. She had married three years after my disappearance but apparently had not been happy. The computer reported a divorce four years later. At thirty-five she had married a second time and had a child. I wondered what that really told me. It was precious little information. Then I had an idea. "Computer, find her last passport and show me her photo." Some five seconds later the face of a wrinkled old woman appeared on the screen. I looked closely at the image. I thought I saw a faint resemblance to Marianne. But the old woman had little in common with the pretty girl I had seen just a few days ago.

Explanations

Heinz Fricke, the Head of the Division of History, could be proud. His team had made possible a comprehensive history of humankind. With careful attention to detail, they had studied, cataloged, and preserved papyrus scrolls, thousands of books, memory drives, computer disks, nanocubes, and other media to successfully map out the many millennia of human history. They had determined which interventions might help accelerate progress by running thousands of simulations to see the impact each might have on people and their evolution. If progress accelerated too greatly, people would resist, even to the point of causing societies to collapse. Therefore, the Division of History had had to find out how to achieve the greatest possible acceleration with the least amount of resistance, just as Alfred Pestalozzi had explained.

Finding the optimal speed of development had been a

monumental task. Once, there had been some difficulty because interveners in early history mixed up on-going simulations with future interventions. Then there were other variables, such as the fact that the human race itself was constantly evolving. Humans became neurologically stronger, and their ability to cope with the progress increased over time. So the Division of History had to proceed cautiously in the early days of humankind and could only accelerate more aggressively in later centuries.

Once someone asked Fricke why he had not brought knowledge all at once to an earlier century. For example, why hadn't he given Newton the task of publishing not only his three laws but also the Theory of Relativity? The Division Head had just smiled and replied that people then wouldn't have been able to cope with that much progress all at once. If the Division of History had forced a faster pace, more people would have lost heart and become active resisters.

"You know too little about history," Fricke explained. "For example, resistance to nuclear power or universal education didn't simply focus on abuses and shortcuts in research. The idea itself was so fundamental and powerful it almost caused human development to come to a complete halt. We couldn't hazard such a collapse."

In the end, the interveners did a good job. They were the right people at the right time. Everyone had contributed to the program's success.

For a while interveners went into the past without the possibility of retrieval. This had led, as in the case of Adam and Eve Hamilton, to disaster. Later, retrieving interveners became possible, but most preferred to stay. Being far ahead of their time, they enjoyed high reputations and had no desire to return to a world where they were no more talented or informed than others.

But rarely had anyone made a one-way trip into the future. It had happened only once—with me. Everyone in the Division of History had looked forward to my arrival.

***

Tom Knox escorted me into what resembled a command center for space travel. Dozens of people sat at desks arranged in semi-circles, each with its own holographic monitor. On the front wall, the year 3416 appeared lit-up in large red numbers.

"We monitor interventions here and measure their success," explained Knox.

I looked around in amazement, "Why such an enormous commitment of resources and time?" I asked.

"We want to displace the present year by accelerating the evolution of humankind. We started intervening over fifty millennia ago, as calculated in our time, but have shortened history so much that we are now in the year 3416.

He pointed to the front wall. "With every successful intervention, the course of history shortens and decreases the number of the year in which we live. Our goal is to bring our current state of development back to about the year 2500. Human beings can tolerate that rate of development."

"And achieving your goal requires all this?" I gestured toward the many consoles and the people working there.

"We have interveners at work in several different centuries. If an intervener succeeds in an earlier century, those working in later centuries have to adjust their tasks. This complication requires constant monitoring of history and countless simulations. We transmit information and directions to interveners so they can adapt their behavior."

"Does that mean you're always in touch with the interveners?"

"The Project Manager is. The timepiece you saw shows interveners not only where the project stands by displaying our year here and the year in which they are working, but also allows us to communicate with them verbally. If the bottom of the device is opened, a tiny microphone with an earbud falls out."

"Is communication possible at any time?"

"Of course. Calls go directly to the Project Manager, who, depending on the level of importance, forwards them to the control room or a Division Head."

***

Knox led me to a door that opened as we approached.

"Allow me to present Heinz Fricke, our Head of the History Division," he said introducing me to a slight man wearing a non-descript gray suit.

"Welcome to our world in the year 3416," he said, shaking my hand firmly.

"Hello," I said, a little shy.

Knox remarked dryly, "One hopes 3416 will not last much longer."

I looked back at him and raised an eyebrow.

"We hope this year will be over soon and the display will turn back a year. That is our mission and will signal our success," said Knox

"I hope so too," said Fricke. He looked me up and down, his face revealing no judgment. He pointed to a set of white-cushioned chairs and invited me to sit down. I sat on the edge of my assigned seat while the other two leaned back in theirs. Fricke asked, "How are you feeling about all this?"

"Still a little uncertain but okay," I replied, and then added, "Congratulations on your success. You've altered time."

"Thank you. I've been very curious about you. It's unusual for a scholar of history to have a specimen *from* history sitting before him." His smile indicated that he meant the word as a sort of joke.

I laughed and the tension disappeared.

"I'm not just a specimen from history. I'm a fellow like you, only born a few centuries earlier."

"Of course, of course. I didn't mean to offend. You simply fascinate me," muttered Fricke.

"Your interveners are also just people. They differ little from those living in the period to which they are sent."

"Yes, true. It would be hard to distinguish them from people born in the last few centuries. However, in primitive times, they were quite different, and they had to play a larger role in the evolution of people to help them advance."

His words reminded me of the disk with the Alaker. The members of the tribe had indeed looked much more primitive that the intervener. "So your breeding efforts met with success," I remarked. I couldn't keep a slight smirk off my face.

"You could put it that way." There was a pause. Then Fricke

returned to the topic. "Of course our interveners are people. But they come from the future and possess knowledge far beyond that of the people to whom we send them. Therefore, after a few years of work, some interveners even passed for gods, for example, Schmid, whom the Sumerians called 'Sumid.' "

"So Sumid was one of you," I concluded without surprise. I remembered having wondered, when I first watched the disk, about Sumid and for whom the recording had actually been intended.

"Yes, Schmid had the task of introducing writing."

A ray of sunlight penetrated the window to our right and struck the small table beside my chair. It lit up the austere white room but created little heat. I looked toward the source of the light and saw the contours of the distant mountains once again. A majestic natural monument, just as in my time. The familiar sight boosted my confidence and gave me a sense of security. The significance of the disks I had taken from Bucher now became clear. Given the many questions I had about my new world, I wasn't much interested in dwelling on the Alaker or Sumerians but rather preferred to address my current situation. Nevertheless, I did want to know about the Hamilton couple. I had seen them only briefly on one of the disks.

Fricke hesitated when he heard the name Hamilton. He just said, "An embarrassing story."

"How so?" I asked.

"We sent Adam and Eve Hamilton far back to the beginning of humankind. The two had looked forward enthusiastically to experiencing primal life and volunteered for the deployment. But their enthusiasm turned to frustration. They complained endlessly and claimed we here lived in a paradise lost to them forever. Sure, life in the wilderness was hard. But we had sent along all the necessary tools from our civilization. We didn't understand their whining about a lost paradise. Unfortunately we could not bring them back. Our technology at the time was not sufficient. We don't know what became of them. Our connection with them just broke off."

"An accident?" I asked.

"We don't know."

I felt more relaxed now. Knox and Fricke were taking me seriously and treating me as an equal.

"Can I ask a few questions?" I ventured.

"By all means, of course," replied Fricke.

"Who was Johann Heinrich Pestalozzi?"

"When he was with us, he was a teacher at heart, as was his brother Alfred, whom you got to know. We sent Johann to Switzerland to introduce the concept of the elementary school. He had more success than Alfred did in Africa two centuries later. We still don't know why. Since our transport station is in the foothills of the Alps, various other interveners have worked out of Switzerland. Einstein and Bucher are the ones with whom you are most likely familiar. You'll find a list of all interveners over there."

He pointed to a wall with a long list of names etched on it. Next to each name was a year. I skimmed through names like Galileo Galilei, J. Newton, Marie Curie-Sklodowska, Euclid, Iesu, and more. I was taken aback. Although I was ready for all sorts of surprises, the name "Iesu" gave me pause. I asked, "Okay, who was Iesu?"

Fricke laughed and said, "The son of our Project Manager.

He was interested in philosophy and joined our team as a teenager. He believed that earlier peoples should receive not only technical but also philosophical training. He wished to promote ethics along with science. We took up his idea and opted for an intervention. Even though Iesu did not seem well suited for the mission—like anyone educated in philosophy, he was somewhat quixotic—we sent him back in time. Given that his father was a Project Manager, he got his way. Unfortunately, he died during his mission."

"I see." I was surprised at this new variant of the gospel and said, "But he had tremendous impact."

"Actually, he didn't," was the prompt reply. "At the time of his death, he had few disciples, and his effect would have faded away completely if we had not immediately sent more interveners to deal with humanity's impending brutality. In fact, we managed to slow the slippage in ethics. Among the successful interveners were, of course, Petrus and Paulus. They spread the teachings of Iesu and made sure the lessons found followers."

I hesitated. "So Iesu was the son of your Project Manager. He was born here, and Mary was not his mother?"

"Actually, she was. Iesu was a child in Mary's family, but he was born here with us. The Christmas story is based on an earlier tale having to do with the winter solstice. People needed the tale to explain where Iesu came from. As for the Church's poetic story of Mary's Immaculate Conception—well, we couldn't do anything about that. People have always mystified and sanctified what they don't understand."

I paused again. My worldview had changed radically over the last few days, and I had not yet internalized everything I had learned. I knew that throughout history, from antiquity to modern times, individuals had appeared repeatedly to establish new religions. Even the Romans had documented several preachers, all of whom claimed to be the Messiah. These founders of new religions appeared in every generation up until the time I left the twenty-first century, although the exalted title "Messiah" degenerated over time to revivalists and show preachers proclaiming the "true faith." Using similar methods, they all attempted to recruit followers. Their methods included the assertion that they represented the only possible truth. This truth had to be promulgated with force, and any independent reflection by the followers was deemed harmful. Dissenters were tracked down as heretics and punished. By the twenty-first century, however, gurus, Scientologists—or whatever they decided to call themselves—were less successful. Iesu, on the other hand, had been successful because people in his era were less critical. Therefore, his teachings found fertile ground.

I held my tongue. I didn't want to raise any more questions, didn't want them to subject me to more disturbing information. Nonetheless, I went back to my original question. "Why are you doing all this, anyway?"

"You mean why are we trying to shorten history?"

"Yes. Precisely," I replied. "There must be a good reason for your tremendous efforts."

"Very well. Here's the reason. You see, humankind evolved slowly and steadily over thousands of years according to the principle of chance. Humans reached their present state of knowledge in about the fiftieth millennium by today's reckoning. In other words, it took that many years to reach our current stage of development.

"Then came an emergency. Based on calculations, we determined that the Earth would soon collide with a meteorite that would destroy all life. Unfortunately, we lacked technology to prevent the collision. But we had discovered how to send people back in history via time travel. So we decided to shorten human history by sending interveners, so evolution would no longer be random but guided. Since we could accelerate evolution, we decided to do it. That's how we come to be in the year 3416 today.

"Humanity can now evolve from this point on without intervention, that is, slowly and randomly. If the collision with the meteorite does in fact occur, people will be technically more proficient than they would otherwise have been. Maybe they will be able to prevent the collision and save life on Earth."

The revelation raised all sorts of questions, but I only said, "Hope it works."

"We do, too. However, it's possible that people will still not have sufficient know-how and we'll have to resume interventions in order to accelerate progress. We are hopeful that, on its own, the human race will be able to avoid the danger with multiple interventions."

I remained silent, thinking, my curiosity aroused. At the moment, I was in no position to cope with what I had just heard, but I wanted at least to gather information so that I could think about it later. "One more thing," I said, "Have you had any failed interventions?"

"Yes, of course." Fricke seemed not to take offense at my

question and answered honestly. "In general, interventions have been very successful, but we have suffered occasional failures."

"So in this respect you are no different from ordinary people."

"Hey! We are ordinary people!" Fricke looked into my eyes and continued, "I've already mentioned some failures, such as occurred with the Hamiltons and with Iesu. On our very first mission, we unfortunately miscalculated the location of the Earth at the time of the intervention. The intervener never arrived there. He disappeared in space. That was our biggest failure."

I shuddered at the idea of disappearing in space and refrained from asking any more questions about mishaps. I turned to the names on the list of interveners. "Galileo Galilei," I said, "Wasn't he a failure?"

"No, not at all."

"But wasn't he condemned by the Church because he claimed that the Earth revolved around the sun?"

"That's right. But in his own lifetime, he found fame as a scholar and even had friends in the highest circles of the Church. He enjoyed the patronage of a prince and traveled to Rome four times to promote his theory. The ecclesiastical censors even allowed the printing of his book, *Il Dialogo*. Although later banned, it had an impact."

"Did you know him?"

"Oh yes, Galileo traveled back in time when he was sixteen. I knew him quite well before his mission and took much interest in his fate. As I mentioned, he accomplished a great deal. Only when he turned seventy did attitudes turn against him. That was when he had to answer to the Inquisition. They condemned him, but he was pragmatic. He recanted and only received house arrest. He was allowed to settle near Florence."

"I know. I am familiar with his story."

"How?"

"I viewed the disk he sent Pestalozzi from his exile in Arcetri."

"Interesting."

I studied Fricke and discovered that my revelation did not particularly interest him. Nevertheless, I asked, "One more thing I'd like to know. What happened to him later on during his exile? The report on the disk was recorded during the first year of his house arrest."

"He did quite well. He was there just nine more years—until his natural death. He lived in relative freedom and even published another important work, *Discorsi*. Incidentally, we continued his work. We sent Newton back in history to begin work just one year after Galileo's passing. He also was very successful."

"But Galileo . . . . How did he manage to integrate into society so that everyone believed he was born in Pisa?"

Fricke had a quick answer. "For Galileo, that was easy. For a mere five scudi, he had a Church clerk enter his name and the date '19 Febbraio 1564' in the baptismal record of the Duomo di Santa Maria Assunta. That served as proof of his birth in Pisa."

"Your knowledge is truly amazing," I said. Then I wondered if they knew the rest of the story. "Did you also know that the

Catholic Church removed the work of Copernicus from the Index in 1835—that is, the Church finally officially recognized heliocentrism?"

"I had no idea," answered Fricke.

"And that towards the end of the twentieth century, the Church took another look at Galileo's trial and acquitted him?"

"Really? A mere four centuries later. The Church surely knew how to drag out the process."

"Yes."

"Fantastic!" he clasped his hands together.

"Not really," I snorted. "The Church relinquishes its power and monopoly of knowledge only when it absolutely must."

***

After we said goodbye to Fricke, Knox led me through the whole operations center and showed me each department. He took me up to see the big boss who wanted to meet me in person. We went to the top floor and entered an office with a sign reading "Project Manager." It was empty.

"He'll be right back," Knox said.

I looked around. This room also resembled a command center. A map of the world showing the locations of the various interveners hung on one wall. Knox explained that the Project Manager could connect to an intervener from the console. Once the connection was made, the place and current year would light up on the map. It was also possible to connect to each division so that requests could be immediately forwarded, processed, and addressed. I itched to go behind the desk for a closer look and had just taken a step in that direction when the door opened and a handsome, bearded man entered. He strode up to me, extended his hand and said, "God."

I hesitated, puzzled. Then I shook his hand and repeated, "God?"

"Yes, I'm Vaclav God. Pleased to meet you."

"Are you immortal?"

"No. Not by a long shot. I'm the Project Manager here."

Epilogue

Although decades have passed, I remember well a conversation I had on a pleasant evening about three months after my arrival in the thirty-fifth century—the setting, my thoughts and feelings, and the excitement of a new relationship. The open-air bar on the rooftop high above Bern overflowed with people. They sat in comfortable recliners or mingled in small groups, chatting, drinks in hand. It was a beautiful, warm summer evening. I sat at a low table. In front of me, a partially drunk Sazerac glistened in its glass. I had become familiar with various cocktails in my new world, and this one tasted excellent.

During the first few weeks after my arrival, I had felt lonely here in this city, which had been my city so many centuries ago. I had struggled emotionally. With one exception, it was hard getting to know anyone well. Life moved at a faster pace and seemed more superficial than in my previous time. The residents didn't seem to mind the hectic lifestyle, but it got on my nerves. I longed then, and secretly hoped, to return to my own time, to my brother and my old friends. But I had to stay. Tom Knox and Vaclav God had made that clear. I had to make myself fit in and become a man of this century.

A man of this century? How clearly I recall the dry amusement the phrase engendered. I had to smile. Because of the ongoing project, the numerical designation of the year in which I lived at that moment was constantly shifting backwards. We had already approached the year 3400, and the clock would be pushed back even further because the project had apparently been successful. I didn't know in which century I really belonged.

Only one thing had become clear to me in this confusion of time. The developmental level of the people around me had not changed significantly. People remained concerned mainly with their own affairs. That much I understood.

So, at that time, I was learning to take care of myself. I had settled into a comfortable little apartment. I was trying my best as I undertook the minor tasks entrusted to me. I had made a few new friends and had come to realize that my old-fashioned, twenty-first century ways were well received. Long walks in the protected zone helped me re-gain my equilibrium. The natural world was more primitive and restorative than in my former time. I also knew the area very well. Every hill remained in its original place, just as in earlier times, although the fields were no longer devoted to agriculture. Plants and trees grew wild. I had begun to compare my fate to that of an emigrant at the time of Columbus. Emigrants also had to adapt to a new environment and get along, and they, too, had left their families behind yet still managed to achieve happiness. I was learning how quickly time heals wounds and how quickly people can adjust to a new world.

In a short time, I had become happy and even found myself uncomfortable with the idea of going back. I felt a sense of satisfaction in having solved the riddle of Professor Bucher and humankind's accelerated rate of development. I had landed in another millennium. It was what it was. I had experienced more than most people ever had and, with no worries at all, could devote myself to fresh undertakings in this new world. A crowd continued to bustle around the bar, but I was paying no attention. I sat apart in my comfortable chair and looked up at the starry sky.

Had I actually whirled out to one of those stars and returned at nearly the speed of light? Yes, I had actually traversed the shortest timeline through spacetime while the Earth took a lot longer to reach the same point in space. Yes, I had travelled by time machine!

So much had now become clear. I wasn't thinking just about interventions in human history, about priests from antiquity who became gods, or about saints, who like Sumid could speak with God in a temple. That is, Vaclav God, the project manager. Nor was I thinking about Iesu, who much to my surprise actually was the son of God. Rather, I was thinking about the farmers in my former time who obstructed anything that would promote the progress that humanity so desperately needed. Above all, I was thinking about my brother, mired in twenty-first century knowledge despite his keen mathematical insight. How I would have enjoyed speaking to Michael again about his statistical proof of God. I would have shown him his calculations were correct and there had actually been purposeful intervention in the process of evolution.

My reverie came to an abrupt end when someone called, "Daniel." I turned around.

Tom Knox was walking over to me from the bar smiling. He had two full glasses in his hands. "May I join you?" he asked handing me another Sazerac.

I remember pointing to the chair across from me and gladly taking the proffered glass. The warm night brought thirst with it.

I opened the conversation. "I am constantly amazed at the technology of your—um, our—century."

"For you, no doubt. You're probably still experiencing some sort of culture shock. For me this is all normal."

Leaning back in my chair, I looked up at the stars and pondered. Jana, a new friend, broke away from the crowd at the bar and walked over. She sat down casually, hooked her arm through mine, and asked if she could listen in. I reciprocated the gentle pressure, letting her know that I was glad to have her there. I introduced Jana to Tom Knox, and they greeted each other.

Although I had seen and understood much in this new time, I had only encountered earthly creatures—humans, animals, and plants. I had heard nothing of extraterrestrial life forms, although I certainly found their existence plausible, given all the stars up there. So, I decided that now might be a good time to bring up the topic. I asked, "Are we really alone in the universe, or are there other living things out there?"

Jana didn't respond. Knox paused only briefly and said, "In the small area of space that we have explored thus far, we have encountered numerous forms of life."

"Really?" I was surprised.

"They're not terribly interesting. Most are unicellular and primitive multicellular organisms."

"Not people like us?"

Knox laughed. "No. We haven't found intelligent life anywhere."

"Too bad."

"Why too bad?"

"Wouldn't it be interesting to communicate with beings from other worlds?"

Knox didn't answer. I looked back up at the stars and asked, "Why are there no other intelligent life forms?"

"Think about our own evolution."

"What do you mean?"

"The Earth was formed over five billion years ago. Soon after that, half a billion years later, the first single-celled organisms appeared. Later primitive multicellular organisms arose. Life continued to develop and became more complicated. There was no intelligent life, however, for a very long time."

"Why not?"

"Evolution did go on for a long time. But it was repeatedly blocked. For example, dinosaurs ruled the Earth for hundreds of millions of years, and they ate up everything that evolved. When they became extinct due to the impact of a meteor that made Earth practically uninhabitable for a time, the way opened for new forms of life."

Knox took a sip from his glass and continued. "Intelligent

life on Earth only appeared a few hundred thousand years ago, thus relatively recently given the length of time the Earth has existed. On another planet with conditions similar to ours, life forms might never have arisen or might arise at a very different point in time. Why would intelligent life evolve on another planet, one close enough to communicate with us, during the same period as on our planet? That would be a huge coincidence."

"Makes sense to me."

"Anyway, we haven't bumped into any intelligent life so far."

Knox leaned forward and continued seriously, "Moreover, as you now know, it's not a question of 'random' development of intelligence. We now can distinguish three stages of life. The first is the emergence of life itself, that is, of life that acts without consciousness. The brain is only a nerve center that controls actions reflexively. In the next stage, we have intelligent life. An intelligent being acts consciously by reflecting and making decisions. Such beings explore their environment and begin to understand it. However, their achievements are limited by their own intelligence, that is, limited by the capacity of their brains.

"In humans of your former century, for example, brain capacity was sufficient to grasp the theory of relativity, although many people could not imagine how the universe might work based on such rules. People couldn't visualize a fourth dimension. But shortly after your former century, interveners led people to influence their own development through genetic engineering and efficient education. This enhanced their ability and created the prerequisites for understanding the ultimate relationships of matter, energy, and time. It was during your era that this third stage of development, the stage of 'self-generated intelligence,' began. Many rejected the technology back then. Of course, they didn't know that they themselves were already a product of it.

"Only through self-generated intelligence have we arrived at the current state of human brain capacity, which, much earlier in your history, we had brought about through selective breeding. Now we're excited to see how this development will continue to push forward in your former century. It will, we hope, impact us and bring us closer to our goal."

Knox had paused in his lecture. His enthusiasm had overtaken him, and he flushed.

I had enjoyed the convivial atmosphere under the stars and the fascinating information. After a while, I broached my next question, "Can all the movements of the stars above us, all these forces, be expressed mathematically? Can we see paths that lead into the future?"

"Aren't you really asking whether we can predict the future?"

"I suppose so. In a way."

"At the simplest level, that would be possible with Newtonian physics. But the uncertainty principle of quantum theory is relevant. So chance plays an important role. We don't know which path a particle has followed or when the particle will break down. Numerous variations are possible, all real and true in some respect. We can't calculate chance. It's part of the laws of physics. So, although we know the physical laws that can determine the future, we don't know the future. The prediction of the future has its limits because of the undeniable, inherent principle of uncertainty."

"So, the ancient oracles who prophesied the future can't be replaced by a mathematical calculation," I interjected.

"Right. Although one can, in general, understand random chance through statistics, the math can't be applied to individual cases. Unfortunately, there were always people who said they could foresee events in a world line. Such frauds exploited the stupidity and superstitions of people."

I had a follow-up question. "Are we humans ever masters of our own destiny? Do our lives simply run their course according to the laws of physics? The application of those laws might differ randomly, but do we have any control at all?"

"You're asking about free will?"

"Exactly. If we had no freedom to choose, we wouldn't be responsible for our actions. Each would follow a predetermined path. Even criminal acts would be predetermined, which would mean people should not be punished for them because the people had no free will to follow or not follow the law."

"Are you saying that people are responsible for their actions only if they have the freedom to make their own decisions?"

"Yes, that's what I'm saying. But are humans free?" I pressed.

Tom Knox sipped his drink. He sensed my determination. "I'll try to answer the question of free will this way. Our brain consists of millions of memory cells, neurons that communicate with each other. Millions of perceptions and millions of experiences programmed into the brain influence the outcome of this communication. The question becomes whether the same input always produces the same result. In other words, if the stimuli on multiple brains are exactly the same, so that the brains perceive exactly the same events and experiences, will the same reaction always result and in the same way? If the reaction were always the same, then we could predict the behavior of humans.

"If, on the other hand, the results of identical stimuli and experiences were not the same, the person would be free to determine his or her behavior." Knox paused for breath. "We simply can't answer the question of free will because, unfortunately, we aren't in a position to influence two people in exactly the same manner. First, no two people are exactly alike. Second, there are too many factors in any decision-making process. But we can entertain the question as it applies to lower organisms, for example, a single cell organism, a snail, or a fly. If we control every stimulus to the brain, or rather to the central nervous system, of primitive animals, the resulting behavior is always the same. For example, a snail always withdraws into its shell when its tentacles touch something."

"So the snail has no freedom of choice?"

"That's right. It doesn't decide but reacts as a reflex according to its preprogrammed survival behaviors."

I remember that I was not wholly satisfied with Knox's explanation. He pressed on.

"As I mentioned, the human brain evolved over thousands of years. It's much more complicated than that of a snail. Nevertheless, it makes most decisions unconsciously and without real choice. By far, most of its actions and reactions emerge from the subconscious. Also, we are strongly controlled by reflexes. But people differ from snails because we have consciousness. The part of the brain where consciousness is located has developed in such a way that it allows choice among different options. Because people, in the course of evolution, have apparently always striven toward awareness, mutations of the brain favored this direction. Humans are, as I said, intelligent beings."

"So do we have free will?"

"Sure, but just in the small area of consciousness."

We became silent. Then I said slowly, "So apparently one can understand the brain and free will in scientific terms."

"Right. The laws of physics explain and determine everything in the world that has occurred since the Big Bang."

"Just since the Big Bang? What about the Big Bang itself?"

"How it happened, what caused it, and what was before it—we don't know exactly. We have developed physics and technology so robustly that we are able to jump through time. But reality outside of this universe and time, on the other side of the Big Bang, there we remain ignorant."

"So you don't have any idea?"

"The further we push our knowledge, the more we have to admit that we don't know much."

"Well, we had that much figured out even back in my century." With some satisfaction, I took a sip from my glass and continued, "You fabricated the gods of antiquity; you appeared as angels during the Renaissance; and you were the 'ordering principle' of my century. Come on, are you religious or what?"

"Religious? We know that this universe and all that lies within it must have had a beginning and been made subject to laws. We haven't got to the bottom of that yet."

"Well, Tom, is there a higher power?" I was goading him, but he seemed not to notice.

Knox shrugged. "We have no evidence. We know there's no super brain that communicates with seven billion people. That's how many live on Earth. No super brain advises and controls those seven billion individuals with their highly conflicting demands and divergent wishes. Such a god, one who aids both friend and foe and with whom one can communicate in prayer—that god doesn't exist. Over the centuries, science has progressively left less room for a higher power and has pushed the concept further and further back. Currently, the unknown higher power exists only before the Big Bang. We can explain everything that has emerged in the world since the Big Bang. Scientists are, however, addressing the question of how the Big Bang happened and what existed before it. Whether displacement of some higher power will continue and whether, in the end, there is still actually room for a higher power—well, faith is an individual thing."

"So Vaclav God is not 'God'?" The question sounded strange.

"No. In previous centuries, interveners correctly referred to Vaclav as 'God.' After all, it's his name. Perhaps the Hamiltons used the word casually. Certainly Iesu did and even called Vaclav 'Father.' Thus the name became associated with a being of great power. The name lodged in the minds of people. But in reality Vaclav is no more a god than was Schmid, or Sumid."

A realization washed over me. I reached for my drink. "Vaclav God just provided the name?"

"Yes. His name has served as a generic term, just as the

name Caesar referred to all Roman emperors who followed him, morphing, of course, to 'Kaiser' and 'Tsar' as the Empire split apart."

I took a sip of my excellent drink and placed the glass back on the table.

***

And now, dear distant friends, let me remind you that Vaclav God encouraged me to write this report. But he winked and said no one would want to publish it. I wonder what instructions he would have given me if he had known it would reach your hands.

Printed in Great Britain
by Amazon